POINT OF FORK

A Novel

By

Fred Hardy, Jr.

Point of Fork is a work of fiction. Names, characters, businesses, institutions, places, events and incidents are products of the author's imagination or are used fictitiously. Any resemblance to actual persons, living or dead, or locales is entirely coincidental.

To Jo

- -If 'tis wrote against anything, - - 'tis wrote, an' please your worships, against the spleen! In order, by a more frequent and a more convulsive elevation and depression of the diaphragm, and the succussations of the intercostal and abdominal muscles in laughter, to drive the *gall* and other *biter juices* from the gall-bladder, liver, and sweetbread of his majesty's subjects, with all the inimicitious pasions which belong to them, down into their duodenums.

The Life and Opinions of Tristram Shandy, Gentleman
Laurence Sterne

PROLOGUE

The boy awoke just as a terrified shriek stopped in his throat. He lurched upright in his bed and looked around the room for assurances that it had only been a bad dream – the same grisly nightmare as two nights before, and two weeks before, and two months before. Ever since the week before his eighth birthday. Ever since Dad had left for good in his new 1953 Hudson headed for Pittsburgh and a new job with U.S. Steel. He could hear the soft drone of the fan and feel the breeze hit his moist skin as the whirring face oscillated in his direction. He knew he was awake. Through the open window he could see the West Virginia Mountains and the coal tipple silhouetted above the treetops, silent against a sky brightened by the waxing moon.

Still trembling, he looked intently around the moonlit room. The two mismatched wooden chairs cast long shadows on the floor – bare except for a worn scatter rug. The large oak dresser with the cracked mirror revealed two half-open drawers. Five feet away his little sister Lela was sleeping on the daybed, her fine blonde hair shining in the moonlight. He watched as the tattered bedspread rose and fell with her rhythmic breathing. The boy felt like peeing, but he didn't want to leave the house. Still it was reassuring to feel the soles of his feet touch the floor. Outside the back yard was nearly as bright as daylight. The old bluetick hound rose stiffly to his feet, shook himself, and followed the boy down the worn path toward the two-seater. One seat would have sufficed for their small family, but since neither the boy nor his dad hit the hole with any regularity, one seat had the number 1 scratched in pencil behind it, and the other was designated number 2.

By the time he returned to the house, the pungent odor of lime and stale urine in his nostrils had given way to the lingering aroma of baked bread and cabbage cooked in ham hocks, dinner from the night before. It was a good smell. The boy glanced toward the door of his mother's room. He wouldn't awaken her. Crawling softly back into his bed he tried to forget the nocturnal images that had been shaking him with increasing frequency. Reverend Belcher's bony left finger quivering as it drilled an accusatory hole through his heart. The thin red cheeks puffing and his green eyes glaring behind wire-rimmed spectacles as he pulsated a hoarse rhythmic chant and pounded the pulpit with his right hand. Words he didn't understand – awful words like "abomination," "perdition," "contagion," and "conflagration." They were meant for him. They were a judgement for his "iniquity."

Then the race. Always a terrified scramble from the church door down the steep hill with the dogs at his back and Reverend Belcher astride a black horse whipping them on. He could hear the shouts: "Hellfire will swallow you up. There shall be no escaping the awful judgement of the Lord!" Steeper and steeper the descent becomes as the boy loses control, and the dogs gain ground. Gnarled black trees and tangled thickets fly by as he fights to maintain his balance. Several times a yelping dog is trampled beneath the pounding hooves of the gaining horse only to regain its feet and rejoin in the chase. Then the cliff. No escape. A vast smoking valley with muffled shrieks and hideous groans rising from the flames. "Where will you hide now?" the preacher bellows as the black horse whirls to a dusty halt. Above him the yellow eyes of the dogs and their snarling teeth awaits the preacher's command. Then rocks crumble and fall as the ground gives way. The boy feels himself slipping toward the gaping abyss and hears the hoarse hideous laughter of Reverend Belcher. He begins to fall . . .

Chapter 1

The patient rose haltingly to his feet as the doctor returned to the small examination room. "Keep your seat, Colonel. The angiogram confirmed what we expected. Three major blockages. We should be able to restore reasonable blood flow to the heart with bypass surgery; less invasive procedures at this point are not a viable option."

"What's the timetable for recovery? The academy closes in six weeks; I need to be back at the helm for opening in September. "

"You're 66, Colonel. Maybe a little young for retirement, but you've had a full career - first in the Marines, then in your law practice, plus a good thirty years as president of Point of Fork Military Academy. "

"Thirty-two, Max, thirty-two. And you can call me Brad. I was at PFMA for ten years before your parents left you with us - a snot-nosed kid with a bad attitude and a short fuse on a one-way street to nowhere. "

"Don't think I've forgotten that day either. No kid could ever have felt lower. Leaving home for the first time, repeating the ninth grade, and no hope of seeing my family or girlfriend until Thanksgiving. I think the girlfriend was probably history before my parents arrived back home to Atlanta. No great disaster in the cosmic scheme of things. As it turned out, my life was probably saved on that hot September day. I know this; Max Jarvis isn't the first guy who owes his second chance in life to you and that school. You've done more than your share for Point of Fork, and the academy has done a lot for the country, the State of Virginia, and thousands of messed up kids like me. But the school can go on without you. It's got to. My office will call you tomorrow and schedule the procedure. With proper rest and therapy, I think you can look forward to a long and active retirement. But you can't go back to Point of Fork. It'll kill you. "

Colonel Bradley Harrington eased his brown Mercedes sedan out of the Henrico General parking lot, took a left, drove through two traffic lights, and stopped for the third at Patterson Avenue. When the light changed, he turned right and pointed the car west on what quickly became Route 6 as he headed out of Richmond toward Point of Fork. It was still late morning, and he decided not to stop for fast food. No more of that. He would be back at the school in little more than an hour and could have a salad plate sent to his office from the mess hall. He cracked the window on the driver's side and followed the road as it dwindled to two lanes - thinking about nothing.

About halfway back, he felt a sharp twinge at his chest and briefly took his foot off the gas waiting for the angina to subside. He was ok. He would *be ok.* But what a kick in the ass; it had finally come to this. A nondescript childhood in the backwater town of Bluefield in southwest Virginia. Enlisting in the Marines at seventeen. The University of Richmond on the G.I. Bill after storming the beach at Saipan. Then Law school at Virginia where he had met Louise Cabell - a true Virginia blue-blood of the DAR and Daughters of the Confederacy. Folks back in Bluefield could never really take it in. Little Brad Harrington - a nobody from nowhere - son of a non-union miner who had died penniless of black lung the summer before his boy's senior year in high school - now hanging out his shingle in Roanoke with all of the best connections. Then Point of Fork - the challenge and opportunity that seemed to come out of nowhere following a dinner conversation with a client who served on the school's board of directors, to assume the helm of America's most prestigious college preparatory military school.

Prestigious. Not then - not during the late sixties at the height of the anti-war and anti-military movement. No, plenty of people had wondered about his leaving a comfortable, if mundane, law practice and going into education. Military schools - once a proud bastion of Southern education - were closing every day. Even PFMA had seen significant decline in enrolment. But Colonel Bradley F. Harrington would take the helm and steer the ship through the troubled waters of the sixties and into the heady decades beyond. The school would not only survive but flourish as never before.

Then the awards, the recognition. The triumphant return visit to Bluefield for the first time since enlisting as a teenager. The appointments and citations - both for him and for the school. He had done it. He had done it alone against great odds and in the face of conventional wisdom. He had done it when others doubted - as they always had. *And he would do it again.*

The Colonel turned into the driveway of the President's Home and parked the car along a line of blooming dogwoods. Through the living room window he saw Louise rise from her parlor chair and go to the front door. A waive of angina - much sharper than before - hit him as he shut the car door.

Point of Fork Military Academy sits on a three hundred acre parcel of land overlooking the confluence of the James and Rivanna Rivers in Virginia's Piedmont. A grant from King George II to the Page family, the land on which the academy now stands has never been bought or sold. Across the James to the north is the town of Columbia. Except for the occasional news footage showing the flooding that occurs every few years, most Virginians have neither seen nor head of this forlorn, rotting village of some two hundred dispirited inhabitants. Technically, the town still maintains its designation of city (the nation's smallest and among the oldest) dating back to the boom days of the colonial canal system when it was Virginia's largest municipality west of Richmond. Tradition has it that when the state capital was moved inland from Williamsburg, Columbia was Richmond's closest rival losing out by only one vote. But for Columbia it was all downhill from there as first the canal system and then the railroads petered out, and the town gradually dwindled into abject dereliction. The stores and shops along Main Street as well as the mills and taverns of years past have long been boarded up or fallen down.

Of Columbia's nine churches, only two hold services today - both largely sustained by the academy across the river. The Point of Fork Baptist Church is attended by a few locals but largely by academy faculty and staff; in fact, all but one of the church's deacons are members of the academy's administration - reflecting the staunch Southern Baptist tradition and affiliation of PFMA. The Academy's six Catholic families and some two hundred Catholic cadets attend St. John of the Cross in

Columbia along with some two dozen locals. One of the town's taverns has been converted to a thrift shop, and there is an old filling station and convenience store across the street. The only other occupied building along Main Street is the old Columbia Hotel - now converted to apartments mostly for welfare families. Once a grand edifice on Columbia's largest hill, the hotel still sports its imposing portico, but is fast falling into decay and has not been painted in years. The dark interior smells of urine and rot. Traces of the old flowered wallpaper can be found in some of the rooms and hallways, much of it covered by graffiti, but bare beams are now exposed throughout most of the sprawling building. A two year old child drowned two summers ago in the hotel's crumbling swimming pool that had not been operational since the 1950's and is now surrounded by weeds, overgrown boxwoods, and volunteer Virginia pines. Two women living in the hotel work in the academy's kitchen and are among the fifteen town residents who cross the river daily to work as laborers at the school's maintenance shop, the kitchen, or on the grounds crew.

The President's Home, a three-story Greek revival mansion, was once the proud seat of Point of Fork Plantation, then nearly six thousand acres over half of which was comprised of fertile lowground along the two rivers. Like many stately antebellum Virginia homes, both it and its sister mansion, Glenn Arvon on the James, were reputed to have been designed by Thomas Jefferson. Several of the old oaks still surround the home, and even now massive elms defy the Dutch elm disease that has taken so many stately trees throughout the country.

The school itself is of an ascetic military design and stands in bleak if stalwart contrast before the mansion. Founded in 1851 as a classical academy, the school was neither military nor Baptist until after the Civil War during which several alumni had fought valiantly with General Jackson for their Commonwealth and the Lost Cause. The school's founder, Dr. Thomas Page of Point of Fork, was the uncle of Thomas Nelson Page, a well known attorney and gentleman author who wrote popular novels and stories romanticizing life in the Old South. Dr. Page had envisioned a boarding school where the local gentry could groom their young sons for a university education and as future leaders in society. Most of the academy's earliest graduates had attended the University of Virginia or William and Mary. A few had ventured north to the Ivy League institutions. For almost a decade women scholars graced the academy's classrooms as day students, but that came to an end in 1870 when, succumbing to the economic distress of Reconstruction, the school was reorganized as a military academy under the auspices of the Baptist General Association.

The academic quadrangle is surrounded by a scattering of buildings interspersed with an incongruous mixture of shrubs and hardwoods. These include the mess hall, the old gymnasium, the new field house, the Military Science Building, and three barracks that house about two hundred cadets each. There is also the sparkling new Harrington Center for Computer Technology - the most comprehensive facility of its kind in secondary education. Over half of the academy's twenty-two buildings have been restored or renovated within the last dozen years. The academy grounds are scrupulously attended by a crew of a dozen or so local black men – nearly all well advanced in years. The incongruous sight of these white-haired relics shuffling about the campus in the early morning is a quaint if vaguely disturbing reminder of a day long forgotten throughout much of the South. Esau and Folley, who have both outlived any tangible service to the academy, have been permanent fixtures since they began working at the academy as teenagers during the Depression.

Having withstood the anti-military sentiment that closed many military schools during the sixties, the academy now thrives. Harrington had defied the conventional wisdom of the time and maintained the tradition of strict military discipline. His first official act as president in 1966 was to supersede the board's wishes and integrate the academy. No academician, he had nevertheless cajoled or blustered his way onto virtually every educational committee, task force, and school organization in the country. The athletic teams, traditional powerhouses even during the lean years, were made even more potent; the Titans were the best teams money could buy, as many opponents learned the hard way while "Prometheus," the PFMA Titan, stalked the sidelines. Harrington had been bold - often peremptory in his initiatives both within the school and on the outside. And he had won plaudits - many plaudits. He liked that and made few gestures toward false modesty. Like Churchill, the hero of his childhood, Bradley K. Harrington was a survivor and a winner. He even liked a good victory cigar. But there was little victory enfolding Colonel Bradley F. Harrington today. No one knew it, but his ticker was going bad. And so was the school.

Chapter 2

Francis Marion "Frank"Crawford, Jr. arrived at Point of Fork in January of 1978, early in Colonel Harrington's second decade as president. Although he had consistently tested out at above-average IQ, Frank had never excelled at school, and following his parents' acrimonious divorce, he had proceeded to flunk every freshman class except P.E. for the first semester at Charlotte Country Day School. His father, one of the most successful civil engineers associated with Charlotte's building boom, had made his fortune as a young man by landing the city's sewer project. Recently he had been elected to the Queen City's council. But his wife caught him laying pipe on the wrong side of town one evening, and her rancorous accusations were heard clear back to Raleigh truncating his incipient career as the boy wonder of the state Democratic Party. Frank Senior was relegated back to slide rules, concrete, and re-bar; the boy was soon on his way to Point of Fork.

Frank Senior had become acquainted with his son's new school through several of his football teammates while attending Virginia Military Institute where he had lettered for three years. *En route* to a 9-1 record under the leadership of legendary Coach John McKenna, the Keydets had marched over traditional in-state rivals Virginia Tech (at that time the state's "other"military college) and a hapless UVA squad, then in the throes of one of its record-setting losing streaks. When McKenna departed VMI for Georgia Tech after Frank's junior season, he took VMI's winning tradition with him forever - as well as the team's sophomore quarterback and most of the defensive line. New coach Vito

Rigazzo, left with no true quarterback, moved Crawford from his halfback position during spring ball, and the team finished a disappointing 2-7 the following fall. Frank Senior didn't connect on many passes that season, but his status as the team's signal-caller did manage to cement many future business connections *via* the famous VMI "Network" that would serve him well in both his business and in his short-lived political career.

Frank Junior shared his father's six foot frame but showed little of his athletic proclivities. His face had many of the same features, but what had passed as ruggedly handsome in the father was bulky and ungainly in the son. He had his father's wavy blonde hair and the dark green eyes, but a vacuous stare and a somewhat weak chin spoiled the effect. When young Frank Crawford arrived in his mother's Oldsmobile, his natural awkwardness was exacerbated by his status as one of only a dozen new cadets in a system that had been in full swing for a semester. Most of the September cadets had risen to the rank of Private First Class and had become more-or-less accustomed to the discipline and military protocol of the school.

Crawford's roommate, Luis Carbonell, was the son of the Vice-President of Venezuela. PFMA boasted a large contingent of Latin Americans - or the "Spic Patrol" as they were fondly labeled by many of their classmates. Language, culture, and to some extent their superior intellectual and even financial standing tended to alienate the Hispanic cadets from the corps and created social ghettos from which only the most assertive or urbane emerged. Carbonell, despite his sophisticated upbringing, had shown little interest in his previous roommate, Sonny Morris of Aiken, South Carolina, and just before Christmas Leave, Sonny was booted for stealing a bag of pork rinds from the PX.

Crawford didn't begin much better than his predecessor. Within a week the "Spic Patrol" and eventually the whole of D Company had been fully advised of the new cadet who picked his nose throughout Study Period and beat off every night in the top bunk. Carbonell, a popular, assertive youngster, reveled in his roommate's insecurity and exploited it at every opportunity. Ultimately this would prove to be a mistake.

- -

Frank Crawford passed all of his classes for his first quarter at PFMA; in fact, the only D he made was in Health I - not as rare a situation as it sounds considering the record of Captain R. Dunston Brady, the academy's sole health instructor and track coach. Brady was among the youngest faculty officers at PFMA having graduated from Baptist College (now Charleston Southern University) in 1975. A less than mediocre student at North Rowan High School, Brady had failed the tenth grade and had also been forced to repeat at least one course in summer school on two other occasions. A gawky almost anorexic lad with a sunken chest and a whining nasal voice, young Dunston had shown some talent for running in ninth grade PE, and by his senior year managed to place sixth in the North Carolina State Meet in the two mile run. There he caught the eye of Howard Bagwell, the track coach at Baptist College. Bagwell encouraged Brady to enroll there and come out for track as a walk-on. Baptist College had no football team and only a token basketball team at that time, but the track team was the talk of Charleston. In the dual role track coach and athletic director, Bagwell had recruited a team that regularly struck terror in the hearts of Clemson, the University of South Carolina, and any other school foolish enough to schedule a no-name school with a big-time track budget and very little compunction about the academic background of any athlete who knew his way to the finish line. Brady ran track for four years at Baptist but was no factor on a team of thoroughbreds. His one crowning moment was making All-Conference by running the third leg of a championship two mile relay team featuring three Jamaicans - two of whom went on to become Olympic medalists. After his fifth year Dunston Brady received a B.S. degree in Physical Education and was duly licensed to wreak revenge and misery on the academic world that had so abused him in the past. To this task he was well suited. Deferential, even obsequious to his superiors, Brady viewed society entirely within the context of ass kissing. In his limited world vision, all of humanity was divided into two groups – those whose asses he was required to kiss, and the others who were requires to kiss his. To those in the first group he paid meek and servile obeisance. From the second group he exacted the same - as could be attested by all future ninth and tenth graders who had the misfortune to take the required Health course at PFMA.

Athletics are compulsory at Point of Fork, so when Frank Crawford arrived at mid-year he was placed on Captain Brady's indoor track team. This or swimming offered the only logical choices since the winter season was already underway and these teams did not make cuts. The track team boasted over 100 members. Because many of PFMA's football players were naturals for track and field, the Titans had a nucleus of about thirty sprinters, jumpers, hurdlers, and throwers who insured a state championship nearly every year. The remaining seventy participants were put into the distance events with the hope that perhaps a half dozen runners would emerge to compete in those events with minimal embarrassment. Frank was no more enthusiastic about running than he had been about other sports, but dutifully found himself jogging near the back of the pack down the long country roads of Cumberland County – at least until the line of runners spread out sufficiently for a half-dozen or so to peel off at Byrd Creek and enjoy a smoke or two under the bridge. There he became acquainted with Bill Williamson, one of the least popular seniors in the corps, who, because he had amassed only twenty demerits in his four years at PFMA, had attained the rank of lieutenant in Frank Crawford's company. Frank was a natural suck-up and cultivated a friendship with Williamson, whose parents had refused to sign him off on a smoking permit, with a reliable supply of Marlboros.

Frank normally arrived at practice about five minutes late – occasionally a minute or two later, which put him in danger of being placed on report. His roommate Carbonell, was always early to wrestling practice. Wrestling was his second favorite sport to soccer, which he and his fellow Hispanics dominated. The soccer boom in the United States was still in its incipient stages during the early '70s, and PFMA's "Spic Patrol," who came from a culture that played the sport from their infancy, ran circles around the exclusive prep schools whose players were a generation away from knowing a "soccer mom." In wrestling Carbonell found his natural agility, aggressive disposition, and compact physique ideal for take-downs and reverses, and was one of the league's best in the 160 pound class. By his skill and flair, Luis had won several fans who regularly came to the matches, among them Captain Brady's wife, Rae Ann.

Chapter 3

Rae Ann Ralston Brady was originally from Richmond, the only daughter of Jack Ralston, a vice-president of Phillip Morris, the capitol city's largest employer. Her father had served two terms on the city council before being unseated by a maverick populist of sorts named Howard Carwile. Carwile was a local shyster in the seediest sense of the term, who had set a local record by running for office unsuccessfully six times in a row. Although he had no coherent political philosophy or agenda, he finally hit a public nerve when he began running against the established "Richmond Forward" political coalition on literally all issues. An ungainly man with thick bifocals, a sallow complexion, and a voice and speaking delivery humorously reminiscent of the Kingfish of the Amos'n Andy show, Carwile's large head and dour countenance presented the aspect of a stature much larger than his 5' 8" frame. Every Sunday afternoon, Carwile's half-hour radio show came on the heels of the last of the church broadcast on WXGI, and his political hellfire and brimstone did not take a backseat in terms of intensity to the fervor of his Baptist predecessor. For the entire thirty minutes that he had purchased – often to the point of being cut off in mid-sentence – Carwile thundered the gospel of political turmoil and confusion. Referring to Richmond Forward as a "calumnious cohort of chicanery," and to Ralston as a "pusillanimous purveyor of pecuniary provincialism," Carwile was not taken seriously until an unlikely coalition of reactionaries, blacks, pre-libertarians, and other disenfranchised constituents of the early sixties began to view him as some kind of champion for the underdog. Carwile won by less than fifty votes but went on to serve for three terms while setting a city record for casting the lone dissenting vote in 278 roll calls.

Thoroughly humiliated, Jack Ralston never returned to public service. He concentrated all of his efforts on manufacturing cigarettes of ever-increasing nicotine content and retreated to the tranquil solitude of his home near the end of Lock Lane in Windsor Farms. Richmond's most aristocratic neighborhood, Windsor Farms with its towering oaks and spacious Georgian-styled homes meanders its way back from Cary Street to the banks of the James River. Crouched among the ancient boxwoods, the homes with their tastefully landscaped lawns sit well back from the quiet shaded streets of the neighborhood.

An indulgent parent, Ralston always gave his only child the best of everything. Rae Ann had a horse on her ninth birthday and a Corvette on her sixteenth. She attended St. Catherine's School where she excelled in field hockey more than her class work. Although not a homely girl, Rae Ann could be said to have been on the plain side. With straight dirty-blonde hair and a bland face that evinced little expression, she possessed few of the charms necessary to attract the guys' attention at Miss Donnan's Cotillion – not until her ninth grade year when she began to fill out her evening dress in ways that could no longer be overlooked. Rae Ann added a final touch by fashioning her hair – with the aid of Lady Clairol - in the style of Mary Travers of Peter, Paul, and Mary, the popular folk group. The effect was to almost completely overshadow the plainness of her expression. Almost completely, and within a couple of years her figure had matured to such striking proportions that the boys over at St. Christopher's were filling the locker rooms with tales of imagined conquests. All were unanimous that with a bag over her head Rae Ann Ralston could contend with anything *Playboy* could put on its centerfold.

These changing attitudes were not lost on Rae Ann, nor were they entirely unwelcome, but to the frustration of many a young swain, her virginity had withstood several evenings parked in the latex-encrusted driveway of "Blue Shingles," a remote abandoned mansion that had seen the fall of many a maidenhead. She had even managed to survive a passionate nocturnal visit to West Point, a small municipality east of Richmond, equally known for its malodorous paper factory and the mysterious blue light that was said to appear along the railroad tracks during the late hours of the evening. Rae Ann managed to hold onto her virginity until the summer following her senior year about an hour or so after her Cousin Leah's debutante party. Nearly two hundred couples had been invited to the Country Club of Virginia, and the one-and-only Four Tops had been procured for the evening's dancing and entertainment. Outside, two beef quarters were turning on a spit where the young couples lined up between sets for a slice or two on a hot roll. Even longer lines could be seen at the two bars located on either side of the patio. The escort who had been selected for Rae Ann had just graduated from Washington and Lee and would be entering the University of Virginia Law School in the fall. At first glance Ted Henning was not impressed with his date's unremarkable face. But taking a broader view as his gaze fell lower, he was encouraged. And after seven Scotch and sodas and three hours on the dance floor, he had seen and felt enough. Rae Ann had downed her share of gin and tonics, but she was in full control of her faculties as Ted's GTO glided past the lamppost in front of her darkened house and came to a stop under a massive sycamore overlooking the river.

Ted Henning knew his way around an evening dress; although W&L was an all-male college, nearby women's schools such as Sweetbriar, Hollins, and Southern Seminary supplied a steady inventory of ladies of impeccable pedigree and various virtue for all social occasions. With the gentle rush of water through the canal locks subdued by strains of Johnny Mathis' "Chances Are" over the car radio, Rae Ann offered only perfunctory resistance. Alcohol and hours of anticipation on the dance floor had heightened Ted's craving, and more than once during a slow dance a desultory hand or leg had wandered into that demilitarized zone of a lady's defense with no palpable opposition. Nor was his impatience abated when first one and then two erect nipples flowed out from beneath the loosened dress. With only the faint green lights of the dashboard to reveal the promise that lay before him, it was abundantly clear to Ted Henning that, while he was no sexual novice by any standard, he had now elevated his game to a new level. And that was not all that was elevated. In the ensuing contortions and exertion little concern was paid to torn fabric or a broken zipper here and there, nor did either of the lovers notice as the music faded and the dashboard lights dimmed and finally blinked off.

Not until Ted had found his cummerbund wrapped around the GTO's Hurst shifter and had managed to get only a few weak clicks from the starter did he realize that he and his date were at the end of a deserted road at one in the morning with a dead battery. Rae Ann's home was about a mile up the hill, but using her phone or one of her neighbors' in their state of dishabille was out of the question - too risky. Ted raised the hood and tried shaking the battery terminals. He turned the ignition again; no luck. He slammed his hand on the steering wheel in frustration. The nearest pay phone that Rae Ann could recall was five miles away – a good two hours walk. Suddenly, for the first time that evening, the black formal shoes that Ted had rented began to pinch his feet. Then, through the steamed windshield he saw a light materialize. It was coming toward them. For one moment of panic Ted feared that he had parked on the railroad tracks running along the riverside, but no, this light was moving slowly up from the river's bank. Wiping the fog from the window, Ted was able to make out the forms of three large men. Each was carrying a handful of fishing rods in one hand and a stringer of catfish in the other. The men were black.

"You need hep?" The men appeared to be in their twenties. One of them looked quizzically at the couple's attire and smiled as he made eye contact with his friend.

"I could use a jump; you got any cables?"

"Deed you does," chuckled the third man. "Looks like you's all juiced out sho'nuff." Both of his companions rolled their eyes. "Naw, we don't got no cables."

"You two looks pretty steamed up. Don' tell me you been dancin' at the Sahara Club." The remark drew a cackle from one of his companions and a stare from the other.

"If you gentlemen have transportation nearby, we could use a wrecker. I have forty dollars on me and would gladly pay you to call an all-night station. I can use my Triple A card to pay him." The fishermen looked at each other.

"Eddie's truck's parked right up the hill 'hind them bushes. How 'bout you goin' with him? Clarence and me will stay wit da cah." Rae Ann's eyes widened, and she shook her head vehemently.

"No, I trust you. Here's forty; we'll wait for the wrecker." All three of the men smiled but without mirth. As they trudged up the hill toward the hidden truck, Ted could hear the men talking in muffled tones. He glanced at Rae Ann, whose expression of terror had now hardened to one of indignation.

"You just forked over your last forty bucks, and we're no better off than before."

"The wrecker will be here in a few minutes."

"In your dreams! That forty bucks is on its way to the first whorehouse or nip joint in niggertown. Take my word for it; you'll never see it again. We might as well start walking." The couple had nearly made it to the Cary Street when the headlights crested the hill. Ted flagged down the wrecker from Boulevard Exxon and led the driver to his GTO.

Rae Ann showered and was in her bed by three o'clock. No one was up. Her parents had been to the same party and had imbibed copiously. For that she was thankful, but she remained distraught as the effects of the booze began to wear off and the events of the evening swirled in her head. Before drifting off to sleep, she promised herself that never again would she give in to a one-night stand. She meant it at the time, but promises are made to be broken, and Rae Ann had crossed a threshold from which there was no return.

- - - - - - - - - - - - - - - - -

That fall, Rae Ann Ralston matriculated at Meredith College in Raleigh, North Carolina. Ted came down from Charlottesville twice during the first semester taking a weekend break from law school. The dating hours for freshmen at the all-girls' school were strict, but those two-hour quickies at the Brownstone Hotel were worth it; Rae Ann had a world-class body, and her face - - she had a *world-class* body.

That fall Rae Ann's cousin Leah introduced her to her sorority sisters and to several fraternity guys from N.C. State. It was at a frat party there that she met two football players who had crashed the party. Over the next several weeks she was invited to a number of post-game gatherings by various members of the Wolfpack team. These were not fraternity parties. Most were held far away from campus at the Riverside Motel near the Dupont plant. Players faced loss of scholarships for drunk or disorderly conduct if their indiscretions became public, so the Riverside's remote location and the fact that the police showed little interest in what went on there made it the ideal venue for the uninhibited flow of beer and testosterone. Rae Ann had never been interested in football, but she couldn't help noticing that the guys at the football parties offered assets rarely available at the Sigma Chi house. What many of them lacked intellectually was more than offset by iron pectorals, bulging biceps, and massive deltoids.

On the Saturday night following the Maryland game, Rae Ann waited in her room for Ted Henning, who had promised to arrive no later than 7:30 following an afternoon session with his Constitutional Law study group. She was not excited; several of the State players had invited her to a four-keg blast at the Riverside starting at eight. Ted would never understand her attraction to "those Neanderthals" as he routinely referred to all athletes with the exception of squash players, golfers, or the like. Also she was not inclined to introduce her jock friends to the hero of Lock Lane riverfront. The only regular at the Riverside who even remotely resembled Ted was Al Feathers, the team manager, and he was tolerated only because he had access to the test files at the Phi Gam house.

By 8:30 Rae Ann had waited long enough. She met a cab outside, and within twenty minutes arrived unescorted at the Riverside. The late October evening was cool, but a small bonfire had been built from downed limbs and a couple of wooden benches. One of the kegs had already been emptied and unceremoniously heaved into the river by Al Delgado, the team's All-Conference offensive guard as well as the ACC shot put champion. Rae Ann wore skin-tight herringbone slacks. The effect of her long legs was accentuated by high-heel leather boots. Her platinum hair fell to the shoulders of an open brown sweater covering a white Villager blouse beneath which danced the sassiest set of tits Nick Zunich had ever seen – and he was an avid connoisseur of the raunchiest skin magazines in print - domestic or foreign. Nick brought her a large cup of beer. Nick had at least one thing in common with Rae Ann – he was a truly remarkable physical specimen from the neck down. Actually he *had* no neck; his blocky head with its flat face and a nose that had been broken too many times to count seemed to be attached directly to his bullish shoulders. Nick was feeling lucky; already that afternoon he had managed to set two school records – one for the most tackles in a game (11) from the outside linebacker spot, and another for the most consecutive monosyllabic answers in a post-game interview. He had NFL written all over him.

By eleven o'clock most of the couples had migrated toward the motel rooms. Only two couples and a half-dozen dateless players remained. Rae Ann had quaffed four cups of Schlitz, but Nick was way ahead of her. He excused himself for a trip to the river "to drain his lizard," and when he did not return after five minutes or so, Rae Ann went looking for him. She was about thirty yards up river when she was thrown down from behind near a clump of cottonwood trees. Nick Zunich had made his twelfth tackle of the day, but this time he was also going to score for the first time in weeks. Rae Ann, with some initial reluctance, had acquired a taste for rough sex during previous excursions to the Riverside, but Zunich had not satiated his blood-lust nor his passion for punishment from earlier that afternoon. She felt her right arm twisted to an excruciating position behind her back. Her hair was in the mud, her slacks were torn roughly to her ankles. Two crashing blows landed with a sickening thud to the temple and jaw. Several times, her ears ringing, she drifted into various states of consciousness, and each time she saw a different face before her: Nick Zunich, Frank Martin, Jerry Bedricci, Tyrone Brown . . . .

Rae Ann's sedation wore off just after Doctor Gillman left her private room. Her parents had not yet arrived from Richmond, and only a nurse and Ted Henning were in the room. Ted had been delayed earlier by a four car accident just above Creedmoor, and in his haste and frustration he had made a U-turn and tried a detour that only led him farther out of the way. What should have been a fifteen-minute inconvenience turned into a two-hour delay. With much difficulty Ted had extracted Rae Ann's whereabouts from her roommate, and by the time he had arrived at the Riverside, a near panic had ensued. Two of the less inebriated players had heard the screams from their open first-floor windows. After hauling Harold Coffin from Rae Ann's semi-conscious body they were in a state of near hysteria. They didn't need this trouble; the Carolina game was a week away. Ted pulled up in his GTO at this point and after much wrangling convinced the frantic players to let him take Rae Ann to the hospital. "No police, no press, no trouble." Her father was a powerful man with connections all over – especially in the nation's largest tobacco producing state; he wouldn't want this getting out, and he could keep the whole matter out of sight.

"Don't try to talk. I know you're hurting, but the doctor says you'll be fine in a couple of days." Rae Ann tried to form a word but felt a sharp pain in her swollen jaw.

"I know this wasn't your fault. Those animal rapists will pay somehow – I don't know how yet, but – "

"Fuck off, asshole!"

State lost to Carolina the next weekend by a score of 31-17. It was a depressing day for the Wolfpack faithful closing out any hope for a bowl bid. Nick Zunick had six tackles in the first half but tore his ACL early in the third quarter ending his season as well as any real hope for a pro career. Rae Ann recovered and was able to return after Christmas for her semester exams. Her father withdrew her from Meredith after her last exam and enrolled her in Baptist College, where she would continue her studies and eventually resume an active but less turbulent social life. It was there, in the fall of her junior year, that she met Dunston Brady.

Chapter 4

When the Colonel got out of bed at 6:30 the next morning he felt no trace of the angina. That was often the case. Usually the first pangs would start to hit him just before lunchtime. Without shaving he tossed on a PFMS sweat suit and drove his car around to the back of the field house. When the immense field house was in the planning stages, Colonel Harrington had stipulated that a small private dressing room be set aside for the academy's president. It had a one-stall shower, a sink, a toilet, and two spacious lockers – both of which always had two clean towels folded on the top shelf. There were also two doors, one on each side of the room. The one on the left led directly into the back of the faculty's sauna/steam room. The door on the right opened into a small private corridor that led to the swimming pool. Next to that door a set of scales was positioned that the Colonel had requisitioned years ago from the old gym's training room after the new field house had been completed. It was the type that has a sliding lever in the back to measure a person's height. The large sliding weight was set on 150 and the small one on twenty-six. When Colonel Harrington stepped up, the balance hit the top with a clank. "Shit!" He tried shifting his weight to the backs of his feet. Nothing. He moved the weight to twenty-seven. Still nothing. Twenty-eight. The balance eased down and settled in the middle of the aperture. "One seventy-eight! No wonder I'm at death's door. I was never an ounce over one fifty-five in the Marines." The Colonel slipped into his swimming trunks, grabbed two towels, and started down the hall to the pool. No one was up this early, so he skipped the shower. On the deck he went through his usual stretching routine, a truncated version of the morning exercise he has learned at Parris Island boot camp.

After twenty laps and his morning ablutions, the Colonel took his uniform from the second closet checking to make sure that Folley had shined his shoes and brass. When he got to his desk ten minutes later, his usual breakfast had been dropped off by the cadet guard - a bowl of raisin bran, a glass of skim milk, a small glass of orange juice, and a thermos of black coffee. His secretary, Mrs. Stickley, would not be in for an hour. He poured a cup of coffee and opened the top drawer of his desk. He drew the manila envelope from the drawer and shook out the white business envelope inside. "Marvin and Cale, Attorneys at Law." Opening it, he stared once again at the two-page correspondence. The Colonel could feel the chest pains starting already. The phone rang.

"Colonel, this is Max Jarvis."

"Max. I thought your secretary was going to call."

"Well, I wanted to speak with you myself, and I knew you'd be in early. I had a more thorough look at your test results, and I want to move the timetable up for your procedure."

"I love that word, 'procedure.' You cardiologists love euphemisms. That bad, huh?"

"I'm not saying that, Brad. I do think we need to get right on this, though. I want you in here for bypass surgery next week – maybe as early as Tuesday. My secretary will call you later this morning."

"You like giving orders, don't you, Max? I don't recall your being crazy about taking them a few years back."

"I don't know what you're talking about; I was a model cadet."

"Yeah, sure – like that prank you pulled your senior year."

"I've told you a dozen times, Colonel, I took a bum rap for that "Three Gents" caper. I don't know who was responsible or how it got done, but I had nothing to do with it."

"Whatever you say, Max."

"I'm not kidding! I was totally innocent – at least that time - but I got stuck with the punishment. Say, speaking of punishment, is that guy, Captain Brady, still around? I remember that he liked to lay it on us. I'll never forget him standing over me in the mess hall - a real Point of Fork moment - ordering me to eat all of the turnips on my plate. And then when I mumbled some comment under my breath, he made eat five more helpings."

"Sure, he's still here."

"You're kidding! I thought you would have sent him packing years ago."

"No, it's not that easy, believe me – especially since he's been here so long. Don't forget, he was at the academy before I got here. But I'll bet I get a call from parents every week on that guy."

"Yeah, I guess so, and I'm sure no one else is going to hire him."

"I wish. Say, weren't you here with a cadet named Frank Crawford?"

"Sure, I remember him – a real "toad" as you guys used to say. Lived over in "D" Company and hung around with Bill Williamson and that whole weird group."

"Anything else? Do you remember who else was in that bunch?"

"Yeah, there was McBride, and Phillips. I think Jerry Stevenson used to be with those guys a lot. It wasn't a real club or anything; they were all kind of pals with that French instructor, Captain Reardon. Why? What's he up to?"

"Well, I can't really go into it, Max. Let's just say he's one of those alumni we get now and then who tries to stir up trouble for the school."

"He may be an alumnus, Colonel, but he's not a PFMA graduate. Remember? He got kicked out his senior year. I think it was for stealing. His roommate's watch if I remember right."

"That's right; I had forgotten. One of our Sp - - Hispanic kids, Carbonell. In fact we had to put Crawford on the bus that same morning. Bermudez was so mad we were afraid he'd try to kill him."

"I doubt Crawford would have gotten much sympathy from the corps – maybe from Williamson and that bunch. What's he up to anyway?"

"Well, it's a law suit. At least that's what he's threatening."

"That was fifteen years ago! What could he bring up now? Don't tell me his self-esteem has been shattered and he wants his damned diploma!"

"No, I really can't go into it. I doubt that it will amount to anything. We get these things all the time."

"Well, I hope the school's not in trouble – not over that loser."

"The school *is* in trouble, Max. The CEO's got a dying heart and a former hooligan for a surgeon."

"Thanks for the vote of confidence. My secretary will call you later this morning."

"OK, Max. Thanks for calling."

- - - - - - - - - - - - - - - - - - - -

When Dr. Max Jarvis hung up the phone, he looked at his watch. Twenty minutes until rounds. He picked up the test results on Colonel Harrington and shook his head. One more problem. One more issue to deal with. At thirty-five, a man should be looking at his best years – the most productive professionally and the most satisfying personally. Security and stability - he had earned that. Yet it seemed that whenever he had managed to steer himself out of the backwaters and dangerous shoals of life toward the clear deep blue waters, he could never seem to catch the trade winds of prosperity. Always he was drawn inexorably toward some issue, some back current that threatened to sweep away everything he had labored so long for and shatter it against the pounding reef of disaster. And the most pathetic part was that it was always so avoidable; invariably he had done it all to himself.

He put down the report and unfolded the blueprint. Was he overreaching? Probably, he always did. He had gone to William and Mary from Point of Fork on a basketball scholarship. At the time he assumed that he would be starting no later than three or four games into the season. The "Tribe" was not exactly the UNLV of the East. Basketball players actually went to class, and W&M had rarely finished in the top half of the ECAC – one of the weakest conferences in the NCAA. At 6'3" he was actually the team's tallest guard, and he had averaged eleven points and eight assists coming off the bench at Point of Fork, the nation's third-ranked team. But it didn't happen here. And after seeing less than a minute per game, he and Coach Parkhill came to an agreement. Max had to admit that he was a step too slow for the college game – you can't coach quickness. Traces of that deficiency had been evident even at PFMA – it was clearly the reason that Luther Jackson, now a freshman at North Carolina, had started in front of him. Because his college grades ware good, a partial academic scholarship was arranged. Along with a work-study program, Max's college fees for the last three years would be less than $2,000. His father, who worked at the Coca-Cola plant in Atlanta, couldn't afford even that, but he would take out a loan and Max would pay it back.

That financial obligation was miniscule compared to the debts Max had accumulated at the Medical College of Virginia and later as an intern and medical resident with the Navy in Alameda, California. And he was hardly past the interest on those loans when he took out over a hundred grand for the house off of River Road. But he had to be crazy, and First and Merchant's Bank had to be even crazier to go for the deal that he had talked them and four junior partners into. Richmond's first comprehensive state-of-the-art cardiac care hospital would be located just off of River Road – a choice location in the city's westward expanding affluent population and less than three miles from his home. Even if the ambitious project paid huge dividends – and there was every reason to hope that it would – the bank would own him until he was a grandfather.

On Max Jarvis's desk sat a family portrait taken only last Christmas. He thought he still looked like a kid seated next to his wife, Johanna. Two years younger, she somehow looked more serious – much more the adult with her unfailing practical expression. "Do we have to do this?" she had asked. "We already have all we'll ever need in life. How many families have what we have? A beautiful home, a dependable income, a place at the river. Security, Max! And we have no way of knowing what expenses lie ahead for Justin."

Yes, Justin. Max studied the two boys in the portrait. Brett was twelve – the prototypical All-American boy with the untamed shock of blonde hair. The deep green of his eyes was his mother's, but their self-assured, almost cocky twinkle was all Dad as was the sturdy frame just beginning to take shape. In Brett Max saw a future fulfilling all of the aspirations a father has for a son. Already a dauntless spirit had begun to emerge showing a nimble wit, a glib turn of phrase, and an audacity that in time may necessitate a dose of PFMA. Max knew Brett's devotion to his younger sibling, but Justin's expression of pure adulation toward his brother touched him to the point of tears.

Justin was ten now. Months before he was born, the parents had been warned of the difficulties that lay ahead. There had still been time to take measures – to terminate the pregnancy, as it was so antiseptically suggested. No, even Johanna, with all of her practicality, had refused to entertain that option. Down's babies often survive well beyond their teens – some for decades beyond. And wasn't Max the one who always said that the measure of a life was its quality, not its duration? Besides, who was more prepared than a doctor to provide and care for a special child? But it had been tough at times; with all of the rewards – and they were many – there had also been extra demands, the frustrations, and the implacable limitations. Those would always be there. As would the remarks – often unintended, sometimes well-meaning, as well as the ever-widening gap between Justin and the other children his age. But Brett was a perfect brother; with Brett, Justin was never left behind. Max had no idea at what point Brett had begun to realize that his brother was different. He and Johanna had tried to explain it early on, but somehow Brett had seemed always to understand, and his commitment to Justin was of a nature that transcended familial affection. In a way even more than his parents, Brett would always be there for Justin.

Once Max had convinced Johanna that the hospital plan was a winner, he had her total support. Now if only he could convince himself! He had done his homework. Research into the demographics, the location, and the need for the facility all combined to show a favorable outlook. His partners, four of the best cardiac men in the area, were willing to stick their necks out – although not nearly as far as he had. Doctors are supposed to be smart. And the bank. Banks don't just lay out thirty million bucks without checking around to see that deal is a money-maker. Of course to Max it was not the money – not all of it. It was medicine, and doing something meaningful for mankind. And yes, prestige. He wasn't afraid to admit it. His father had worked forty years at the Coca-Cola plant with hardly a promotion. When he retired he was making seven dollars an hour, and when he died suddenly of a heart attack two years later, he had less than a thousand dollars in his bank account. No way would he leave Johanna looking to her son for support as his father had. He had plans for his family, and with hard work, creativity, and a little guts he could make all of the parts fit into place.

Whatever obstacles presented themselves would be overcome. He would do whatever it took. Thirty million dollars – to Max the number was beyond comprehension.

Chapter 5

At his retirement two years previously, John Reardon had risen to the rank of Lieutenant Colonel having served PFMA for over forty years. Only two faculty officers in the school's history had served longer. Because of his seniority Reardon had been the chairman of the Foreign Language Department since the early eighties. Colonel Harrington, who had rarely darkened a classroom door since his graduation from law school, considered him a master teacher. Reardon, who had never married, came to Point of Fork immediately after earning his Bachelor's Degrees in French and Divinity from Bob Jones University in Greenville, South Carolina. His appearance had changed little over four decades. He was one of those individuals who begins to look old in his early twenties and looks much the same many years later. He was about 5'6" in height with a slight build and a somewhat stooped posture. His face had been pockmarked by adolescent acne, and his salt and pepper hair – now thinner and more gray than black – was combed straight back – just as it had been since high school.

Until his retirement Reardon was part of a small group that remained somewhat aloof from campus affairs for decades. They were dubbed "The Three Gents." All three had arrived at Point of Fork as young instructors in the early 1950's. Because of their close friendship and their gliding manner of walking, the cadets assumed that they were gay. In addition to Reardon, who taught French, there was Shelby Pleasants, the school's librarian, and history instructor, Jubal F. Taliaferro? They had much in common. All were the products of genteel Southern upbringing, all presented themselves as serious academicians, and curiously none had ever acquired a driver's license. By the time Colonel Harrington arrived as the academy's ninth president, all three appeared to be well beyond their middle ages with their thinning white hair and expanding girths.

They say that horses sweat, men perspire, and women glow. Observing Shelby Pleasants, one might conclude that he had done none of the above-mentioned bodily functions at any time in his life. Whatever muscle he might have nurtured seemed to have remained so unutilized that his entire anatomy from the face down had taken on the atrophy of a flaccid sag. Long before the age of forty, gravity had consummated its victory over Pleasants' entire mortal frame, and age had prematurely frosted his head with shining locks of silver. Hearing his soft voice, one might conclude that this was also the result of infrequent use, but that was by no means the case. Pleasants was a rumor mill. His quiet, cozy library with its fireplace and plush reading chairs provided an intimate ambiance for subtly interrogating cadets about events within and surrounding the academy and its personnel. Over the years his soft voice and disingenuous wheedling had extracted hundreds of scandals of varying degrees of veracity. Irrespective of their accuracy, these tales were artfully embellished by Pleasants and disseminated back into the corps.

Pleasants had grown up in Farmville, Virginia, a small town barely fifty miles from the academy. He had attended Hampton-Sydney College, a distinguished liberal arts school in his hometown, and had come to PFMA as an English instructor immediately after graduating. These events conflict with a persistent rumor perpetuated throughout the PFMA corps that Pleasants had served gallantly in the U.S. Army during the Korean conflict. The apocryphal tale, started by some campus wit and actually believed by many of the more credulous cadets, asserts that prior to a tragic war injury, the soft-spoken librarian had been endowed with a deep, booming voice. A hand grenade was said to have rolled into a trench endangering Pleasants and all of his comrades; whereupon, the dauntless Virginian placed his helmet over the bomb and sat on it, protecting his fellow combatants, but immediately divesting him of both his manhood and his resonant bass voice.

At Hampden-Sydney Pleasants had been no better than an average student, but he maintained hopes nonetheless of someday attending law school at the University of Virginia as his father had. Originally Pleasants had planned to work at the academy for two or three years, perhaps take a few summer courses at UVA, and save some money toward law school tuition. This dream never came to fruition, and as years passed his law ambitions gradually receded into lassitude. In fact, Pleasants' academic and intellectual growth had ended altogether upon his departure from college. He would be loath to admit it, but even as the school's librarian, a post he took over in 1960, it could be truthfully said that after earning his degree at Hampden-Sydney, Shelby Pleasants never read another book.

In contrast to his friend and colleague, Jubal F. Taliaferro was every inch a scholar. Descended from the Taliaferros (pronounced "Tolliver") of South Carolina, he had graduated *cum laude* from Davidson College at the age of twenty. He had then embarked on a career as a "professional student" earning two Masters degrees simultaneously from Duke University. He had just entered a doctoral program in English at the University of North Carolina when his father's fatal heart attack brought his academic career and his family fortunes to an abrupt halt. Less than a week after the untimely death, it was learned that the entire Taliaferro fortune had been dissipated in several unwise investments. The family home, after four generations, would have to be sold, and Jubal would have to find employment. He had few employable skills and no prospects when he appealed to his friend and former classmate Dean Rusk, a promising newcomer to the State Department who would later serve as Secretary of State in the Kennedy and Johnson administrations during the early years of the Vietnam War. Rusk had connections to the Page family of Point of Fork and even had two cousins who had graduated from the academy in the late 1940's. Taliaferro was hired over the phone.

The Three Gents were all hired as tactical officers, which meant that in addition to their teaching responsibilities, they lived in barracks apartments. Except for their living arrangements and maintaining general order within their companies, tactical officers had no military responsibilities beyond those of the other faculty officers. The school tried to maintain at least a dozen unmarried men on the faculty to live in the barracks, and as many of the young faculty found wives over the years, the constancy of Three Gents was considered a material asset in preserving this quota. Although each of the men brought certain liabilities to the school because of their idiosyncrasies, all had something of value to offer the program as well. Reardon, a skilled magician, was a consummate performer, and his predilections as a showman served a worthy purpose at various events during the year. Pleasants was the most effeminate of the three with his dulcet voice and prissy gait. Yet his aloof demeanor combined with his silver hair somehow created for many the illusion of a scholarly, even pedantic intellect.

Although the Three Gents regularly dined together at their corner table in the faculty section of the mess hall and showed little interest in most campus affairs beyond their immediate sphere, Taliaferro was clearly the least sociable of the three. So great was his disdain for society that he rarely took the trouble to bathe, preferring to mask his pungent odor with copious splashes of Aqua Velva. He was openly hostile to the faculty children whose whining voices and rambunctious play tormented his meals. The three were invariably the first to arrive at mealtimes, and with his cutting wit Taliaferro could be counted on to ooze a constant and caustic seepage of commentary on the families of his colleagues as they filed through the serving line. On occasion, when provoked beyond his endurance, he would throw his fork down on his plate, explode to his feet, and after muttering a few choice imprecations, stalk from the dining facility. Invariably, however, he would make a detour through the kitchen grabbing a copious plateful of edibles. He never deprived himself of nutrition as was amply evident in his expanding waistline. In fact, he frequently waited until finishing several generous helpings before departing the room in a huff. He also had a friend in the larder, Louis Johnson, who was faithfully rewarded each Christmas and at the end of every school year with a carton of Pall-Malls for providing serving trays stacked high with meatloaf or pastries. By the 1980's the incipient paunch, which Taliaferro had brought to the academy as a young man, had expanded to fifty-eight inches. With a head roughly the size and shape of a cinder block, and his wavy gray hair combed sternly back from his massive forehead, Taliaferro gave the visual impression of immense inert bulk. To compensate for this ballast, he had developed a side-to-side amble accompanied by a steady horizontal thrusting of the arms that served as counterweights. The cadets called him

Major Maytag.

But in contrast to his friends, Jubal Taliaferro also brought significant assets to the academy. He was a genuine scholar and, at least during his early years at the academy, was a fine instructor. Also, whether out of duty, anti-social nature, or pure curmudgeonry, he was a relentless and fastidious tactical officer. His apartment was located above the front entrance to the company. When his massive bulk was not standing sentry at the doorway, his apartment door was left ajar, and Jubal Taliaferro had excellent hearing. No cadet from other companies entered D Company without his authorization. And the saying around campus went that you couldn't even fart on the third floor of D Company without Major Maytag finding out about it.

- - - - - - - - - - - - - - - - - -

Reardon seemed to have spent a relatively contented if uneventful career at Point of Fork. Once or twice he had toyed with the prospect of seeking a pastorate at a small rural church, and several times he had returned to his mother's church in the mountains of North Carolina to work with the young people and occasionally serve as substitute minister during the summer. Reardon was a fairly accomplished musician who could play both the piano and the organ as well as sing a fine tenor in the choir. But after his mother's death in 1968, he was never invited back to preach.

Captain Reardon was one of four ordained Baptist ministers in addition to Chaplain Findlay, who served on the academy's faculty or staff. Several times each year he was called upon to preach at chapel, and his musical skills were cause enough for Colonel Harrington to designate him the school's entertainment director. This involved several duties such as serving as master of ceremonies at various academy functions. The most notable of these was announcing the cadets and their dates as they filed under the arch of sabers at the annual Scabbard and Blade Ball held every April. Reardon, despite his love of all things theatrical, had some misgivings about this part of his assignment. As a Baptist clergyman he had been among those who questioned Colonel's institution of dances at Point of Fork when he came on board back in the sixties. More to his taste was the selection of the cadets' Friday evening entertainment. Often this was simply a 1950's vintage movie shown in the old gymnasium. These he carefully screened ahead of time for anything lewd or suggestive. Should anything untoward be found in the screening, Reardon was always poised in the projection room to block out the offending scene with his hand – to the clamorous boos and cat calls of the audience.

At least once each month the movie was replaced by a live show of some kind booked by Captain Reardon. With extravagant fanfare he presided over these attractions, which included magic acts, hypnotists, tumblers, acrobats, and the like. Despite his distaste for other sports, Reardon had a predilection for wrestling in all of its forms, and one of his biggest hits each year was the Mr. Moto Wrestling Extravaganza. Mr. Moto had been one of the more popular "bad guys" of the Mid-Atlantic Wrestling Federation during the early 1950's. Although born of Chinese parents in Cincinnati, he had donned the flag of the Rising Sun and performed a mock-Japanese ritual before each bout exploiting the still smoldering "anti-Jap" sentiments of that time. Moto and his troupe of has-beens, their bellies sagging, pranced and cavorted about the ring admirably, slamming one another to the mat to the delight of a raucous corps. Mr. Moto himself served as the referee until the final match, a tag-team bout in which his partner, the Asian Avenger, would invariably distract the referee allowing Moto to break a chair over his opponent's head and finish him off with his patented "sleeper."

The crowd's frenzy was heightened by the throw-by-throw account delivered by Captain Reardon who had graciously agreed to serve as ringside announcer. Despite his physique, which was far from strapping, he claimed to be an aficionado of the sport and was the PFMA matmen's number one fan, always in the front row shouting encouragement to his favorite grapplers. He even owned an ancient wrestling singlet, which he showed only to a few selected cadets. Reardon claimed to have worn it when he won the 135 pound state championship as a schoolboy in 1951.

Whether his scholastic exploits on the mat were apocryphal or not, there is no doubt that Captain Reardon was the hit of the show one winter evening when a wrestling bear had been engaged to take on any and all comers. The muzzled and de-clawed black bear had routinely dispatched each of the school's starting linemen one-by-one, along with several members of the wrestling team and a scattering of dare takers. Somehow Reardon's arm waving and other flourishes at the conclusion of the show caught the attention of the bruin, who broke away from his handler and charged the master of ceremonies from behind. What ensued was one of the most brutal annihilations in the annals of the squared circle. After the first vicious take down, Reardon was pounced on, picked up, thrown over the ropes and out of the ring, whereupon the bear pursued him into the crowd and grasped him in a vice-like bear hug. The cadets in the audience assumed it was all part of the act and ignored the frantic pleas of the bear's handler for help. It was not until the whitened Reardon lost consciousness and was tossed like a rag doll into a ring post that the crowd realized anything was amiss. By then the bear had become bored with his ill-fated adversary, and was lead quietly back to his cage. Reardon suffered a concussion, three broken ribs, and massive contusions from head to toe, but was back in the classroom the following Thursday. The next week some campus wag put the following announcement in the school newspaper: "Wanted – Date for Scabbard and Blade. French Instructor Seeks Companion Who Can Dance Close but Follow and not Lead. Hairy Legs Need Not Apply."

Chapter 6

When Rae Ann Ralston entered Baptist College, she made a concerted effort to make a clean break from her past life and put all of the unpleasantness of the past year behind her. In a decision that showed her characteristic decisiveness, she stunned her family by abandoning her English major to study nursing. She also privately forswore all sexual promiscuity and especially her predilection for jocks. The first time the new co-ed was spotted on her way to Biology 102 in her tight sweater and mini-skirt, Rod Higgins, the campus stud, made a move to cut her out from the pack. He was much encouraged when she accepted his invitation to see *Irma La Douse* at the drive in, but the evening proved for him to be one of frustration and futility – as was also the case for several of his disappointed classmates. A first classman from neighboring The Citadel had entertained high hopes upon spotting the striking coed in town. But faring no better, he confided that Rae Ann Ralston was a frigid bitch who would ultimately take her virginity and other considerable assets to the grave.

This, of course, was not possible, but she did in fact curb her concupiscence admirably until mid-way through her senior year. By that time the young gallants of Baptist College had long ago abandoned all hope of enjoying the hottest body in Charleston and were reduced to making jokes about the girl with the Cadillac body and the VW face. In truth any one of them would have publicly recanted his wisecracks on the steps of his frat house just for the chance to slip his hand under her sweater one time, but ironically that honor fell to perhaps the least likely candidate on campus.

At age twenty-two, Dunston Brady was a virgin. In deference to accuracy it must be admitted that few opportunities to relinquish that status had presented themselves, but when they did, he lacked assertive confidence to carry the day. Brady's stork-like features and meek demeanor did little to arouse the libido in the opposite sex except for those whose carnal appetites remained permanently excited. And even in these rare cases, his response was invariably so tentative that all efforts ended in confusion or embarrassment. Such had been the case four years earlier on the evening following the State Track Meet in which Brady had finished sixth. In the stands that afternoon had been one Beth Franklin. She competed for cross-town rivals, South Roan, and had been eliminated in the semi-finals of the 440 earlier that day. Beth may not have shown Olympic speed on the track, but she was definitely known locally as "fast" – in fact world-class - in the back seat of a car. Around the town of Spencer her hair-trigger sex drive was said to be instantly activated whenever a Y chromosome appeared on her radar screen, and she had long ago lapped the field of her schoolmates in terms of sexual experience and proficiency. Her willing ways were the talk of the football team, the track team, even the chess club; and her exploits were fully recorded (and embellished) on men's room walls all over town.

When Dunston Brady crossed the finish line, he was in a state of near-exhaustion, having run twelve seconds faster than his previous best. His rubbery legs giving way, he immediately collapsed in a sweaty heap on the track's infield. His coach was not only shocked but nearly euphoric as the unanticipated point Brady had scored for the team meant that North Rowan would go into the mile relay with a chance to win the team championship. The spent runner was so delirious that he was totally unaware as an ecstatic Coach Frailey pumped his hand, which fell limply to the ground the moment the coach trotted off to exhort the relay team to win one for the old Green and White. That was not to be; nor were the designs of Beth Franklin as she walked onto the infield to attend to the abandoned athlete. As he gradually came to his senses, Dunston found his head nestled within the ample cleavage of a girl he had never seen in his life. He also became aware to his mortification that he was rapidly reaching a state of full arousal. This did not escape Beth's practiced eye as Brady's jock was stretched to the breaking point offering meager resistance to his rising tumescence. Disoriented and embarrassed, his attempt to roll onto his stomach only left him further entwined in Beth's yielding lap, a place where he again found himself under more intimate circumstances seven hours later.

Dunston could not honestly remember if he had asked Beth to the party during the confusion of those unsettling moments on the track's infield, or if she had invited him. All he knew was that he was alone in an upstairs bedroom with a girl named Beth – somebody – who had just thrown off her bra revealing a set of knockers to rival any he had pored over in the *Playboy*s he kept hidden in the top of his closet. As her hand slid expertly to his groin, he knew more-or-less what to do and had every intention of following her lead to its natural conclusion. Once again he found himself as stiff as a shaft of re-bar, but now to his horror he felt a sudden deflation on hearing the unmistakable purr of the slow steady release of his zipper. Like a beach toy that has been punctured, his manhood shriveled at the first touch of her hand to a limp mass the size of a tiny gherkin. The extremity that had risen so earnestly to greet the wrong occasion that afternoon was now as limp as a breezeless flag in this, its moment of truth. Beth, however, was not a lady to be easily discouraged, and she lent all of her considerable experience and expertise in attempting to resurrect the flaccid member. But all efforts were futile, and when the hopelessness of the situation became obvious, she threw on her blouse and stalked from the room unceremoniously abandoning her dysfunctional lothario to his abject discomfiture.

After that humiliation Dunston Brady abandoned forever the life of the young libertine and sought only Platonic relationships with the opposite sex. When he arrived at Baptist College, his teammates on the track team found him to be more than a little sanctimonious when the locker room conversations turned raunchy, but this seemed consistent with his personality, which was clearly odd in a number of other ways. Brady, who tended to avoid even friendly social interactions, made no attempt to respond to their derision. He found his carnal comfort in solitude – either with the skin magazines he purchased across town or in the shabby strip joints on Bay Street. In both cases, Dunston protected his anonymity by going alone and choosing times and locations where encounters with people he knew would be unlikely. Several times he noticed a short, secretive man sitting alone or with one of Bay Street's ubiquitous b-girls in the dark recesses of the Erotica Club. The stranger had both the face and the physique of a frog with his compact stubby build and his wide mouth and bulging eyeballs. Brady had also seen the same man – perhaps in his early forties - at least once at Teddy's Book Store glancing furtively in all directions before bounding out to his car, a late-model Firebird.

Dunston meet Rae Ann Ralston during their junior year. Human Sexuality was required course both for his P.E. major and her nursing curriculum. Both of these sexual dysfunctionals took a purely academic approach to this course, coldly ignoring the light humor and repartee that both the professor and the students seemed to enjoy. Rae Ann had resumed dating but had rebuffed all advances on her person since the night at the Riverside with Nick Zunich. For his part, Dunston's only sexual confrontation since Beth Franklin had been two months earlier at one of Bay Street's nameless strip joints. Dusky Sommers of the Harlem Review had been doing the midnight show's finale before a sparse Monday night crowd. Dunston, who was returning from the rest room, was caught off guard as he crept past the tiny stage and turned toward the aisle leading to the back row. Too late he realized that he was being dragged up the two steps by the tawny stripper. Blushing and paralyzed with embarrassment, he stood motionless as she draped her arms over his shoulders and began her grind to the delight and cat-calls of the audience. Dunston turned to escape only to have his hand jerked back and thrust roughly toward the woman's crotch. Hid adrenaline rushing, he mustered the strength to tear himself loose and beat a hasty retreat into the street.

Dunston's attraction to Rae Ann was not motivated by the prurient drives that inflamed most of her suitors. While it was difficult for any male to overlook such nubile splendor, his attention was snared by the long platinum hair that fell gracefully to her shoulders. After only two dates with Rae Ann, Dunston was subjected to his first interrogation. He and hurdler David Smith were the last to leave the locker room after track practice and were headed across campus toward their dorm. "You going out with Rae Ann Ralston tomorrow night?"

"Yeah, we're driving to Columbia to see The Temptations."

"Columbia! That's a long trip; I guess she'll be taking an overnight." Brady offered no comment. "I wouldn't mind a night on the road with those legs, but I hear she's a prick-teaser. You're not cutting that stuff, are you?"

"Knock it off, Smitty. You're getting out of bounds."

"Well, I hope for your sake *you're* getting out of bounds. Tell me the truth, Brady. Does she at least let you tickle her twat? You getting any stinky-finger?"

"Forget it, Smitty, she's not that kind of girl."

"Well she damned-well oughta be with that ass of hers. What a waste!"

"Not everyone spends their life looking for a one-night stand. If a relationship develops that means something, it won't be based on sex; it will be based on mutual interests and shared dreams."

"I'd settle for a relationship with her tits. Most guys wouldn't mind sharing what's hanging between their legs with that piece."

"Don't call her a piece, Smitty. I don't appreciate it."

"No, and you obviously don't appreciate a good piece of ass either. There's no hope for you, Brady." And, at least for that weekend, Smitty was right.

But there is always hope – even for those who are not actively seeking it. And that hope was to manifest itself only six weeks later on the calm shores of Charleston Bay. Water somehow seemed to be a common denominator that would figure prominently in the calculus of Rae Ann's sex life. Whether it be chance or some primordial longing that water aroused in the deep subliminal recesses of her psyche, for Rae Ann it seemed to act as an aphrodisiac. From that first time by the James River with Ted Henning, to the brutal assault by Nick Zunch at the Riverside Motel – and for many occasions to come, the influence of water on Rae Ann's sensuality was a constant.

Had it been with anyone but the tractable Dunston, the idea of parking on the lonely shores of the bay would have sent up a phalanx of red flags for Rae Ann. She had learned from bitter experience what was to be expected. But this unoffending suitor presented no threat, and with the full moon weaving its chain on the waves, both young people were content to relax and enjoy the warm breeze and the gentle lapping of the water. They talked of school and the shallowness of life at Baptist College. Rae Ann expressed the view that campus life for her had been even worse when she was at Meredith. Carefully avoiding the particulars, she alluded vaguely to that semester three years earlier in Raleigh and the way she had been treated and regarded there.

"Like a piece of meat." Dunston was slightly put off by the indelicacy of her description.

"Some people are like that. Who were they, N.C. State guys?"

"Yeah, jocks mostly, football players - animals with the IQ of an ape."

"Yeah, we've got our share of them on the track team. Not just the Negroes either. I had to put a stop to David Smith a few weeks back."

"Who's David Smith?"

"A guy who runs the high hurdles. Calls himself Smitty - real jerk with a big mouth. Thinks he's God's gift to women, and likes to talk like they were all put here for his personal use."

"What did he say?"

"I'd rather not go into it."

"Was it about us?"

"*His* version of us. Or *fantasy* would be more like it. He thinks an evening together that doesn't end with me pouncing on you is a waste of time." Dunston was a little surprised at his own choice of words.

"You have never treated me that way; that's what I've always appreciated about you."

"I never have and I never would."

She looked at him quizzically. "You wouldn't want to?"

"I don't mean that, but I know the type of girl you are, and I respect you for it." Both were quiet for a few moments, and Rae Ann allowed herself to rest against him. They shared a chaste kiss.

"Do you treat all girls the way you treat me?"

"You're special to me, Rae Ann, but I'd never take advantage of any girl. I wasn't brought up that way. I was taught to respect ladies."

"I appreciate that." Rae Ann pulled Dunston toward him and lay back on the car seat. She kissed him deeply. Dunston felt a strong stirring, and after a long silence

Rae Ann asked, "Are you a virgin, Dunston?"

Dunston's silence was sufficient to answer her question. Following her lead, he rolled over as she pulled him closer. As his leg slipped between her thighs, he felt her wrap her right leg around him drawing their bodies even more firmly together. His head was swimming, as he remembered the night with Beth Franklin. Would it happen again? He was as hard as a locust post. Rae Ann began to draw deep breaths, and he fumbled behind her for the zipper. There was none; she was in a jumper, which she threw over her head in a flash. Contorting his skeletal frame into a fetal ball, he clumsily worked his way out of his slacks.

"We can't," she moaned, "it's the wrong time of the month."

"Do you men the dangerous time or the impossible time?"

"Do you have a rubber, Dunston?"

Hearing the word "rubber" from Rae Ann's lips shocked him. Dunston would have preferred the term prophylactic, but in fact he had a rubber. He had possessed several over the years, all of which he had allowed to crack and deteriorate in his wallet. The one he had now was a French tickler that he had paid fifty cents for in an adult book store. It was a novelty, clearly marked, "not for the prevention of pregnancy," but in the dark and in his immediate state of urgency this was overlooked. He was still rock-hard and did not want to lose it as he had with Beth Franklin.

Rae Ann had heard of and even seen ribbed condoms, but she was shocked that Dunston would have this model in his possession. In her state of arousal she was not inclined to protest, and spreading her suntanned legs, she guided him in. It was all over in thirty seconds. By the time Dunston had shot his wad, Rae Ann was just getting hot. She kept him going for five more minutes until he had shriveled down to two inches, and when he withdrew, the French tickler was nowhere to be seen.

He reached over to try to retrieve the lost rubber but received a sharp slap on the hand. With some pain and much effort Rae Ann finally extracted the condom – or most of it. Obviously it had not served the purpose for which it had been intended. The evening was over, and a few weeks later it became apparent that life as they had known it was over as well.

Chapter 7

Colonel Harrington survived the surgery, but Max was not pleased with what he had seen. It was clear that the heart disease had progressed farther than Max had diagnosed. With medication, proper rest, a low-fat diet, and a carefully orchestrated rehab program, the Colonel could look forward to a limited but reasonably comfortable retirement. But there were many things that he could not do – certainly not for the foreseeable future and probably never. Max checked on his patient in the recovery room. He was coming out of his anesthesia and clearly was uncomfortable. He advised the family to go home or to their hotels as the Colonel couldn't see anyone until the morning. He would have them notified if there were any change. Before leaving, Max left word that he was to be called immediately at the first sign of any unforeseen developments.

He got to the house just as Johanna and the boys were pulling up in the Pathfinder. They were just back from Brett's Little League game, and Justin was trying to tell him how Brett had done. Justin really didn't understand baseball, but he knew that his older brother, whom he adored, was always the center of attention whether on the pitcher's mound or on the base paths, where his speed and daring drew both the praise and the reprimands of his coach – depending on the outcome. Justin was allowed to sit next to Brett on the bench when the team was at bat, and was always first out to greet his brother when he crossed the plate.

Johanna, whose turn it had been to help work the hot dog stand, had brought back a basket of leftover franks that would serve as dinner saving her from the need to prepare a meal. Max slathered on a glob of mustard and took a huge bite. "You keep serving us these, and we'll all end up like Colonel Harrington."

"How did the surgery go? Is he going to be OK?"

"OK for now, I guess, but I'm concerned about his recovery."

"That bad?"

"Well, he could be OK if he follows his regimen, but good luck on that. I know he has every intention of going back to Point of Fork in the fall. He can't do that if he wants to pull through."

"Have you talked to Louise?"

"I plan to, but I don't hold much hope of her keeping him in check."

"Well, she'll just have to. The Colonel is just like the rest of you men. You think the world's going to come to an end if you're not constantly on guard and ready to step in to solve every crisis. Colonel Harrngton still thinks he's storming the beach at Saipan. How many times have I had to hear that story?"

"Four less than I have. I think he still relives that battle every Veteran's Day parade at PFMA. The last time I thought my feet would freeze off while I stood at attention. By my senior year I practically knew the damned speech by heart."

"You guys just live to be heroes!"

Max looked across the room. Brett was helping Justin to put a puzzle together.

It was designed for a four-year-old, and they had done it a dozen times every evening this week. Justin would scramble the nine pieces, and Brett would carefully guide him, putting the picture of an airplane together to the delight of his brother who would beam with pure joy before scrambling the pieces again. With only two years separating them in age, the boys were obviously different in many respects and yet strangely similar in others. Max and Johanna had always been honest with Brett concerning Justin's limitations. At twelve, Brett could not remember a time without Justin, and over the years he had learned, in a general way, both the immediate and long-term implications of Down syndrome. Almost instinctively Brett had developed the ability to make Justin a central part of his life. Including Justin in many of his activities had enriched Brett's childhood experience in ways far more profound than any burden his brother's impairment might impose. Max was both proud and amazed at the older boy's response to his brother's condition, and there was no doubt that this had gone a long way toward his own acceptance of Justin.

Almost eleven years earlier, when Max and Johanna first spoke of this with Stan Harding, her obstetrician, there had been an initial numbness. Stan and Max were both practicing at Saint Mary's at the time. Max had a gained a general understanding of Down syndrome in medical school and sought the counsel of every friend and colleague in the field – particularly those in pediatric cardiology. He knew from his own practice that Downs was often an issue there. Abortion was not an option at Saint Mary's but could have been arranged at several facilities in the area. Neither Johanna nor Max seriously entertained that alternative. Although Max had been a Catholic all of his life and Johanna had converted shortly before their marriage, the position their church took on this issue was not the ultimate consideration in their decision to carry the baby to term. Initially the couple had regarded the unborn child as an intruder on their "perfect" young family; yet, even then it was Brett, the already precocious toddler, who somehow convinced the young couple of their need to make a place for Justin in their lives. Watching their alert agile child scoot across the floor, they sensed somehow that the four of them were destined to share an experience that would be both daunting and fulfilling beyond anything "normal" families could appreciate.

After putting the children to bed, Max called the hospital to check on the Colonel. There was no change. At least Max was confident that Harrington was in good hands – you could do a lot worse than Henrico General when it came to cardiac care. For the hundredth time he allowed himself to second-guess his judgement concerning the project he was undertaking. Was he making a mistake? A heart specialist could enjoy a comfortable career right where he was without the risk of signing off on a thirty million dollar note. But no, it was already a done deal. Tomorrow he would sign on the dotted line, and at least then he could forget about any second thoughts. Max would be glad to get that behind him.

"How's the Colonel doing?"

"Resting well, Johanna. I've cleared my schedule tomorrow morning, but I'll run by and check on him before our meeting at the bank."

"Why do *I* have to sign the thing?"

"Believe me, you'll find out soon enough if we screw up. With thirty million bucks on the table, they'll have their hands in everyone's pocket."

"That's fine, but they won't find anything but a house mortgage and a stack of bills around here."

"You got that right!"

"Well, I'm glad the Colonel's resting well tonight; that'll make one of you."

As it turned out the meeting at the bank was far simpler and less formal than Max had anticipated. All of the partners and attorneys were on time at ten o'clock, and the whole thing was over in less than fifteen minutes. Walking out Max felt a little uncomfortable. Shouldn't there have been more to it? Some kind of ceremony – a champagne toast? Construction would begin in six weeks. Thirty million bucks!

- - - - - - - - - - - - - - - - -

The meeting earlier with the Colonel had not gone so smoothly. When Max arrived at Cardiac Care, two nurses met him with complaints. The Colonel had been slow coming out of anesthesia, but once fully conscious and more-or-less coherent, he had done everything possible to make their lives miserable and disrupt the workings of the night shift. First he had refused pain medication, but within an hour he dressed them all down for neglecting to administer it. When he rang the nurses' station and they failed to respond to his satisfaction, he loudly accused them of sadism and threatened a lawsuit that he promised would, "turn this house of horrors on its head."

"He's been barking out orders all night. Kindly remind the Colonel that this is a hospital – not his little kingdom up at Point of Fork – and we're not his little soldier boys that he can order around like minions."

"Relax. I'll talk with him."

"Good luck!"

Checking Colonel Harrington's chart, Max was not pleased with his vital signs, particularly his high fever, but decided against changing the medication at this point. When he opened the door, Colonel was awake.

"Morning, Colonel."

"Don't good morning *me*! What did you use while I was out on the table? A chain saw?"

"A trenching tool, actually. Saved it from my days at PFMA."

"I'd appreciate it if you could lay off the references to the academy in recalling your early development. We don't need the adverse publicity when the malpractice suits start piling up. I would have thought we might have instilled a little compassion."

"Let me have a look at your dressing."

"Like the bloodthirsty Amazon that was just in here? No, thanks. She and Lady Macbeth have been having themselves a ball here in their little torture chamber."

"They're just doing their job."

"Yeah, like tearing the damn dressing off like they're shucking an ear of corn!"

"Actually it's less painful than peeling it off slowly."

"Sure – and a hell of a lot more fun!"

"Whatever you say, Colonel. Glad to see you're in such good spirits."

"Call me Brad, Max. I've told you a hundred times."

"Yes sir!"

"That's right – be sarcastic while you have me here at your mercy. When do I get out of here anyway?"

"Too soon to say. I'd like to keep you here for another day or two for observation. Then if all goes well we can move you into a private room."

"How about going home? How long before I can be back at work?"

"You know what we said. We talked about that before."

"You mean what *you* said. I never agreed to retiring."

"Let me put it to you straight, Brad. One way or the other you're going to retire – either voluntarily or in a pine box. You insist on your way, and within a week they'll be calling Bliley's Funeral Home to your office to pick you up. I don't like being so blunt, but it's that simple."

"Simple for you. Look, Max, I'm not playing hero. I'm not out to prove anything or show the world how tough I am. If you've got to know, the idea of retirement has been an appealing prospect for some time, and I plan to get out as soon as I can. But there's some unfinished business – a problem - that I have to attend to personally. Once I get these loose ends tied up, I'll be more than happy to walk away – the sooner the better."

"That's exactly what you *don't* need, Brad. Whatever it is, I'm sure there's someone on the staff, or maybe your successor, who can deal with it."

"No, that's what I'm talking about. I have to deal with this one myself. Nobody else. Whatever happened on my watch I can clean up. I've put my whole life into making Point of Fork what it is; I don't want to be remembered as the guy who ran it into the ground."

"I doubt that's likely. Can you tell me what it's about?"

"I haven't told anybody – not even Louise. You remember Cadet Crawford?"

"Sure, Frank Crawford. You asked me about him the other day. Said something about a lawsuit. Listen, Brad, if that's what you're worrying about, I've got news for you. You're not the only lawyer in the world. The country is crawling with competent shysters – every one of them ready to separate any poor fool from his hard-earned money. Just ask some of my colleagues who are facing nasty divorces or even nastier malpractice suits."

"I wish it were that simple. No, this is personal. I've got to handle this one myself. Get this done and then I'll be off to the old folks' home for bridge and canasta."

"You'll never make it. Besides, what's the saying? 'A lawyer who tries to represent himself has a fool for a client.' What does Crawford want anyway?"

"He lives in Richmond now. He's been seeing a psychiatrist there, some woman named Dunnigan."

"That figures. He should have seen a shrink fifteen or twenty years ago when it might have done him some good. What did the guy tell him – that he's an asshole and has always been an asshole just like his classmates tried to tell him at Point of Fork?"

"You're closer than you think. Crawford's never gotten his life back on track since he was dismissed from PFMA. Fired from jobs, a couple of DUI's, arrested for indecent exposure, two divorces, you name it."

"Why am I not surprised?"

"Well he started seeing this Dunnigan shrink about a year ago, and guess what she says? All of his psychological pathology dates back to his time at PFMA."

"No way – I knew Crawford from the time he got here, and he was already one of the most screwed-up guys in the corps. Always hung around with Captain Reardon and his circle of losers – Williamson and that bunch."

"Well, he'll use that part in court. Seems that this Dunnigan claims to have used hypnosis to uncover all these suppressed memories – long-forgotten homosexual encounters with Reardon and others – supposedly over a period of years right under our noses at Point of Fork. Post-traumatic stress disorder they call it. Now she claims he's revived a full and detailed recollection of everything that supposedly happened. Says he's ready to go public with a twenty million dollar law suit if we don't settle right now for five."

"What do you plan to do?"

"Probably the smartest thing would be to pay the bastard. The school can afford it, and I'm sure the board would prefer to keep the allegations out of the news media."

"No way that would ever happen."

"Of course not, and even if we could keep it quiet, I can't stomach the idea of that toad getting the last laugh on us. No, we lose either way; my instinct is to call his bluff. I'm guessing he'll probably go forward with the suit, but I wonder how far he's willing to go public himself."

"Unless he's changed, he's the type to back down when things get nasty."

"Yeah, but the academy's going to be the loser if he doesn't – no matter who wins in court. Like my old law partner used to say, 'Don't get in a squirting contest with a skunk.'"

"Has Crawford hired anyone?"

"Yeah, Marvin and Cale. They're good, and they don't mind getting down in the mud and flinging it around."

"Plus, what does Crawford have to lose?"

"That's just it. Where he's coming from there's no way to go but up."

"Colonel, get some rest. We'll talk about your recovery schedule in a day or so. I've got a meeting in a half-hour. This afternoon I'll check around discretely and see what I can dig up about Crawford. Maybe I can find something that could help."

"Remember – not a word about the law suit to anyone for God's sake. No one knows."

"Don't worry."

"Right, 'don't worry' – isn't that what you told Coach Weaver when he put you on Brown against Staunton Military? What did he get that night – thirty?"

"You've got a good memory."

Chapter 8

Crawford's case was the type that Marvin and Cale liked – high profile with the chance for a big payoff. The potential for negative publicity provided the type of leverage that promised a high settlement, and if the case went to court the firm would be on the front page for months. Dan Marvin would handle it himself. His client, to be sure, was not the most attractive; but he had worked with slime balls more revolting than Frank Crawford for far less incentive. And then there was the academy itself. He couldn't wait to get Point of Fork in his crosshairs.

Three years earlier Marvin had come out on the short end of an encounter with the academy that had left a bad taste in his mouth and an unhealed bruise on his ego. Despite its refurbished buildings and cutting edge technology, Point of Fork Military Academy was in many ways an anachronism. The curriculum was traditional, the discipline was stern, and the school had somehow seemed to have rebuffed nearly all of the educational reforms of the previous decades. During the late sixties, when military schools were dropping like helicopter pilots in Vietnam, Harrington had resisted the trend to de-emphasize the military tradition of his school. He sensed – providentially as it turned out – that there would always be people seeking the singular qualities that schools of this type had to offer, and he made no attempt to soften or apologize for this dimension of the school's program. Visitors to the campus were often astonished at the sense of quiet and order both on the grounds and in the classrooms, which they interpreted as a picturesque vestige of traditional Southern deportment. But beneath the academy's façade of old Virginia courtliness was an austere military protocol that permeated every facet of life at the academy. Even corporal punishment, which the school had officially banned since the seventies, lurked in the shadows. It remained enough of a real or perceived presence on campus (in the imposing person of Commandant Buck Bristow) to put the fear of God into cadets who would have openly laughed at their high school principals. By no means did this preclude small or even serious escapades of cadet mischief, but the way the system dealt with these misadventures caused any would-be miscreants to think twice before exposing themselves to the consequences that the system had firmly in place. When a cadet crossed the line, the likelihood of his getting caught was high. And when he was caught, little concern was given to the effect of the school's discipline on his self-esteem. Offenders faced an implacable Commandant and an unbending system of penalties.

This is where Dan Marvin's nephew had found himself three years earlier. It had begun as a rather minor infraction – what they call a "category two" on the academy "stick sheet" - normally worth eight or ten demerits. Ed Marvin was in the ninth grade and had been dissecting a frog in Captain Burch's biology class. The students were labeling the organs, and when Jim Murphy left the table next to him to ask Captain Burch a question, Ed took advantage of this opportunity by taking a huge glob of frog eggs with his scalpel and leaving them on his classmate's seat. When Jim returned with his tray and sat down, he immediately realized that he had been had. Jim, who was now pretending to be absorbed in his dissection project, was unable to suppress his laughter and soon became the target of a flying liver. Captain Burch looked up just in time to see Murphy try to push Marvin's head into his own specimen tray, and by the time he got to the back of the room, both cadets were on the floor. Murphy got out of the scuffle with no more than a formaldehyde stain on his tie, but young Marvin's shirt had been torn or cut with a scalpel. Both cadets were placed on report for horseplay.

When Lieutenant Colonel Bristow read the special report, he assessed the standard eight demerits for Cadet Murphy, but because Cadet Marvin had initiated the incident, he assigned him twelve demerits plus the loss of his next weekend leave privileges. This did not sit well with Ed's father, who felt that his son had been unfairly singled out. He also had counted on his son's presence at a family function that weekend. When he called the Commandant, he was politely received but got no satisfaction. He felt – correctly – that Bristow was not interested in discussing the process whereby his son had received his extra penalty tours and loss of leave. That evening Marvin called his brother, the high-powered lawyer, who assured him that he could obtain justice for his nephew and that he would quickly have the situation rectified.

He was mistaken, and this was not to be his last mistake relating to this issue. After getting the famous PFMA runaround the following afternoon, Dan Marvin made his second miscalculation. He called Harrington at home after supper. The Colonel had eaten early that evening and was already well into his second highball. About three minutes into his diatribe, Marvin began to sense that his thundering was not having the desired effect – particularly his suggestion that Cadet Murphy had taken a scalpel to his nephew and in the process had cut his own shirt. Marvin was unaware that Harrington was himself an attorney. The whiskey may have loosened the Colonel's inhibitions somewhat, but he still knew the law and was not intimidated by Marvin's empty threats. When he had heard enough, Harrington interrupted him for the first time. He calmly informed learned counsel that his nephew would be returning home the following day, and that he hoped his next school would be more to his parents' and their legal representative's liking. Completely nonplussed by this sudden riposte, Marvin began to stammer out his own rejoinder before realizing that the line was dead.

The boy's father called the academy the following morning in a panic. He begged to speak with either Harrington or Bristow about the misunderstanding with his brother the evening before. The lady at the switchboard spoke with a gentle Southern accent. The people he wanted were in staff meeting but would be happy to receive his call after ten o'clock. He hung up the phone somewhat relieved, but immediately his phone rang. It was his son calling from the Richmond bus station. At seven that morning young Ed Marvin had been packed up, handed a box breakfast, and taken to Columbia to meet the bus that the James River Line ran from Lynchburg to Richmond every morning. After several frantic phone calls in an effort to get his son reinstated, the father realized that his efforts were futile. He never forgave the academy, nor did he forget his brother, the famous lawyer, who had blown his son's case. The incident created a permanent rift in the family. Dan Marvin wanted another shot at Point of Fork.

- - - - - - - - - - - - - - -

Marvin's experience with the academy's swift justice may have been at odds with American due process, but it was pretty much the norm at Point of Fork. As a cadet,

Max had gotten a taste of reality on April 1 of his senior year when he awoke to a disturbance outside his door shortly after the 6:15 bugle. Posted on the wall he found a long mimeographed sheet bearing an anonymous poem. Sometime during the night several dozen of these sheets had been left on display at strategic points around campus. About thirty cadets were crowding in to read the poem.

The Ballad of the Three Gents

Shelby is a harmless prude; he lives a life of solitude.
Some folks say that he's a fairy; wife or lover? He hath nary.
When his nation went to war, he landed on the thundering shore
Where he learned that war is hell along the 38th Parallel.
Squatting in a hand-dug trench amid the filthy stink and stench,
He saw a hand grenade roll by and come to rest; he thought he'd die,
But like the champions of old, he did not flinch, this warrior bold,
To save his men and do his best, he gave his all to save the rest.
Scrambling from his safe protection, Shelby ran in the direction
Of the bomb, and with his hat he covered it, and there he sat.
Instantly the fully loaded hand grenade went off – exploded
Sending both his balls, I fear, into the upper stratosphere
There they flew for half an hour until by gravitation's power
Landing on the smoking sand of that distant war-torn land.
Now he lisps just like a fairy in his comfortable library.
There he gossips night and day with young cadets so they will say
Who did what, and when, and where the most delectable affair
Is going on. Then he'll embellish all the facts with pride and relish,
Adding touches here and there, and fabricating with a flair.
What a wonder 'tis to see this master of hyperbole!

Then there's Jubal, if you please. Many times we've seen him wheeze
Trudging up the barracks stairs with a plate of fresh eclairs

Taken from the dining hall and piled so high about to fall.

Stacks of cheese from north Wisconsin, brought to him by Louis Johnson,

Meatloaf, cold cuts, pounds of bacon – anything that can be taken.

Major Maytag, as he's known, is wide of girth and large of bone,

Hot of temper, hard to please, rarely gives out A's or B's.

D's and F's are more his style, his body smells just like a pile

Of cow manure left to rot or stagnant urine in a pot.

Odor riper than a scallion, Aqua Velva by the gallon

Cannot hope to mitigate this putrid pile of spite and hate.

Yet be it said now, in conclusion, there should never be confusion,

Major Maytag, for my dollar, is a gentleman and scholar.

Of all the Gents, and there are three, he's the pride of Company D.

Just as Jubal loves his scrapple, Major Reardon lives to grapple.

Not too wide and somewhat short, wrestling's his favorite sport.

No one from afar or nigh loves to grasp a naked thigh

Like this educated scholar; many times he made them holler.

Rarely has an academician done as much as this magician

For the boys he likes so well; just ask Crawford – he could tell

A string of tales on this old teacher, wrestling fan, and Baptist preacher.

On his face are many dimples left by acne, blackheads, pimples,

But his voice is sweet and gay when he's speaking *en Francais*.

Then he's teaching in his class while he's checking out the ass

Of each and every freshman who might entertain his *parlez vous*.

So now you have in one fell swoop these three fine gents, a sterling group

As fine examples no young lad has ever better models had.

So when you've done the best you could, and life is still a pathless wood,

Do not court with beak despair nor gnash your teeth and pull your hair,

Nor turn to liquor, do not fall into the clutch of alcohol,

Or, worst of all, don't fail to heed my warning 'gainst the loco weed,

The prelude to a life misspent. No! Use your brain and pick a gent

And set you sights on his fine life, for that's the way to quell the strife!

As fine examples burning bright, shining through the gloomy night

> Like guiding beacons heaven-sent streaking through the firmament,
> These noble pillars of our nation lead to victory and salvation.
> Nowhere can you learn more sense than from the lives of these Three Gents.

Within minutes tactical officers were deployed around campus tearing the offending lyrics from walls and tree trunks, but the damage had been done. An investigation was launched, and suspicion immediately fell on Max Jarvis, the editor of the *Counterattack*, PFMA's prize-winning literary magazine. No one else had a key to the copy room where the ditto machine was located, no other suspects were identified, and no one was forthcoming with a confession. Because of the scandalous nature of the prank, Colonel Harrington handled the matter personally, calling the culprit into his office. "This so-called 'poem,' Cadet Jarvis is a disgrace to you, to this academy, and to our corps of cadets."

"I didn't write it, sir; like I've said all along, I don't know who did or how they got into the copy room."

"Well, I don't think elves snuck in there and did it, do you?"

"No sir. Like I said, I have no explanation."

"I've looked at your record here, Cadet Jarvis. You've done well."

"I've worked hard since I've been here, sir."

"And I see that you come from a good family."

"Yes sir."

"This is very reprehensible, young man, not worthy of you or the family you represent. I'll review this further and send my recommendation to the Commandant. You may report out."

"Cadet Jarvis reporting out, sir."

After Max reported out, Harrington had Mrs. Stickley run off twenty copies of the poem to send to selected friends. Max was assessed fifty demerits. It took him three weeks to march them off.

Chapter 9

When Max got home from the bank, it was too early for lunch. Johanna was just getting off the phone with the boys' school. "How was the meeting?"

"Short, nothing to it, really."

"Nothing but thirty million dollars. That was the school."

"Don't tell me the boys are getting expelled."

"Don't laugh. Brett got sent to the principal this morning for fighting."

"Fighting? Over what?"

"Ms. Banks says some kids had been teasing him about his brother. Brett had just walked Justin to his special class, and a couple of them decided to make a few remarks. One of the boys, the Brooks kid, got a cut lip, and Brett tore a hole in his slacks. She let them all off with a warning; it's so unfair!"

Max looked at his wife. Like her, he had endured the sting of unfeeling remarks directed toward the children, intended or otherwise. "I know it's not fair, but those kids don't know any better; they're children. I hate to admit it, but I might have done the same thing in the seventh grade. We've got to expect some of this, and so does Brett – comes with the territory. I'm proud in a way that Brett's protective of Justin, but when kids are cruel, he's going to have to learn to walk away. I've explained it to him before, and he's just going to have to learn."

"I wonder if it's too late to reconsider and send him to St. Christopher's."

"We've been through all of this before. St. Chris is a great school, and I know a lot of Brett's friends go there, but he wants to be with his brother. Public school won't hurt him; generally, I've been impressed so far. I imagine he'd face pretty much the same teasing at St. Christopher's. I'll talk with Brett tonight."

There were about a half-dozen Point of Fork classmates with whom Max had maintained fairly close contact over the years. That afternoon he got on the phone and managed to reach four of them. Without going into details, he asked them what they remembered about Crawford and the crowd that hung around with Captain Reardon. They all remembered pretty much the same thing. Reardon, they recalled, had always been considered strange by most of the corps, and the label of "queer" had been applied with some frequency over the years. There was considerable circumstantial evidence, but in all the years he had been at PFMA, nothing even approaching proof had ever come up. There was his bachelor status – always a red flag at boys' schools – but then there had plenty of bachelors over the years – including one or two that had to be quietly whisked away in the night when their behavior aroused suspicions (or more) on campus. All four alumni recalled Captain Antonelli, the math instructor who didn't return after Christmas Leave of his first year at the academy. Supposedly the parents of an unnamed cadet had threatened to sue the school after their son, his advisee, had reported Antonelli's giving him an open-mouth kiss during an advisee conference before leaving for vacation. An assembly had been called on the day cadets returned to school, and Colonel Harrington explained the "unfortunate incident" as a cultural misunderstanding based on the kissing practices in Antonelli's family who were first-generation immigrants. The practice, Harrington asserted weakly, was "common within the cultures of many Mediterranean countries."

But nothing beyond innuendo had ever stuck to Reardon. There was his somewhat effeminate demeanor, his peculiar interest in wrestling, and most disturbing, the persistent rumors that Reardon, an aficionado of muscle magazines and a photographer of the Polaroid persuasion, had approached a number of well-built cadets over the years to pose for him in bathing suits. Harrington had once approached Reardon and questioned him on this issue, but went away convinced that the veteran instructor was guilty of nothing worse than being a harmless eccentric. Reardon assured him that nothing untoward had ever taken place and that his interest in those cadets was purely aesthetic. The Colonel strongly advised however that, "for the sake of appearance," he find his photographic subjects off campus – as far away as possible – and so far as Harrington knew, that had been the end of it.

In retrospect, Max's former classmates were generally of the opinion that Reardon was probably a closet homosexual who satisfied his longings vicariously through magazines, wrestling, or whatever.

"Maybe the poor guy slipped into Richmond after dinner for the midnight show at the Lee Art Theater," suggested one alumnus. "We don't know what he did in his off hours, but if he had been hitting on cadets, something would have turned up over forty years. The guy's a weirdo – we always knew that - but I think he's clean."

"Yeah, I agree. I think the guy was just odd."

The most concerned was Tom Hatch, now an orthodontist in Knoxville, who had recently been appointed to the PFMA board of directors. Tom had been considered a "lady-killer" during his school days with his rugged good looks and his boyish grin. But the dark, wavy locks that had begun their inexorable retreat during his senior year at the academy had now receded to the point that he had long forsaken all methods of parting his hair to hide the expanding devastation. For years his dome had been totally bereft of its last strand. "The last thing the school needs is a sex scandal, for Chrissake. It really doesn't matter whether it's true or not; if anything comes out in the public, we look bad."

"You've got a point there, but I really doubt that he ever did anything overt."

"Probably not, but there were stories. If you really want to follow up on this, you ought to call Crawford's roommate."

"Carbonell? I know everybody's coming out of the closet these days, but don't tell me *he's* gay!"

"No, not him. But I remember he said something that sounded disturbing to me the last time I saw him."

"When? I thought he went back to Venezuela for good right after he finished at Georgetown."

"That's right," Tom recalled, "and I wouldn't want to leave Venezuela either if I had his connections. He's been making millions in the beef export business ever since and has never been back. I looked him up two years ago when Alice and I took our second honeymoon in Margarita. We were in Caracas for one night, and he met us for dinner."

"What did he say?"

"Nothing that specific; I mean our wives were there."

"Did Luis marry that girl from D.C.?"

"No way! He ended up with one of those Venezuelan beauty queens."

"What are you talking about?"

"Beauty queens. It's like a national obsession down there. The whole country is into turning out winners for Miss Universe and Miss World or whatever."

"You're shitting me!"

"No way! They start them when they're little girls and train the most promising prospects for the international contests. It's all highly organized there – and big business. It's like their national identity is all wrapped up in cosmetics, aerobics, and silicone."

"So what does Mrs. Carbonell look like?"

"Let me put it this way. Imagine a body like Coach Brady's wife with a face to match. And she can't be over twenty-five."

"When's the next plane to Venezuela? I'm calling my travel agent. No – seriously – you say Luis thought there might be something to Crawford's story?"

"Not exactly, but I could tell he was uncomfortable about the subject when we were going over old times and Reardon's name came up."

"I'll give him a call."

Before dinner that night Max went by the hospital to check on Colonel Harrington. He was asleep, so Max decided to let him rest. The nurse at the station said he had been doing better and that his fever was now down to normal. When he arrived at home and saw the driveway empty, Max remembered that Brett had a ball game. In less than five minutes he was at the ball field and had found a parking spot near Johanna's station wagon. Walking to the bleachers, he could see Brett out on the mound. The team was ahead 6-0, and there was a man on first. Brett's pitch was hit on the ground to the shortstop who stepped on the bag for the force at second to retire the side. That turned out to be the only pitch Max would see his son throw that day. Todd Farinholt, a hefty towheaded youngster with good control but nothing on the ball, was brought in for the final two innings, and Brett was moved to third base, where he fielded a routine grounder and threw it to first for the final out of the game. Johanna drove the boys home, and Max stopped by the Peking duck for a take-out order.

After finishing his homework, Brett watched *SpongeBob* with his brother before bed. He would have preferred ESPN, but this was Justin's favorite cartoon show and thus a sacrifice that had to be made. As devoted as he was to Justin, Brett occasionally wished he could have had a normal brother who could do more of the things that he liked to do. Then he would hate himself for even entertaining such thoughts. Before he fell asleep, there was a soft knock at his door. His dad came into the darkened room and took a seat at the corner of the bed. "Sorry I missed most of the game today; I had some things to take care of."

"I pitched a shutout 'till they put Todd in."

"I know. I saw your last out. How did you do at the plate?"

"Two singles. Scored both times. I think I could play better if they left me in as pitcher instead of moving me around."

"I doubt it makes a lot of difference with your hitting. Besides, they have to let everyone play – those are the rules."

"I could pitch every two or three games for the whole game and play third the rest of the time."

"I doubt Coach McGinnis would go for that, and I don't blame him. He needs you in there as often as the rules allow. Speaking of rules, Brett, I understand there was a problem at school today."

"Kenny Brooks called Justin a halfwit at recess. I told him to shut up, and he said, 'make me.' So I did."

"Now remember, Brett, we've talked about this before. You are going to hear things you don't like about your brother. Sometimes people don't mean them or don't understand, but even when they do, you just have to take it. Don't say anything; don't *do* anything - ever."

"It ain't easy to just stand there and keep your mouth shut."

"I know. I never said it was. But you've got to understand, Brett; your brother is special, and we've been blessed in a special way. Lots of people don't understand that, and some never will, so there's no use trying to explain. But we know. And as long as you and your mom and I understand that, nothing anyone else thinks or says matters."

"Should I tell Ms. Banks?"

"I wouldn't. What would it accomplish? Would it change what Kenny Brooks thinks or says?"

"But it's so unfair! Justin never hurt anyone in his life; who's going to take up for him if I don't?"

"It may not seem fair, but that's the way it's going to be. I won't have it any other way. The next time I hear of you fighting at school, you're going to wish Kenny Brooks was all you had to contend with." Brett silently met his father's eyes.

"Dad?"

"Yeah, son."

"Is Justin ever going to do things like a normal boy?"

"Some things, but not everything. And he'll pick them up more slowly. Justin will never play Little League like you do, but you can teach him about baseball. I've seen you two roll the ball back and forth already. I'll go by Disco Sports this week and get a glove for him like yours; he'll like that."

"But he can never really play in games like I do."

"Actually he can. They have these Special Olympics for children like Justin. He's just about old enough to participate. Maybe you and I can start him out here at home and sort of be his coaches – train him for the hundred meters and the softball throw."

"Let's start tomorrow after supper!"

"OK. I'll pick up the glove after work." As Max shifted his weight to get up and leave the room, he felt a small hand at his elbow. Brett always delighted in sharing these few special moments after bedtime with his dad and wanted to savor them as long as possible. When Brett began to breathe deeply and regularly, Max eased himself off the bed and walked softly to the door."

"Night, Dad," came a soft voice.

"Goodnight, son."

Chapter 10

Abortions were not legal in 1971; Roe vs. Wade was still two years away. Although Jack Ralston was opposed to the procedure in principle – and had said as much in his disastrous run for local office - he had tacitly made it clear to his daughter that he would provide the means for her to end the unfortunate pregnancy. All she had to do was give the word. Rae Ann was not showing yet, but almost surely would be by the time of any wedding - even in early summer. After meeting Dunston for the first time, Ralston's concerns were not allayed. He could see nothing of promise in the ungainly young man with the stork-like features and the nasal voice. He told his daughter of his concern that one evening's indiscretion could forever relegate her to a life of mediocrity and unhappiness. His wife was more blunt. "Where did she find this sap?" she asked her husband. "Ted Henning is finishing law school, and I understand he's going in with Battle & Associates. This Brady character looks like some sort of pathetic simpleton or a refugee from Auschwitz, and the way he creeps around reminds me of some kind of pervert."

"He doesn't make much of an impression. Maybe there's more to him than meets the eye."

"I certainly hope so. His fawning and sniveling give me the creeps. And that whining voice of his! Can you imagine the figure he'd make at the Country Club?"

"Not really. Honestly, I hate to even think of it." But less than two months later, there Brady was as the man of the day. Just inside the grand portico he stood stiffly receiving guests to his wedding reception. In his rented cut-away, he looked for all the world like Ichabod Crane in Disney's *Legend of Sleepy Hollow*. The wedding had been a tasteful one – just a mile away at St. Stephen's Episcopal Church.

Surprisingly, even at this late date in her pregnancy, the bride's splendid figure did not betray her. Not even the trace of a bulge was evident as her father walked her down the aisle in her satin wedding dress. The bride's side of the sanctuary was filled to overflowing with Richmond's most prominent families. Half of Windsor Farms seemed to have turned out. Across the aisle the Bradys made every effort to fit in. Their modest contingent from North Carolina was well scrubbed and dressed in their Sunday best. The one uncle, who had shown up proudly donning his new NASCAR jacket, was discretely directed to a seat in a remote corner. The evening before, at the rehearsal dinner, there had been one awkward moment. Rae Ann's cousin, who had made one too many trips to the bar, in an unguarded moment let slip an unfortunate comment about the Beverly Hillbillies coming to town. But only one of the visitors from Spencer responded to the insult, and apologies quickly laid the unpleasantness to rest. Most of the Bradys were strict teetotalers and simply chalked the remark up as but another example of the degrading effects of strong drink.

It was actually Jack Ralston who landed his son-in-law the job at Point of Fork. Dunston had interviewed for several P.E. openings in both of the Carolinas, but nothing had materialized. Point of Fork was then near its lowest ebb. Although Colonel Silas Freemont was still the official president of the academy, he was nearing eighty and in fact had never taken more than a passing interest in the school. Like his father, who had preceded him at the post, Freemont came to Point of Fork after retiring as pastor of Brook Road Baptist Church in Richmond. In recent years it had been his custom to leave the academy for Boca Raton, Florida on the weekend after the Thanksgiving Day football game with Staunton Military Academy. The Florida trip, ostensibly for fundraising purposes, lasted through Spring Leave, whereupon he would return just in time for the parade season.

It was at the Mother's Day Parade that Rae Ann's father had paved the way for Dunston's employment at PFMA. Representing Philip Morris, who had contributed a generous donation toward restoring the Memorial Cannon, Jack Ralston was at the podium taking the review of the corps as an honored guest. Later at the reception Colonel Freemont happened to mention the need to fill an opening in physical education the following fall – preferably with someone who could be an assistant in either the track or soccer program. By fortuitous coincidence there was also an opening for a school nurse. The rest was history. The Bradys arrived with their infant daughter Caroline that August taking up residence in #6 Faculty Row, a diminutive two-story Tudor style townhouse with two bedrooms, a small living room, a kitchen, and a tiny living room. Each townhouse contained two adjoining living units. These modest dwellings housed the youngest faculty families, and served as a considerable inducement to marriage for bachelors, most of whom were obliged to live in the barracks. By this time it was becoming evident that Rae Ann would deliver a new little Brady in the fall.

Rick Wagner, then an assistant football coach and math instructor, was the first to meet the newly-arrived couple. Rick had played offensive guard at PFMA under the current head coach and athletic director, Mutt Billingsley, before going on to star at

Eastern Kentucky. After only four years as a high school coach, Wagner had risen to head coach at Science Hill High School in Johnson City, Tennessee, where his team had pulled off one of the most stunning upsets in the history of football in the Volunteer State with a 31-21 victory over perennial powerhouse Dobyns-Bennet of Kingsport. His return to PFMA the next season was with the understanding that he would replace his former mentor upon his retirement two years hence. This opportunity represented the fulfillment of a dream Rick had harbored since the day he taken his diploma ten years before.

Rick and his wife Kate, who lived at # 3, helped the Bradys move into their new home. That evening they brought over a six-pack of Coors, and Rick regaled the new couple on the ins and outs of life at PFMA. Rick was consummately gregarious by nature, and having been both a cadet and more recently a faculty officer, he could recount the history of the academy about as well as anyone. Perhaps the most famous tale was the fiasco that had occurred two nights before the 1965 Thanksgiving Day feast that traditionally followed the Staunton game. By tradition the visiting football team, as well their corps and faculty, were the guests of the host school for Thanksgiving dinner, and over the years a competition had developed between the two food services that rivaled the game itself in intensity. By early November cadets and faculty began to notice a sharp decline in both the quality and quantity of the meals as Stu Bonesteel, the Mess Sergeant, began to hoard funds and provisions for the gala event. Vienna sausages, fish sticks, and mystery meat began to show up frequently as entrees for dinner while toast and hardboiled eggs became the standard fare for breakfast.

Over the years Sergeant Bonesteel had made contacts whereby he was informed whenever an Army refrigerator truck had broken down on the highway or a railroad car transporting food had derailed. Often he would hop into an academy truck and drive as far as Philadelphia or even Cincinnati for a load of frozen cod (with the heads still attached) or sixty cases of hot dogs. Cadets seeking a clandestine smoking place, claimed to have found crates of the stuff stored for months in the underground tunnels that crisscrossed the campus to provide a conveyance for the academy's water and electricity. Once Bonesteel had pulled into the academy at four in the morning with a particularly fragrant cargo, and the school enjoyed sheepshanks three times a week for a month. But the Thanksgiving debacle of '65, as it came to be called, was in a class by itself. Sergeant Bonesteel had acquired forty live turkey chicks at the beginning of the school session, which he kept in a large pen behind the mess hall. The whole lot had cost him less than twenty dollars, and the cost of feeding them was negligible. This allowed him to splurge on jumbo shrimp, caviar, and other *hors d'oevres* and garnishes for the traditional Thanksgiving meal. He had enlisted a dozen enthusiastic cadets with farm experience to help with the slaughter before dawn on Thanksgiving morning.

As the day approached and Bonesteel warmed up to the occasion, he began the practice of bringing a pair of turkeys into the mess hall every day and placing them in a small cage in a corner of the dining room. These cages were surrounded by corn stalks, pumpkins, and other seasonal decorations; and to make the theme complete, a double-bladed axe was ominously suspended with bailing twine two feet above the cage. Several staff members and their wives objected to the noise and odor, but the mess sergeant was having none of it; besides, the cadets were getting a kick out of feeding pieces of cornbread and other table scraps to the doomed fowl in order to fatten them up for Thanksgiving. One of the most offended was Mrs. Bonita Le Few, the wife of Major Allan Le Few, chairman of the History Department. Although the Le Fews had been at Point of Fork for almost twenty years, they had never really assimilated into the academy community. Both were from aristocratic Williamsburg families and had been married in Bruton Parish Episcopal Church, where they still attended services at least twice a month. Mass at St. John of the Cross was out of the question, and the local Baptists might as well have been snake handlers to the cultivated Le Fews. Bonita, in particular, felt alienated and stifled by a lack of social and cultural refinement at the academy, which she attempted to address by organizing the Fine Arts Club for faculty wives.

On the Tuesday evening before Thanksgiving, the Le Fews were enduring a dinner of corned beef hash at the corner table most remote from the turkeys. No one saw how the first bird got out of the cage – maybe Boesteel had carelessly forgotten to latch the door. But in the melee that followed, the tom exerted a great flutter of wings in an ungainly attempt to flee to the rafters. The commotion and effort lifted the giant bird only four feet – enough to dislodge the axe and send it falling with fatal accuracy just at the tom's mate stuck her neck out to exit the cage. Seeing the bloody carnage that immediately ensued, the terrified tom ran and flapped across tabletops throwing up plates and huge masses of hash with his powerful wings and legs. The hen, her head completely severed, ran blindly around the large room spurting up dark geysers of blood and bumping into tables as the panicked diners made their frantic ways toward the doors. But the Le Fews were trapped in the most remote corner; the only route of escape was to charge directly through the confusion of overturned chairs and tables, blood, and corned beef hash. Showing more courage than common sense, Major Le Few led the way for his wife, who followed as best she could in her high heels on the slippery floor. The tom, taking to the air again with his last rush of adrenaline, managed only eight feet and landed with a giant flutter of wings on top of Bonita Le Few's head. As the bird struggled frantically to disengage its talons, it tore out huge tangles of snarled hair. Blinded by the flapping wings, Bonita slipped on a pile of corned beef hash and landed in a large pool of turkey blood. Her husband, who had raced several strides ahead, returned with a chair, and in a riot of blood, feathers, and hash, managed to bludgeon the panicked bird to death.

The Le Fews threatened a lawsuit against both the academy and Sergeant Bonesteel, who was placed on administrative probation by Colonel Freemont. It took a full day for the grounds crew to restore the mess hall to some semblance of order. Esau and Folley, who presided over the operation from a distance, gawk in wonderment at the chaotic scene. "Look like th'Devil had a fit in heah," whispered the former; the later just shook his head and chuckled, unable to conceal his smile.

Two days later the Thanksgiving feast went on as scheduled following a 28-7 drubbing of Staunton. Despite the fracas two days before, many in attendance said it was the best feast ever. The Le Fews were not in attendance, nor did they grace the mess hall for the remainder of the school term. With her nearly shaven head, Bonita would not face the stares and snickers of the faculty families, many of whom regarded the Le Fews as elitist snobs.

- - - - - - - - - - - - - - - - - - - -

At the conclusion of his epic, Rick noticed that the last beer was gone and offered to make a quick trip to Kroger's before it closed and pick up another six-pack. Dunston, who had drunk only papaya juice, offered to drive him to the store. "Your husband is very quiet," observed Kate after the men had left.

"It's not you," Rae Ann responded. "He doesn't make friends quickly."

"Doesn't drink, either, does he?"

"Not really. Dunston's sort of a health freak, to tell you the truth. He runs eighty miles a week, and he's very particular about what he consumes. At our wedding reception he forced down two stems of champagne, and I thought we might not make it to the airport.

"Well, he seems nice. I hope he likes it here at the academy. Most of the people are really friendly; it's like a family – especially for the young couples."

"Well, socializing is not really Dunston's strong suit, but I'm sure we'll get along fine. What do people here do for social life, anyway?"

"Nothing very elaborate; I can tell you that. There's not a lot here, as you can see, and not many of us could afford to live as high rollers anyway. Most of us young couples and families get together on weekends, and there are always ball games and such here at school."

"Dunston is going to be on the track staff."

"The track team's really good. We all make a trip every spring to the state meet;

it's a real event. Donnie Lawson's been the head track coach forever; your husband will really like him."

"I hope so."

"I think you'll like Margaret Layton, the head nurse."

"I already met her. She seems very professional. My only concern is having to stay on call in the infirmary two nights a week, but it beats working the night shift at UVA."

"Plus I think you only have to stay there if someone's admitted for overnight. I don't think it's that often."

"That's what they told me. Other than flu season, it shouldn't be too bad."

"In the summer most of us cook out on the lawn behind the row. Bring your own burgers or whatever, and everyone brings along a side dish to share."

"Sounds like fun."

The men returned with the beer, only three of which were consumed before calling it an evening. Moving had taken a lot out of the Bradys – especially Dunston.

At six the next evening the Bradys joined eight other couples out on the Faculty Row lawn for the nightly cookout. Two grills were being fired up as the couple was introduced to their neighbors. The Bradys set up a play pen next to several others in the shade. Earlier three plastic kiddy pools had been tossed out on the lawn and filled, and eight toddlers were already racing from one to the other creating their best splashes. One sturdy lad of perhaps eighteen months sported a sagging diaper swollen to three times its normal size, and three of the youngest kids were totally naked. Several of the men and two of the wives went to one end of the lawn where a volleyball net had been set up, and played while the burgers and hot dogs were being grilled. After dinner most of the couples sat out in lawn chairs and had a beer or two while the children wound down. Although Dunston maintained his usual reserve and nursed his papaya juice, Rae Ann had four beers and was a bit wobbly as her husband helped her into the house. Her enchanting totter was not lost on the men as she faded into the twilight.

Chapter 11

On the morning of Colonel Harrington's release from Henrico General, Max stopped by for a final visit. The Colonel had made a remarkable recovery considering his slow start, and Max had agreed that after a couple of weeks he could return to his office but only for an hour or so at first. "Only routine stuff – Lieutenant Colonel Frazier can handle any emergencies. Let him and Mrs. Stickley take care of whatever strenuous tasks come up."

"You're trying to make me into a figurehead."

"That's the deal, remember? You can finish out the year and preside over graduation. They'll need you this summer to help with the transition – let Frazier take care of as much of that as possible. Then the new guy – whoever they get - takes over in September."

"I want to talk to you about that."

"No, we've already talked about it, and I'm holding you to our agreement. Otherwise I call Louise right now, and you're in here for another month."

"There's one piece of unfinished business - - "

"You mean that stuff with Crawford. Like I said before, let the new guy wrestle with that. You don't need to be dealing with him and his allegations while you're recovering. If you'll listen to me and do as I tell you, you might be around to see your grandson graduate from the academy. Otherwise you won't make it to Christmas."

"What about the other part – what I talked with you about yesterday?"

"I don't know, Colonel. I'm up to my neck with the hospital project. I just don't know if I can justify taking on another obligation."

"Board of directors? *What* obligation? You come to the academy twice a year, meet for a couple of hours in the morning, sit down to a big feed at lunchtime, and go home. Big obligation!"

"I'm sure there will be board meetings this summer to find a new president."

"No, not more than one – two at the most. I'll be appointing a search committee that will start the process. Of course, this will be short notice, but at least the time of year is in our favor. How about it? Have we got an agreement?"

"Why do you want me on the board anyway? I figure that over the years you've already got the thing packed with all of your old cronies anyway. What do you need with another rubber stamp?"

"I like the way you put that; you always had a way with words."

"OK, but you know what I mean. I assume they're going to pretty much go along with your choice – or a least the kind of guy you want."

"I wish, but it's not like you think. The academy by-laws require that the Baptist General Association appoints a third of the board – basically all clergymen. Then at least a fourth of them have to come from the armed services. There are quotas for alumni, patrons, the founding family - everything under the sun. Get the picture?"

"Sure, but except for the Baptists and the Page family, you still have pretty broad latitude in terms of appointments."

"Some, but not as much as you think. There's always politics. We're even starting to get pressure for more minorities and women on the board?"

"At Point of Fork? I never thought I'd see the day. Times, they *are* a-changing!"

"Save the sixties rhetoric for your generation. The point is that I need every friendly face I can get on the board until the new guy is chosen. The Baptists will be pushing for a preacher like my predecessors. I made them pretty mad when I started dances at the academy, and a few of them are still sore at me for letting the blacks in."

"You're kidding - that was decades ago. Before I even got there. Most of those people are long gone by now, and attitudes have changed a lot since then."

"Some have, but you'd be surprised. Point of Fork is still an old fashioned place in a lot of ways."

"Right, and in a lot of ways that's good – although I probably wouldn't have admitted that when I was a cadet."

"I'm sure you wouldn't have. There's also a bunch that will push for someone with a military background."

"Do you think we could survive another Harrington?"

"You've still got a smart mouth. No, actually I'd like to see an academician or possibly someone from the business world as the next president of the academy. No retired officer, no lawyer, and definitely no preacher."

"You got any names?"

"Yeah, a few. And I'm all for the committee going out and finding more candidates. I just don't want the school turned into one of those Bible-thumping religious academies like we see popping up all over creation. The religious program's an important dimension of the school, but it's never been our driving focus."

"And I always thought you were a good, solid, born again Baptist!"

"Don't laugh. I've always valued the academy's church affiliation, no matter what some of them think. If you check, you'll see that I've maintained and even expanded the chapel services and religious program during my tenure. Don't forget - I'm still a deacon at Point of Fork Baptist. I just don't want to hand the school over to a bunch of Holy Roller fanatics. And believe me, that's just what some of them are licking their chops to do as soon as I'm out of the picture."

"Why do you say that?"

"Believe me, I know. I hear from them almost every day. You would have thought last year's book fair was a symposium on blasphemy and pornography to hear some of them tell it. I even saved one letter claiming I was in league with Ol' Scratch himself for poisoning the minds of our youth."

"What were you selling, *Hustler* magazine?"

"No, they were all citing the usual suspects – Joyce, Salinger, Richard Wright - anything they could lift a few cuss words out of or a salacious line or two. I tell you, some of those people are sick. One guy nearly had a hemorrhage over a mythology book we had on sale. Oh, and you'll love this; I have been challenged at least a dozen times for allowing Sunday Mass on campus for the Catholics."

"You sure didn't have them when I was there."

"No, but we should have. Anyway, you get the picture. There are plenty of people and church groups out there who would jump on any opportunity to push their own agendas. I'm certainly not opposed to change – I instituted plenty of changes of my own, and we are probably overdue for some fresh ideas, but I don't want to see the academy transformed to something totally alien to its tradition."

"OK, you've made your point. Here's the deal. You stick to my rehab schedule and follow my guidelines, and I'll fill the vacancy on the board."

"It still has to be approved; I can do that by mail. I'll let you know when it's official."

Chapter 12

Unit #5 on Faculty Row was occupied by Vernon and Lynda Philpott, a young couple who had been at Point of Fork for a year when the Bradys arrived. Lynda was of dark complexion and was decidedly unremarkable in appearance other than a demeanor vaguely evoking a residual hint of her days as a flower child at Richmond Professional Institute - now Virginia Commonwealth University. Vernon was a trim 5'7" in height with a bright red head of hair that featured a cocky cowlick in the front. The son of a Trenton, New Jersey ophthalmologist, he had met his wife while a student at RPI. They rarely socialized with the other young couples on the Row, but Vernon had been among those present when Rae Ann made her rather stunning if ungainly departure on the evening after the cookout. A Chemistry instructor, he had been returning that night from his classroom where he had been making an inventory of lab supplies for the coming year. As he approached two colleagues who were folding up lawn chairs, his attention was arrested by the shapely silhouette disappearing into the lighted doorway. "Who's the new couple?"

"The Bradys – Dunston and Rae Ann."

"He must be the new P.E. guy."

"That's right, and she's a nurse. She'll be working in the infirmary."

"The cadets get one look at that strut of hers, and we'll have an epidemic on our hands."

Philpott had a good eye for nubile young women. In addition to his work at the academy both he and Lynda were photographers and ran a small business doing weddings, family portraits, and the like. Vernon was also a regular at academy sporting events where he photographed action shots to sell to the players a few days after the contest. He had quickly learned that his most reliable income did not come from the stars whose scampers into the end zone appeared regularly in the local papers, but from the role players and reserves. He actually became something of an expert at catching the nuances of interior line play, and when a seldom-used reserve was sent in, Philpott's zoom lens was trained on his number for the precious play or two that would guarantee an easy twenty-five bucks.

Less financially remunerative but far more interesting professionally were Vernon's efforts in Charlottesville, where he would haunt "The Corner," about three blocks of various stores, shops, and restaurants, which cater mostly to students from the University of Virginia. There he approached attractive coeds for whom he offered to do "portfolios" at his own expense proposing to sell them to magazines and modeling agencies for a percentage of the profit. There was never any profit, and he had few takers, only two in the last year. But the occasional sessions were gratifying enough to offset the effort and a few embarrassing put-downs. Vernon would take a series of shots in evening dresses or swimsuits and return them to the girls for approval before suggesting the potential to earn "real money" by doing a series of nude or semi-nude shots.

Recently Cherie Winston, a tall brunette sophomore from Chicago, had agreed to a series of "art" photos. Vernon booked a room at the Cavalier Inn, which he had refurbished in the décor of a cheap New Orleans whorehouse. Cherie was immediately suspicious but proceeded reluctantly after Vernon's repeated assurances that the session was to be strictly professional. The bulge she noted in his pants warned otherwise, and she became increasingly wary as his manipulations of her poses became more intimate. Finally, after several dozen shots, Philpott abandoned all pretenses of professionalism, backing her up to the headboard as he threw his belt off. The terrified coed grabbed a satin sheet and made for the door, but Vernon, a black belt in *Tae Kwon Do*, was nimble and blocked her exit. He apologized profusely until she became somewhat quieter, whereupon he mildly chided her naïveté regarding the "standard arrangements" for sessions of this nature.

Rae Ann Brady first met Lynda Philpott during the second week of school at the Fine Arts Club meeting. Bonita Le Few had invited Sylvia Rentz, a local poet, as the guest speaker. Several of Ms. Rentz's poems had been published in *Virginia Cavalcade* and *The Dominion Quarterly* as well as two slim volumes she had published through Vantage Press at her own expense. Ms. Rentz chose to read from her latest book, *Exotic, Erotic!* Although the sensuality of her themes was sufficiently shrouded in esoteric symbolism, the subject matter was still too *avant-garde* for the tastes of the twenty-six faculty wives who had convened in the parlor of Heritage Hall. Several shifted uneasily in their chairs, most applauded politely even if not enthusiastically, but Rae Ann was simply bored. She panned around the room restlessly looking for some clue in the faces of these unfamiliar women until her eyes met the steady gaze of Lynda Philpott. Lynda's smile was almost a leer, and to Rae Ann's astonishment her right hand appeared to be palpating her right breast. Rae Ann immediately turned her attention to the reader, but her curiosity getting the better of her, she glanced back furtively several times only to meet the same direct stare. Each time Lynda smiled broadly still cupping her breast in her hand causing Rae Ann to blush uncontrollably and to resist the urge to look across the room in her direction again.

Adding to Rae Ann's discomfiture was the fact that she had previously accepted her next-door neighbor's invitation to walk back across campus to the Row with her. Rae Ann could think of no plausible excuse to renege at this point without further embarrassment, so she found herself alone with Lynda as they made their way home. Crossing the darkened football field, they turned silently toward the townhouses. "Does your husband coach?" Lynda asked.

"Yes, he'll be working with track and cross country. He was a runner in college."

"I'm not surprised. He looks like a runner – so tall and lean. Vernon never played sports in school, but he stays in shape with karate. He just got his license as an instructor and is starting a karate club here this year. Vernon always likes to stay fit."

"I guess everyone here is involved in sports or clubs at school. There's not much else to do here in Cumberland County. Colonel Harrington has asked Dunston if I'd be interested in sponsoring some sort of dance committee or club for the cadets."

"You'd better take it – I can promise you there's no social life around this town."

"Do the folks here party or anything?"

"Oh, I suppose the ones who have been around here for centuries get together, but Vernon and I don't really fit in with their clique. You've seen the people tonight at the Fine Farts Club, as I call it. They're definitely not our type."

"How about Charlottesville or Richmond? Do you and your husband go into town for shows or concerts or whatever?"

"Let me put it this way. Vernon and I have an open marriage – always have. We both have our own friends we have met around the University or at the Quest Book Store downtown. We're very discreet. Sometimes we go into town together depending on the arrangements we have made." Rae Ann was becoming nervous again, and they were still a hundred yards from the Row. She looked and saw that Lynda was again massaging her right breast. "Vernon and I know several open-minded couples whom we meet with regularly. We'll do a threesome, whatever. But obviously Point of Fork is very conventional – too inhibited for that."

"Dunston and I are as conventional as they get."

"Hey, that's cool. Neither of us are pushing anything. I know Vernon has told me he likes your looks, though; and I'm game for anything. I thought I'd test the waters just to check – no offense intended."

"None taken," Rae Ann mumbled as she approached steps to her porch. She hurried inside and closed the door."

"How was the meeting?" Dunston called from upstairs."

"OK I guess, not the most exciting. A local poet read from her new book."

"What was it about?"

"I don't remember."

- - - - - - - - - - - - - - - - - -

Vernon removed the glass from the wall separating the two living units. "What did they say?" Lynda asked.

"Nothing interesting."

"Did she mention our conversation tonight?"

"I don't think so. Guess they're not swingers."

Chapter 13

Lieutenant Colonel Ron Frazier had been the Academic Headmaster at Point of Fork for twelve years when Colonel Harrington suffered his heart attack. His informal manner and brawny appearance tended to conceal his scholarly background. He had graduated *summa cum laude* in English literature at Davidson College before earning his doctorate in education at the University of Virginia while serving at the academy. As a practicing Catholic he realized that he had little chance of succeeding the Colonel as president of the academy although he was well qualified for the job. In the past Harrington had made it clear to Frazier that he would support him as a candidate should he choose upon Harrington's retirement to defy the odds and tradition and apply for the position. On the Friday afternoon that Harrington returned to his office, Frazier was retrieving a purchase order from the Colonel's desk as the Colonel came in. "Making yourself right at home, I see."

"Hey, Brad. Yeah, I even leaned back in your chair and threw my feet up on the desk a few times while you were gone. We weren't expecting you back before Monday."

"I just wanted to come in this afternoon and have a look at my mail."

"It's all piled up on Mrs. Stickley's desk. I've taken care of the day-to-day stuff; everything's in place for graduation."

"How about that Crawford business?"

"There's a letter from Marvin and Cale."

"I can't wait. Stick around and we'll have a look." The Colonel went next door and retrieved the letter.

May 19, 1997

Dear Colonel Harrington:

On behalf of my client, Francis M. Crawford, Jr., a warrant is being sworn out against John A. Reardon, formerly of Point of Fork Military Academy, for psychological injuries sustained while a student at Point of Fork Military Academy between the years of 1978-1982. We are also initiating civil action against Point of Fork Military Academy, Commandant Bristow, and you as president of the academy for the resultant psychological damage, loss of income, and other hardships incurred as a result of the impairments sustained by my client while in your care. These can and will be fully documented at the appropriate time.

Both actions will be filed in Cumberland District Court on the date of June 15, 1997. Should you wish to contact me in order to discuss Mr. Crawford's case, I may be reached at the address above. However, I must caution you that while my client may entertain overtures toward reparation, the harm done to Mr. Crawford is both extensive and profound; therefore, the amount of reparation offered must necessarily be substantial in order to even enter into such discussions.

Enclosed are copies of psychological reports relevant to this case that have been filed by Doctor Marion F. Dunnigan,

Sincerely,

Daniel M. Marvin, JD

The enclosed psychological report enumerated Crawford's many difficulties, both personal and professional, since leaving the academy. Dr. Dunnigan's analysis basically concluded that all of these problems were the result of latent psychological injuries stemming from her patient's exposure to the homosexual activities of Major

Reardon and his secret cadet club called "The Brotherhood of the Sword." These experiences, she determined, had caused severe injury to her patient even though the memory of his trauma had been suppressed at the conscious level for many years. It was Dr. Dunnigan's finding, on the basis of extensive (and expensive) psychoanalysis, that her patient would require a comprehensive program of therapy over a long period of time in order to recover any semblance of normal function.

"Ever heard such crap?" the Colonel blurted. "I never knew of any secret clubs on campus, and if there *were* any perverts running around, I would put Frank Crawford as the leader of the pack!"

"I'm sure you're right," Frazier responded shaking his head. "I always knew Reardon was odd by any measure, but we almost surely would have known if anything like this had been going on."

"Well, obviously this is a holdup. They want money."

"Are we going to roll over?"

"Not if I can help it, but I'm still going to talk with them and find out exactly what they're after. Everything else here OK?"

"Just like you left it."

"I'm not sure how to take that. Are you planning to throw your hat in the ring to take on this mess I'm leaving behind?"

"I doubt that I could get the job – wrong religion, you know."

"Frankly, I'm not sure you would want it, but for whatever it's worth, I'm ready to back you all the way if you want to give it a go. I can promise you, though, the Baptists on the board will go ballistic."

"I'll think about it. Maybe we need to go down to the river some bright morning and let Chaplain Findlay give me a good dunking."

"Not a bad idea. With what I've been going through, I could probably use a splash or two myself – just to be safe."

Over the next week Colonel Harrington submitted and received approval by the executive board of the board of directors for Max to complete the vacated term of the late John Matthews. In the same letter he also officially tendered his resignation, due to health reasons. A special meeting to discuss possible candidates and to form a search committee for a new president was scheduled for the following week on the Monday morning after graduation. Harrington called Max to let him know about the meeting.

"It couldn't come at a worse time for me, Colonel. We're taking bids on the equipment for the hospital, I've got patients coming out of my ears at Henrico General, and Justin's got the chicken pox."

"Brad, remember? Call me Brad."

"OK, Brad. I thought you said meetings would only be twice a year."

"Normally that's right, but we need to get on target to install a new president this fall, and time's critical. The meeting shouldn't put you out too much. It's right there in Richmond at the Omni, and I don't expect more than half of the board to show up since the regular meeting was a few weeks ago while I was in the hospital. Mostly local people."

"Couldn't I be among those *in absentia*?"

"Of course you could, but I'd like for you to be there – especially since it will be your first meeting with the board. Just be cordial and stay in the background. I'll make sure you're not put on the search committee."

"Any idea who they want to look at?"

"No, but I suspect a number of them will have ideas of what they want. I'm sure some specific names will come up."

"How about you? Do you have anyone in mind?"

"Ron Frazier, our Headmaster, has applied. He would be my choice."

"I had him for senior English and liked him a lot."

"He's a good man. He's really sharp, and he understands how the academy operates. Plus he's always been totally loyal to the school."

"Maybe there'll be no need for a search committee."

"Don't count on it. Like I've said before, there are plenty of special interests on the board. Plus, don't forget: Frazier's a Catholic."

"Do you really think that will be a problem?"

"You wait!"

"Really?"

"Watch me run for cover after I place his name in nomination. I'll need a flack jacket."

"Speaking of flack, what's the latest on Crawford?"

"He's got a couple of lawyers threatening to sue us out of business."

"From what I hear, he's hardly worked a day in his life. Probably needs the money."

"Well, I hate to say it, but if the school can afford it, I'm inclined to settle with him."

"Don't give in to that toad! You know he's concocted this whole thing."

"Of course he has, but I sure don't want to drag the school through a nasty court fight. I'm meeting with his attorneys next week. It'll make me sick, but if we can come to a reasonable agreement, I'll ask the board to settle."

"Do they know about this?"

"Not yet. I'll tell them in person at the meeting."

"I hope this isn't shaping up into an all-day affair."

"Relax. The rest of them are as busy as you are. We'll be out of there by noon."

"OK, I'll arrange to make it."

"Thanks, Max. I hope Justin feels better soon."

"Me too. With Down syndrome these things are always more serious. There's always the added potential for complications."

"He's in good hands. Give my best to Johanna."

"Will do. See you next week."

Chapter 14

The Colonel could not have been more wrong. Over thirty members of the board showed up for the meeting. Harrington, with somewhat uncharacteristic modesty, had managed to minimize the fanfare surrounding his final graduation exercise insisting that the day should be entirely focused on the graduating cadets. But the trustees were not to be denied on the following Monday morning as one panegyric followed the other citing the academy's growth in prosperity and stature during the Harrington years. A resolution was unanimously passed setting aside a weekend the following fall for a more ceremonious sendoff from the academy. After a perfunctory protest or two, the Colonel suggested several speakers appropriate for the occasion.

In the time since his announced retirement, nearly fifty unsolicited resumes had reached the academy, of which only one was considered viable for serious consideration. After discarding a host of retired military officers who were obviously looking for a comfortable sinecure to supplement their retirement, along with the unemployed Ph.D.s and several preachers who were between congregations, the board decided to interview a Dr. William Marshall, Academic Dean of Episcopal High School in Alexandria, Virginia. Several Baptists on the board expressed grave concern that Dr. Marshall would most likely be himself an Episcopalian. The Reverend John Leatherwood of Tazewell, Virginia protested, "We don't need no Whisky-Palian runnin' this school. Fact is, I think we need to go back to the days before dancin'n whatnot when the Word of God was the way things were ran at Point of Fork." Colonel Harrington shifted in his seat stifling the rejoinder that had nearly escaped his lips.

The only other name bought up before Harrington's nomination of Ron Frazier was Rudolph Dillard, the dean of a small financially beleaguered Baptist college in South Carolina. There seemed to be little enthusiasm for this candidate. Harrington had seen to it that several key board members would speak on behalf of Frazier when his candidacy was announced, and indeed their endorsements were ringing. But the most eloquent testimonial came unexpectedly from Dr. Ray Dalton, pastor of First Baptist Church of Roanoke and a ranking member of the Baptist General Association. As expected, several of the board members had expressed reservations over Frazier's Catholicism. Again the Reverend Leatherwood was the most vehement citing the academy's "loss of direction and mission" since the days when the school was run by Baptist clergymen. "We need a man who will uphold the Christian principles on which the school was founded a hunnert an' fifty yeahs ago. Not some modernistic humanist with a fancy degree who worships statues on Sunday morning."

"I consider myself a Christian," said Dr. Dalton, "and I'm a Baptist clergyman, as you know, but I can't think of a more exemplary Christian than Ron Frazier."

"Depends on what you count as a Christian," Leatherwood responded.

"OK. Let me tell you what I call a Christian. On September 2, 1973 I was sixteen years old, and I had just failed most of my tenth grade classes the year before at Marion High School back in southwest Virginia. My father and I had just unloaded my footlocker, an electric fan, and a few other belongings into room 38 of Ross Hall. It was to be my first time away from home for anything longer than a weekend. My mother was so upset at my leaving home she couldn't bear to make the trip. We stood together for a few minutes outside of Ross Hall while he reminded me again that Point of Fork could be my chance for a new start in hopes of making something out of my life. He told me he had confidence in me and he knew that if I put my mind to it and took advantage of this opportunity, there was nothing I was incapable of doing. We shook hands, and even now I can still see that blue '64 Ford pulling out onto the circle and heading out toward Marion and his job as an electrician in the coal mine. It was the last time I would see my dad alive.

"Dad got as far back as Christiansburg before a truck pulled out in front of him on old Route 11 and drove him off the highway. When I came back to the academy the next week I was behind in all of my classes, I hadn't learned the first thing about the military, and I didn't know a soul. Captain Frazier, who was a second-year teacher and a coach on the JV football team, took it upon himself to help me catch up in his freshman English class, and to find me tutors in the other courses. He even let me 'play' on his football team although I couldn't tackle my little sister. I'm surprised the head coach didn't fire him for actually sending me in for a whole offensive series against Woodberry Forest where my missed block probably caused a fumble leading to our only loss of the season.

"I didn't know it until years later when my mother told me, but there would have been no way for me to return to the academy for my last three years if he hadn't personally found the funding for my tuition – some of which eventually came from his own pocket. He also played a big role in securing an academic scholarship for me at the University of Richmond. Ron Frazier was more than a teacher and a coach for me during my adolescent years. I know that throughout his career at Point of Fork he has left his mark on the lives of hundreds of other young men, but for me he was a father. If I have contributed anything to my fellow man during my church ministry, it was largely through the influence and Christian example of Ron Frazier."

Frazier's nomination was approved for consideration with only two opposing votes.

At the end of the meeting Colonel Harrington brought up the issue of Frank Crawford. Like the Colonel, the board was inclined to contest the issue so long as adverse publicity could be avoided or minimized. Neither Harrington nor the board had the stomach for a nasty public court battle. If a reasonable settlement could be reached, they felt that to be the most prudent course.

- - - - - - - - - - - - - - -

Max didn't get home until 9:30 that evening. He had had to excuse himself from the board meeting after lunch to attend to patients. Then later that afternoon Johanna had called in hysterics because Justin's temperature had suddenly shot back up to 104. He had her bring Justin in to Henrico General and had him admitted. By the time Jack Reese, Justin's pediatrician, arrived, Max had already administered medication and the fever had dropped below 100 degrees, but they decided to keep Justin overnight as a precaution. Meanwhile a disagreement with a medical supplier over a contract for the new hospital had taken so long that Max hardly had time to check his son's progress in the pediatric section.

When he finally got home, there was a message to call Colonel Harrington, but first Max had to deal with Brett, who was upset over leaving his brother at the hospital. Brett had gone to his room to finish a history assignment for the next day. "You OK, son?"

"I'm fine, Dad – just worried about Justin."

"Doctor Reese says he'll be fine. We can probably bring him home tomorrow. Want to meet me tomorrow at the hospital when your mom comes to pick him up?"

"Sure, Dad. Can we go to Chuckie Cheese for supper?"

"We'll have to see how Justin's feeling and make sure he's not contagious anymore. But if you can talk your mom into it, I guess I can stand Chuckie Cheese for a special occasion. For the life of me, though, I'll never understand what you boys see in that place."

"Dad?"

"Yeah, son."

"I get scared when Justin gets sick like this."

"Your mom and I worry too, but we all have to understand that he's going to have these episodes from time to time."

"Is it the Downs?"

"Sure, that has a lot to do with his other health problems. He's always more likely to catch infections, and you remember the operation for his heart when he was little."

"Not really, I guess I was too young, but you told me about the hole in his heart. What did you call it?"

"Atrial ventricular canal defect – but it's really just what you said – a hole in the middle of his heart."

"Is that what Colonel Harrington has?"

"No, he's more like most of my patients. Too many pork chops and Scotches until his arteries are clogged up like an old sewer pipe."

"Is Justin's heart all well now?"

"Absolutely – I assisted in the surgery myself. Closed 'er up tight."

"Then there's nothing to worry about."

"Well, I got to be honest with you, Brett. Justin's always going to have problems. The outside of his heart's weak too. He could develop difficulties with his breathing, plus you know how nearsighted he is. The good thing is that basically Justin's as strong as a horse. He's got a good constitution, and he's always got plenty of doctors who can take care of his problems."

"So he's not going to die, then."

"We all die someday, Brett. And people with Downs generally don't live into their old age. But Justin will probably be a whole lot older than I am now before he goes anywhere."

"Even though Justin's nearsighted, he can catch the baseball when I throw it to him now. I'll show you tomorrow night."

"I know you've been practicing with him, and I think it's great. I'm really proud of you, son. When's the Special Olympics?"

"Next month. Mom says he's going to ride the bus to Charlottesville with the Richmond team, and we'll meet him up there."

"Sounds like fun to me!"

"Then we meet him back here, and we're all going out to eat."

"Not Chuckie Cheese!"

"Anywhere you guys say."

"I'll hold you to that."

By the time Brett was getting ready for bed it was after ten, and Max was hesitant about awakening Colonel Harrington, so he waited until the next morning. The Colonel was just heading out the door for his swim when the phone rang. "Morning, Brad."

"Max? Congratulations!"

"What are you talking about? I haven't won the lottery, have I?"

"Not that I know of, but I have the high honor and distinct privilege of informing you that you were appointed to the presidential search committee yesterday afternoon."

"No way! I'm up to my eyeballs with the new hospital. And don't forget you promised to protect me from things like that."

"How am I supposed to protect you when you don't stick around to defend yourself?"

"I had patients, Colonel, *sick* patients. Some of them are worse off than you were. You told me the meeting was going to be over by noon."

"Well, I was wrong. And I could hardly tell the rest of them that I had promised to keep you off the committee; it would sound like we had a special deal."

"I thought we did!"

"Well, what's done is done. And you can see we need some sanity in the group. Half of them would bring in Jimmy Swaggart if we let them."

"As far as I'm concerned, a Baptist would be the best choice all things being equal. I mean, it *is* a Baptist school."

"No problem there as far as I'm concerned. I just don't want someone coming into Point of Fork and trying to turn it into Liberty University."

"They haven't contacted Jerry Falwell, have they?"

"Not yet, but I wouldn't put it past some of them."

"How about that guy, Leatherwood? He isn't on the committee, is he?"

"He's the chairman."

Chapter 15

Although Colonel Harrington was a lawyer, he had considered calling in the school's attorney in for his meeting with Frank Crawford and his counsel; however, he decided to try a more personal approach in hopes of defusing the situation before it got ugly. He still clung to the unlikely possibility that an appeal to reason, fairness, even school loyalty could lead to an amicable (and relatively painless) settlement. As he sat waiting in his office, he flipped through the 1981 yearbook. Once again he examined the class picture on page 41 and the track team photo on page 88. For the life of him he could not recognize or even recall ever meeting Frank Crawford. The phone rang and Mrs. Stickley announced that Mr. Crawford and Mr. Marvin had arrived. Daniel Marvin was small in stature with dark complexion. His thin gray hair was combed straight back to a point in the back, where it was arranged in a swirl hopelessly designed to conceal advancing baldness. His deeply lined face revealed hollow cheeks beneath high cheekbones. His narrow lips were drawn grimly together forming a tight line. His blue eyes appeared blurred as they stared ahead almost opaquely through thick horn rimmed glasses. In contrast to his client's yellow golf shirt and jeans, Marvin was clad in a charcoal business suit, and despite his wiry build, the lawyer's movements were slow and deliberate almost conveying the aspect of a funeral director. Harrington greeted Marvin and his client at the door.

"Come in, gentlemen. Mr. Marvin, I'm pleased to meet you; please have a seat. And Frank, I'm glad to see you again; it's been too many years since you've paid us a visit. We're always glad to welcome back alumni; I only wish it were under happier circumstances." Colonel Harrington grabbed the limp hand that had been cautiously half-extended. He peered intently into the expressionless face – no recognition at all. "Frank, I've gone over the charges in Mr. Marvin's letter, and I want you to know we take them seriously. You have my assurance that Lieutenant Colonel Bristow and I have already begun to look into these very serious allegations and are committed to taking whatever measures are appropriate to redress any wrongs that may have occurred here at Point of Fork – no matter how long ago. I want to thank you personally for bringing these issues to our attention and solicit any help you can offer toward rectifying any past or current problems here at the academy. Lieutenant Colonel Bristow tells me that - - "

"Colonel Harrington, my client isn't here to reminisce about his days at this academy; it's his recollection of the trauma he sustained here that's responsible for the problems and disabilities he has been going through ever since. I've instructed Mr. Crawford that I will speak for him; in fact, I can't imagine why you insisted on his being here at all. I can tell you that simply being on this campus again has only served to exacerbate the impairments that were inflicted on him here years ago."

"Well, we certainly want to discuss these issues, Mr. Marvin, and for the record, I'm fully disposed to doing anything within reason along those lines. Those who know me will assure you of my thoroughness in these matters, and though I've never had the pleasure - - "

"We've spoken before – over the phone several years ago – in reference to my nephew, Edward Marvin, who was a cadet here briefly. But that's not to the point."

"I'm afraid I don't recall - - "

"I think you'll find there's a great deal you don't recall or chosen to overlook while this school has been under your personal stewardship. I've prepared a copy of the complaint we'll be filing for your perusal. I'll be leaving it with you. If you'd like you can look at it now." Marvin tossed the folder onto Harrington's desk.

The brief was over eight pages long. The Colonel picked up his reading glasses and flipped to the first page, shaking his head as he read. Several times he cleared his throat and looked up either at his accuser or at Marvin, but he said nothing until he had completed the document and returned it to the folder. He laid the folder on the most remote corner of his desk eyeing it as though it contained a vial of anthrax. "I'm at a loss for what to say."

"We're not interested in what you have to say, nor in any belated apologies you might proffer in hopes of withholding from my client the redress that is his due. The damage Mr. Crawford has sustained is severe and totally irreparable. Whatever we can recover in court will be only a token of what he is due. But mark me on this, Harrington: the litigation we'll be initiating next week will certainly result in both the financial and reputational ruin of Point of Fork Military Academy as well as those individuals named in this action." Marvin was leaning halfway across the desk, his dark eyes narrowly focused on the Colonel through the blurry lenses. Harrington averted the glare, his eyes falling on Crawford, who showed no trace of any expression whatsoever.

"Do you actually expect anyone to believe this?"

Marvin raised a hand waving off his client's response. "I can assure you these charges can and will be fully substantiated and corroborated when the case comes to trial. Before we're finished, you will be fully convinced of each of these charges, as will the judge, the jury, and the public - including all of your constituents."

"This is an outrage!"

"Save your indignation for the trial when you'll need it." There was a long pause.

"What do you want?"

"What I want you cannot give. There is no way – financially or otherwise – that you or your institution can even begin to make full restitution for what Mr. Crawford has suffered."

"You can cut through the bullshit. You didn't drive all the way up here to look at the scenery. Give me a number."

"I'd appreciate your controlling your language. We can discuss our business like gentlemen."

"A *number*."

"From you one million. Twenty million from the school."

"You're both out of your minds! You don't even know that I'm worth a million, and you know fully well the academy might not even survive such a large financial loss."

"Again I'll thank you to keep personal affronts to yourself. I don't take the issue of mental impairment lightly, and I'll not tolerate such disparaging remarks either to me or to my client."

"I didn't mean - -"

"I know exactly what you meant. I know it all too well, Colonel Harrington. From the day I started my practice, and even long before, I have had to deal with individuals who share in your contempt for people whom you consider beneath your concern. I believe we've concluded our business for today. You have some weighty matters to consider. Mr. Crawford and I will await your response. The filing date is on the brief."

The Colonel turned toward Crawford. "Frank, I'd like to - - "

"Mr. Crawford has nothing to say."

Colonel Harrington watched through his window as the two walked across the circle toward the parking lot. He had to admit that Frank Crawford appeared to be a basket case. Almost totally bereft of expression. At 6'1" he was only slightly overweight, almost strapping, but he walked as if in a daze. Once he veered off course as though heading toward Ross Hall, his old barracks; and a few moments later he stopped as if to read the inscription at the base of the statue of Dr. Page, the school's founder, before staring off remotely into the distance. Both times his attorney grabbed his arm and redirected him toward the parking lot. The Colonel glared in disgust at the folder on the far corner of his desk. He picked it up gingerly and opened it.

Marvin's detailed account of Crawford's life since his dismissal from Point of Fork brought out even more than Harrington had been aware of. In addition to the failed marriages, problems with the law, and his inability to hold any job for more than a few weeks, there were years of psychological treatment both by Dr. Dunnigan and others in the mental health field. There was no disputing the fact that the poor guy was messed up; you could see that. The question was, "Why? And who, if *anyone*, was at fault?" "How," he wondered, "can a shrink lay a guy out on a couch, put him under hypnosis and determine that it all goes back to his toilet training, or seeing a hog get butchered, or it was something that had happened to him at school? To the tune of twenty million bucks, no less! Sometimes I wonder if they're all a bunch of quacks!"

The centerpiece of Crawford's case was Reardon's alleged club, The Brotherhood of the Sword. Supposedly this secret society existed at PFMA for more than twenty years involving perhaps two hundred cadets in all. Reardon was said to have recruited new cadets through upperclassmen who would invite selected candidates to their secret meetings. These were held in the early hours of the morning in the basement of Memorial Gym. The gym had not been in use for athletics since 1963, when Alumni Gymnasium was completed. For years the building had been relegated to the status of a storage facility, but the basement was too leaky even for that. Even after the old swimming pool was drained, the mold and mildew continued to thrive on the dank, dark walls. Eventually the area was deemed useless and the door to the basement was padlocked. The Brotherhood supposedly met on Tuesday nights. Reardon had one of the few keys to the basement and would be waiting for them, having already set up the four tables – three for members whom he called the brothers, and one for initiates who were called disciples.

Meetings began with a reading of scripture by Major Reardon. Then the Pledge of the Sword was recited:

> I swear by the Holy Bible, by the Constitution of the United States, by my family's name, and by all that I hold sacred and dear, never to reveal outside these walls any of the secrets, practices, or sacred rituals of The Brotherhood of the Sword. I shall defend and uphold this secret brotherhood and maintain all of its principles throughout my private and public life until my mortal remains have been rendered unto dust.

The pledge was allegedly followed by the shedding of the loins, a ritual of purification in which the entire group stripped down to their undershorts. At this point the disciples were ushered by the brothers to the empty swimming pool. Climbing down the rusty rungs to the bottom of the pool, they then performed wheelbarrow races, chicken fights, or whatever stunts the brothers shouted down for them to carry out as their Rite of Inculcation by Ordeal.

Following the Rite of Inculcation, the disciples were sent back to the barracks after first being admonished, on pain of termination (a deliberately ambiguous term), not to reveal anything that had occurred in the unlikely event that they were caught by the officer of the day. Upon returning from Christmas leave, disciples would be welcomed into full membership as brothers.

At the Conclave of the Sword that followed the dismissal of the disciples, Reardon passed out one bottle of Mountain Dew and two Marlboro cigarettes to each of the brothers. These represented the three persons of the Blessed Trinity. The soft drinks, representing the Father as the source of nourishment, were distributed first. The two cigarettes represented the Son and the Holy Spirit respectively – the first because it was consumed and rendered unto dust as Christ was sacrificed as a mortal man on the cross. The second because it burned and gave off light much as the Paraclete had appeared as tongues of fire to inspire and enlighten the Twelve at Pentecost. Then Reardon would read a story or poem that he had brought for the meeting. Some had been composed by the instructor himself. Although not overtly salacious, these were generally of a sensual or quasi-erotic nature and quite titillating for the boys; however, as a man of the cloth, Reardon assured the brothers that nothing conducted in the meetings was in conflict with an enlightened interpretation of revealed Scripture. Readings were followed by philosophical discussions related either to the readings or events on campus.

Meetings always concluded with the Ritual of Unification and Atonement. Here, it was said, Reardon presided as judge and passed sentence on brothers who were deemed to have fallen short of the standards of the Brotherhood during the previous week. Offenses were either confessed or charged by other brothers, and the punishment was one to three whacks on the naked buttocks with a ping pong paddle. Reardon administered the discipline, depending on the nature and severity of the offense and whether it was confessed or brought up by an accuser. Occasionally Reardon himself confessed to transgressions, in which case he received a whack from each of the brothers. After all punishment had been administered, the entire group formed a tight circle with arms closely interlocked and recited the Covenant of Departure into the World.

> As we depart this hallowed place and return to the corruption of the world, we take with us a renewed determination to live as Brothers of the Sword. We swear to uphold the sacred truths of the Holy Word as revealed in Scripture and upheld by this consecrated Brotherhood. May we never by thought, word, or deed forsake our convictions or our Brothers who hold and practice them.

The Colonel returned the document to its folder and threw it down forcefully on the desk. He swiveled on the chair's seat and again looked out the window. The thing was disgusting. Criminal? Certainly perverted at the least. Reardon was a nut case from the word go, but even *he* couldn't dream up anything this bazaar. Still the Colonel wondered of the possible ramifications for the academy. What if people believed the charges? Things like this have been known to happen in boys' schools. A jury might be convinced. And what, God help us, if the charges were true.

Chapter 16

Max was in the back yard with his sons when Johanna brought him the phone. Justin had been working on the softball throw with Brett. Amazingly he had progressed to the point that he could catch the balls tossed underhand by his brother nearly every time. The overhand throws were still a problem for Justin, but he was now fielding nearly half of them. What had amazed both Brett and Max, though, was the unexpected authority and accuracy with which Justin could throw the ball. He was able to put his considerable weight behind it with surprising coordination. With the pop of the ball in his glove, Max tore off the mitt and danced around the yard in mock-anguish while blowing on his palm. "Your poor ol' dad won't have any hand left if you keep burning 'em in like that!" he shouted as Justin squealed and Brett beamed in delight. "I'll bet Justin takes the softball throw hands down. Bret, you and your brother do a dozen wind sprints while I take this call. We still need to work on his hundred meter dash for the next couple of weeks or Justin's going to be sucking wind by the finish."

It was Colonel Harrington. "Yeah, Colonel."

"Did you get the info on the committee meeting?"

"Sure did. Two weeks from Monday at the Omni – then we vote by e-mail ballot the following week. Will you be there?"

"No, don't think so. I think it would be more appropriate and better received if I stay out of this one. Some things could come up concerning the type of president they want that could be awkward to discuss with me there. I want everyone to feel like they can say what's on their minds."

"That sounds pretty democratic of you, Colonel. You haven't been into that Scotch again have you?"

"Oh, don't worry. I plan to know everything that goes on in the meeting within the hour. That's what I've got you in there for."

"Sort of a mole, huh? Make sure nothing deviates from the set plan."

"I'm not counting on anything as a certainty, but we both know Frazier's the best choice."

"Absolutely, but is he electable? I can't see the board choosing a Catholic; too many trustees would be dead set against it."

"You may be right – certainly with a good part the Baptist contingent. But Ron has some friends even in that group, and I don't think the military group is all that hot on a clergyman."

"How about the guy from Episcopal High School and the dean from South Carolina?"

"Dr. Williams doesn't have any strong backing, and I doubt Dillard will even get a vote."

"Who else is out there?"

"Well, Leatherwood's going to nominate a guy named Tommy Benson, a popular preacher from Narrows with a Masters in Education."

"Narrows? Where's that?"

"Out there in southwest Virginia – not far from where I'm from. I've done some checking, and he's actually a pretty good man; I just don't think he's at all qualified for the job. No strong academic background. No real stature."

"Not like an attorney, you mean?"

"Whatever."

"He'll probably get a lot of votes from the preachers."

"Not necessarily. There's at least one other preacher who's going to be on the ballot, Warren Cochran, a Falwell protégé from Lynchburg. With the mail ballot I can easily see the Baptist vote getting spread out so thin our guy will have a clear plurality. That's Ron's best shot."

"I hope you're right, Colonel; is there anyone else on the list?"

"Just one, a retired Marine general with Baptist connections. I definitely see him as a long shot, but we're doing the usual follow-up on him."

"OK, Colonel, I'll be there."

"That's Brad, Max. I'm counting on you to keep Ron's name out in front at the meeting. There will be others speaking for him too. I think he's got a real chance."

"It would be the first time the school's hired a president from inside that I ever heard of."

"First time ever. And, you can take my word, the way things are going we'll need someone who knows the score around here."

"Crawford?"

"Yeah. I'm pretty sure we're going to trial on this, and it could be tough for the school."

"Do you think there's any truth at all to those allegations?"

"Who knows? You tell me; you were at the academy when he was. Did you ever hear anything about Reardon or this so-called club?"

"Oh, we heard about Reardon and his friends alright. But you know how it is around there with cadets. We had a million rumors every day. Nobody took any of them seriously. There were some pretty good ones on you, by the way, sir."

"I'll bet."

"I've been meaning to ask you, Brad – you and Louise never starred in any porno flicks back in the 50's, did you?"

"Real funny! I always thought your class had a lot of sick minds!"

"Just asking. No, I don't think there was really any truth to the Reardon thing. If there had been, you can be sure Crawford would have been right there in the middle of it, but my guess is that he's just taking telling his shrink a story he heard while he was a cadet. I've been in touch with a few of my old classmates. If there was anything to it, they would know. I'll call them and let you know what they say."

"Good. Just don't start letting too much of this out until you get back to me."

"No problem."

"I'll call you a week from Monday after the meeting."

"That's OK. I'll call you as soon as the meeting's over."

"That'll be fine. I'll be in my office."

Chapter 17

By the time Max, Johanna, and Brett drove up to UVA's Lannigan Field, all twelve teams from around the state had arrived. Some groups from the tidewater and southwestern parts of the state had spent the night in Charlottesville hotels. The track and the infield were festooned with banners and other decorations that had been provided by local and national sponsors. A huge Ronald McDonald was stationed next to the javelin runway that would serve as the scratch line for the softball throw. Every detail had been covered to insure that for this day every child would be a champion and that these Olympics would indeed be special.

It was a cool morning for early summer, and many of the athletes were sporting the warmups of their respective teams. Competitors from the Richmond Track and Field Club had reported with their coaches to their venues. Justin and two of his teammates were at the starting line with their coach, Frank Wilson, a Richmond dentist who as a UVA undergraduate had run for the Cavaliers on this very track under Coach Lou Onesty. Frank's son, Mitch, was in the low hurdles. Justin would be competing in the trials of the 100 meters in the morning and perhaps in the finals at two that afternoon. The softball throw was the next to the last event and was scheduled to go off at four o'clock.

Justin smiled and waved to his family as they walked over to wish him luck. He was slated for lane six of the fourth heat. As the first heat reported to the starting line, Justin began to peel off his warmups. "Not yet," warned Brett throwing the jacket back on his brother's shoulders.

"Let's let Dr. Wilson do the coaching," Max interrupted. "Have fun out there, Son; we'll meet you at the finish line." Max slapped his son on the butt, and Johanna gave him a final hug before heading down the track.

Justin gave a good effort in the 100 but did not qualify for the finals. After almost tripping at the start, he regrouped and managed to run a straight line to the finish, catching all but three of the runners. His time of 22.4 was nearly as fast as any he had run in practice. As with all of the competitors, he was nearly mobbed by family, coaches, and meet workers as he crossed the line. Since he would not be competing again until four, Brett suggested lunch across the street at Hardee's and perhaps a little shopping at the Downtown Athletic Store. "I think we should stick around for the other kids," Johanna suggested, and Max agreed.

Although no team score was kept, all of the parents and coaches were in agreement that the Richmond club had acquitted themselves quite well as the day drew toward the final events. Coach Wilson had allowed Brett to take Justin and the two other throwers onto the infield for a warmup. "This one's all yours," he whispered to his brother who returned his grin with an insouciant smile. And indeed, it was no contest; on his first of three attempts Justin uncorked the best effort of the day – almost fifteen feet farther than his nearest competitor. Later as the winner's medal was placed around his neck, the P.A. announced, "Let's have a big hand for our winner, Justin Jarvis, whose toss of 88'10" is a new meet record. And let's hear it for all of the contestants in the softball throw." Brett beamed with pride as he joined his brother and all of the other families at the victory stand.

Max and his family left as soon as the closing ceremonies were completed. It had been a splendid day but a long one – a meal at Chuckie Cheese would be little enough for Max and Johanna to endure on such a special occasion. Back in Richmond, Max dropped Johanna and Brett off at home and drove to the high school to wait for the team bus. He would call home from his car when he had picked Justin up and meet them at the restaurant. He waited for half an hour with no bus in sight. Fifteen minutes later he called Johanna at home. "No sign of the bus. Have you heard from the team?"

"Not a word. You don't think they stopped on the way back to eat, do you?"

"I don't think so. I checked with Frank Wilson before we left, and he said they were coming straight back."

"Are you sure they were coming back to the high school?"

"Yeah, I checked when I dropped Justin off. Besides, there are at least a dozen other families waiting."

"I guess they could have had a change of plans. Maybe one of the parents decided to spring for a team victory dinner."

"I suppose that's possible, but I really doubt that Frank would have changed the travel plans without informing the families. Maybe the bus broke down."

"Maybe. What do you think we should do?"

"All we can do is wait. I'll stay here at the high school; call me on the cell phone if you hear anything, or I'll let you know as soon as the bus gets here."

Max hung the phone up. He drove around to the other side of the high school to make certain that the bus had not come in there. The lot was empty. He drove back to the bus lot and turned off the engine. The phone rang. It was Johanna, and she was hysterical. Someone had called just as she and Max had hung up. There had been an accident – a terrible wreck at the Charlottesville-Shadwell interchange onto I-64. The bus had somehow pulled straight out onto the passing lane and into a tractor-trailer. There were casualties.

"My God, Johanna! Is Justin OK?"

"They won't tell me anything! I don't think they know! They said the injured kids were taken to UVA Hospital."

"Call a sitter for Brett. I'll tell the other families and be there in ten minutes. We'll drive back to Charlottesville right now."

"I don't like this, Max. It sounds bad. What do you think's happened?"

"No way I can know. I'll be right there."

Ellen Hitt, the Jarvis' regular sitter, was at the house when Max drove up, but Brett was in as bad shape as his mother and insisted on riding up to Charlottesville with his parents. "OK, let's all go. Ellen, if you don't mind, stay here at the house and listen for any calls. If you hear anything, call me on the cell phone. The number's on the pad right by the phone."

Bringing Brett was the only right decision under the circumstances, but it made for strained dialogue between his parents as they tried to speculate on the conditions of

Justin and the other children without upsetting Brett any more than necessary.

"Honey, did they say how serious the injuries were? Are all of the kids alive?"

"They said, "Casualties.""

"Yeah, but that could mean anything. Did they say there was any loss of life?"

"They said, "*Casualties*.""

"That charter bus is a big, heavy vehicle. It can sustain a lot of force and provide a lot of protection. It's not like being in a car."

"They hit a tractor-trailer, Max. They said the accident was serious." Max knew that. If it had been a minor wreck, they would have offered some kind of reassurance.

It was after seven when Max approached Charlottesville – still broad daylight with the early summer sun well up in the sky. Two exits before the UVA ramp, they passed the Charlottesville-Shadwell interchange. Max looked across the median and saw the bus. "My God! It's on its side!"

A few seconds later the cell phone rang. It was Charles Hitt, Ellen's father. "Max, Ellen couldn't call you, so she called me as soon as the hospital called."

"Is Justin Alright?"

"He didn't make it, Max." Max froze. He heard himself mumble something as he hung up the phone. Johanna searched his face in disbelief. Max looked at her and shook his head. Brett buried his face in the rear seat.

- - - - - - - - - - - - - - - - - -

The ghastly scene at the hospital was a horrific mass of chaos. Families were crying; some were hysterical as others tried to comfort them. Two of the children had been pronounced dead at the scene, another had died at the hospital; and one little girl, who had lost a leg, was listed in critical condition. Amazingly none of the other children appeared to have sustained serious injuries. Justin had died instantly. The driver of the truck had no way to avoid the crash – he had plowed right into Justin's seat. Justin never knew what hit him.

- - - - - - - - - - - - - -

It was strange. During the funeral Mass neither Max, Johanna, nor even Brett had cried. In fact, Max's grief had found no discernable expression even a full day after the accident, nor would it manifest itself demonstrably until much later that evening. "The Accident," they called it. The bus driver had obviously pulled out onto the interstate without even looking. Tests for drugs and alcohol had come back negative, so what could explain it? Max had no name for his feelings, a complex and unstable chain of emotions that involved shock, disbelief, anger, and self-doubt. A heaviness that would not begin to lift until some sense of emotional order and understanding could be restored. He almost envied his wife and son who had emptied themselves at the hospital, but he knew also that their venting of sobs and tears was only the foretaste of a deep dull hurt that had settled on their lives forever. Although Johanna went about the daily business of receiving condolences without tears, her stricken state was evident to those who loved her, and her sobs in the night went on for hours. Max was unable to sleep until he heard her steady breathing, and several times he was awakened by

Brett's nightmares in his room across the hall. In going in and trying to help Brett back to sleep, Max was not sure whether he was really comforting his son or himself.

Making the funeral arrangements had actually helped. They gave Max something to do that would occupy his mind with details and block for a while the intrusion of the crash scene and events surrounding it that were constantly looping somewhere through the back recesses of his subconscious. Why had he decided to allow Justin to ride back with the team? Several of the other children had returned with their parents. There was a family celebration scheduled at Chuckie Cheese. The coach would have understood. Had he not made such a big production of Justin's gold medal, his son would not have been the last to board the bus and perhaps would not have taken one of the few remaining seats. No telling where he would have sat – probably with his friend, Mitch Wilson. Mitch had survived with only a bruised knee. Scenarios that could have saved his son would turn up whenever Max's mind was unoccupied: at night when he was trying to sleep, in his unoccupied moments alone, and even over the fading voices of well-intentioned friends who stopped by with plates of snacks and prepared dinners that had remained untouched in the kitchen.

Father Burns had been a source of comfort where comfort had seemed impossible. Somehow he had learned of the tragedy and was waiting at the house when the Max and his family returned well after one in the morning. His family minus one. "I'll only stay a few minutes, but I knew you would want to see me when you got back." After a few words and a short prayer, he met privately for a couple of minutes with both Johanna and Brett and finally with Max. It was a truly generous gesture from a friend. He had to know there was little he could do for the moment, but he wanted the family to understand that he was available at any time they needed him.

After the graveside service friends and family met at the house. Johanna went through the motions as well as could be expected, but friends and especially her husband could see the utter devastation clearly written beneath the brave smiles and warm greetings. Seeing his wife and son trying to deal with their grief hurt even more than Max's own personal loss. For once there was nothing he could say or do to help his family. He was speaking with two partners in the new hospital when he noticed Louise Harrington talking with a small contingent from the academy. There were Rick Wagner and Ron Frazier as well as a couple of others that Max recognized. Louise gave Max a long hug. "So sorry for your loss, Max. Brad couldn't come – he's not feeling well, but he wanted me to tell you that we have been thinking of you. He'll be calling you in a day or so when he feels better."

"Tell the Colonel to come in and see me at the hospital tomorrow."

"Don't tell me you're going back to work so soon!"

"I think I need to, really. I don't know how else I can deal with this."

"How about poor Johanna – and Brett?"

"I'm concerned about her, Louise. I don't know how I can help her. Brett – he's going back to school tomorrow. I think that's best."

"I'm sure you're right, Max, but keep a close watch on Johanna. She really needs you now, and I'm sure you need her too. I'll go over and speak to her right now."

Max turned to Ron and Rick. Of course he had missed the board meeting. There were the usual expressions of consolation. "How did the meeting go?"

"Everything went fine," Ron responded immediately, but Max caught Rick's frown. He turned to the athletic director.

"Our man here is going to be the new president, then, right?" Rick shook his head. Ron grabbed Max's arm and attempted a weak smile.

"This isn't the time or place to worry about that business. The board's chosen a good man, and I'm sure we can all work with him. He's got everything it takes to do a great job."

"I'll bet! Who was it, Leatherwood's minister?"

"I'll tell you who it was," whispered the coach, warming up to the subject. "A guy we know absolutely nothing about! A guy they snuck in on us at the last minute to placate all of the military and religious factions. A guy with no background at all in education."

"You man the Marine Corps general?"

"Easy, Rick," Ron broke in. "The man has a lot going for him. He has a background in leadership, he can relate well with most of the school's constituencies; and besides, it's over. The board has spoken."

"I haven't voted yet," Max responded. "I thought we had until the end of the week."

"You do, but it won't make any difference," Rick answered. "This guy is organized. Or his backers are. Even if Ron gets all of the remaining votes, this General Beasley's in. The Colonel told us that."

"So much for my role in protecting your candidacy, Ron."

"Hey – get real, Max. No one expected you to be there. I really appreciate the thought, but I seriously doubt that anything could have changed the outcome. Like Rick said, this guy is really organized. He'll do a great job."

Later that night Max heard his son turning restlessly in the room across the hall. For the past few days he had been leaving the bedroom doors open so he could be with Brett when he woke up in the night. He walked across the hall and sat down on the bed. "Can't sleep, son?"

"I'm getting tireder. I'll fall asleep in a minute."

"Want me to stay here with you for a while?"

"Will you?"

"Sure son." There was a long silence.

"Dad?"

"Yeah, Brett."

"Why didn't you let me put Justin's baseball glove with him at the funeral?"

"We sent the gold medal with him, Brett. I knew he would want you to keep the glove."

"Think so? Does he know I have it?"

"I feel sure he does, Brett, and I'm confident that's the way he feels."

"Does he think the way he used to, or is his mind normal now?"

"That's a really tough one, son. He's still our Justin, but I suppose all of his infirmities are gone now."

"Infirmities?"

"You know, the Downs."

"That's kind of hard to think about. Father Burns said Justin is perfectly happy up there. He's the same brother but without all of his problems. He said he's 'glorified' now. It's hard for me to picture. Do you understand what he means?"

"Sure I do – well, sort of. It's not something we can understand completely here, but we have faith that God is taking care of Justin in the best possible way, and we'll all be together eventually."

"He won't miss the glove then."

"No way. He wants you to have it."

"I'll keep it on my desk forever to remember him by."

"I think what Justin would really like is for you to use it. It's almost brand new and a lot better than your old Wilson."

"You really think so?"

"I'm sure if it."

Max sat with Brett for a few more minutes until his son's breathing became deep and regular. He looked down at the boy and eased off the bed. He listened from his own room to make sure Brett was asleep. After several minutes of silence, Max was satisfied. For the first time he felt tears welling up as he broke into uncontrollable sobbing. He got up and closed the door. He sat on the edge of the bed and bent over. The crying wouldn't stop. He felt movement as Johanna sat up and placed her arm around him, but he couldn't stop. They fell back in bed together, both now shaking and heaving. Neither said a word as they lay together. Gradually the spasms began to subside, and he had nearly fallen asleep in her arms when the phone rang. It was the triage nurse.

"Dr. Jarvis, I know it's a bad time, but you told me to call if there was a problem with Mr. Harrington."

"The Colonel?"

"They just brought him into emergency with severe chest pains."

Chapter 18

Forty-three years had passed since the day Phil Beasley's father had packed his bag and left home. The nightmares of Reverend Belcher and the chase to the eternal abyss had gradually subsided. The nightly phantasm had first been a weekly intruder to the boy's bedroom, then monthly, and eventually, as the boy matured into a man of considerable standing, only a rare interloper on his nocturnal peace. With his father's departure the beatings had stopped as well, but not the guilt – the sense that he had been the reason for the divorce, the poverty, the shame. He had heard it every day that he could remember even while his dad was still around – and every Sunday at the tarpaper church in the hollow, the tiny house of worship with the long name. The Full Gospel Holiness Church of the Risen Christ in Jesus Name was the only church Phil knew for the first sixteen years of his life, and Reverend Belcher was its only preacher. The man who baptized sinners in the icy currents of Contrary Creek and thundered out staccato sermons in Sundays worked as an electrician in the mines during the week.

Caleb Belcher had never finished the eighth grade back in eastern Kentucky where he had learned his trade and received his Calling. His pale skin, blanched by years in the mines, was so tightly drawn across his hollow jaw that his cheekbones constantly shone a bright red. His ice blue eyes contrasted with the coal black hair that was slicked straight back from his forehead forming a ducktail at the neck. At age thirty-five his slight, even stooped frame belied a vigorous physical strength and fierce energy. Migrating across the Cumberland range into West Virginia, he had found work near the town of Jumping Branch, where he assembled a small but ardent congregation. Some were mining families, others were poor mountain farmers, and nearly half at any given time were out of work and on relief. Belcher's contempt for worldly status struck a resonant note with his flock who crossed the mountain every Sunday to hear sermons filled with affirmation that the proud would be justly dealt with on the day of reckoning. Stripped of their privilege and extravagances, the high and mighty would discover too late, as Dives in the parable had, that all on earth is vanity. With horrified eyes they would behold the hopeless, endless torture that lay before them. Then, in the throes of their anguish, the hell-bound would witness the elect – many of them the very ones they had abused in their natural lives - carried aloft to the bosom of Abraham.

Phil's father had been dragged to church for four consecutive Sundays during the scorching summer following the boy's fifth birthday. This was no mean accomplishment for a wife who had submitted to her husband in all things since their marriage six month prior to their son's birth. Barely sixteen at the time of her wedding and eleven years younger than Abner who was also her second cousin, Audrey had quickly descended into a miserable, destitute existence. The only surcease from her wretchedness was the Sunday morning services that she longed to share with her boy. She broached the subject one stifling Tuesday after supper as they sat in the light breeze on their tiny front porch. She was shelling a pile of butter beans, dropping the glossy green buttons into a mixing bowl and discarding the empty pods in a large paper bag. Her husband slouched back in a broken rocking chair, his boots resting on an unpainted wooden rail.

The end of a Chesterfield dangled nonchalantly from his right hand, and a pint jar holding three inches of clear whiskey rested on floor next to the left rocker. The back leg of his chair sprung free from the rocker as he leaned forward to grasp the jar. "He needs to go, Abner, and so do you."

"No. We done been through this before. I'm not takin' my only day off an' listnin' to that ol' fool run on till two o'clock in th' ev'nin'."

"I've asked him to come to dinner after church this Sunday an' have a talk with you."

Abner met the determination in her eyes. His face hardened. "You go along and do whatever the *hail* you want to. Jus' leave me be."

"He's comin' Sunday," she responded evenly with uncharacteristic resolve. Her husband glowered at her in disbelief. "I'll not raise my boy a heathen." For once Abner Beasley knew he was a beaten man in his own home. He sought to cut his losses.

"We ain't havin' no preacher-man for Sunday dinner. F'git it. You tell the reverend to stay put! Think o' some reason, an' I'll go along with you t'church this Sunday. Abner bolted from the chair nearly kicking over the pint jar as he stalked into the sweltering house slamming the screen door behind him.

Seated in the fourth row of battered folding chairs that were tightly arranged on either side of a narrow aisle, Abner and his family endured sermons that ran beyond two hours as the large fan whirred back and forth. Belcher's preaching was in the old style. His rhythmic sentences, each punctuated with the hoarse, explosive "Haah," always reached an emotional crescendo before gradually dwindling to a growling whisper as the sweating preacher ground to a halt. But Abner Beasley's salvation came on the seventh Sunday, a hot day in August when he was served up a plausible excuse never to return to the sanctuary again. On this stifling morning the Spirit had moved Belcher to recall his own salvation form a life of drinking, gambling, blasphemy, and whoremongering when he the Lord convicted him at the age of seventeen. He began with the beginning.

"Friends, ya know that I ain't always lived a holy life. I onest was as close to the pit of hell as most of the damned souls that's a-burnin' an' a-fryin' there right now. By rights I should be with 'em rat now - a-rollin' on those flamin' coals. But the love of **JAY-sus** – Amen - done lifted me out of the squalor an' gave my poor undeserving soul another chanct. A chanct to live for Him.

"Oh, I been to preachin' before. I used to go regular when I was a young boy. My father, rest his soul, was a good Christian man, but he married a woman from Ohio who was a Roman Catholic. An' those priests made him promise to let her take me to that church where they pray to Mary an' other idols against the First Commandment, an' make a pagan goddess outa a woman who was a sinner just like you an' me. Friends, I went to preachin' with her ev'ry Sunday an' even made my First Communion – a blasphemy in the sight of Our Lord! I listened to the priest a-tellin' us how the Pope done took the place o'God Almighty heah on earth, an' we had to believe ev'rything he preached because he spoke for **JAY-sus!** We didn't need no Bible – just follow along with the preachin' of the *whorish* Catholic Church with hits incense, an' hits sprinklin', an' hits preachin' that your *works* are gonna save ya – *not* the blood o'Christ!

"Friends, the Roman Church is the Devil's own church with their fancy music an' their holy water an' such. They deny the sacred Scripture an' spread the Devil's word for anyone who will listen. In fact Satan controls 80% of the world's religions, an' most all of them – the ones what don't preach the full Gospel, can be traced right back to pagan Rome. Just go to half the churches ya see here in town. They try to say they ain't no hell. Well, **JAY-sus** said they's a hell alright. Ya can go ahead an' look hit up for yousef. The Lord spoke twice as much about hell as He did about Heaven. But they tell ya, 'don't worry yousef about none o'that – 'Jay-sus *is* love; he won't let ya burn.' Well, that ain't what th'Bible says. Check hit out for yourself in John 15:6. *If a man abide not in me, he is cast forth as a branch, an' is withered; an' men gather them an' cast them in to the* **fire***, an' they are* **burned***.* Or in Ezekiel 20:47: *Thus saith the Lord GOD; Behold, I will kindle a fire in thee, an' hit shall devour ev'ry green tree in thee, an' ev'ry dry tree: the flaming flame shall not be quenched, an' all faces from the south to the north* **shall be burned therein***.* But Satan don't want ya t'heah none o'that so he's got his own churches – an 'specially the Satanic Roman Catholic Church – out there a-spewin' forth religious filth an' frauds that's written by the Devil hissef. An' all they's a-doin' is trying to lure ya t'hell by sayin' they ain't no hell.

"Well they is a hell, an' by th'Grace o' God I'm here to tell ya 'bout hit cause I done saw hit my *own* sef. I had just turned seventeen, an' by that time I wasn't goin' to *no* church. My mother had passed away two yeahs before, an' I decided they won't no hell noways, so they won't no use to trouble mysef with no preachin' a'tall. In fact hit was of a Sunday mornin' I cut mysef bad on a rusty piece o' barbed wire. I was goin' sucker fishin' at a creek just a hunnert yards from the Baptist church. I remember hearin' the church bells an' laughin' to mysef just before sliding down that bank where the barbed wire done laid my leg open to the bone.

"I bled so bad I liked to die on the spot, but ol' Doc Gill sewed me up an' tole me I'd be alright. Well, I won't alright, an' ten days later that leg was a-swole up to twice hits size, an' Doc Gill said I was about done for. I hadn't slept for two nights, an' was a-sweatin' pints when I was given a vision I'll never forgit. I found mysef a-walkin' late at night around some old grown-up strip mines. I don't know, I guess I might'a been a-coon huntin', but hit was a strange place where I never been before. They was a full moon a-workin' in an' out of the clouds when I noticed a red glow up ahead – maybe a half mile or so from where I was. I thought somethin' might a'been on fire, but as I got closer I could heah all sorts of shouts an' shrieks an' groans. Finally I got to a huge smokin' pit – like an old mine – an' I could heah them screamin' voices real plain now. They was a foul putrid stench a-commin' outa the hole mixed with the smell o' burning sulfur an' coal fumes. I could see the people real plain now. They was millions of 'em an' they was a-jumpin' around on the hot coals, but the flames that was lickin' all around didn't burn them up a'tall. They was just a-fryin'. I could even see their eyeballs a-sizzlin' an' a-boilin in their heads like they was ready to bust, but they didn't.

"Like I tole ya, I could heah them a-howlin'. They was the most hideous, miserable folks I ever laid eyes on. They was a-swearin' an' blasphemin' at God Almighty an' each other. They was fightin' an' a-bitin'. An' leading th'whole thing was the filthiest souls of all. They was Popes an' priests who was out there performing a feverish pantomime of the filthiest sexual perversions the sickest mind could dream of. They was a-tryin' t'do ugly on each other an' with the nuns an' other whores who was out there with 'em. Men with men, women with women, but hit won't no use. The more they tried, the more they was throwed apart by the roarin' flames. But they still kept on a-tryin', an' when they wasn't a-doin' their filthy perversions on theirselves an' others, they was a-fightin' an' bitin' an' a-swearin'. I seen two or three what actually was a-prayin', or they was a-tryin' to; but they won't no hope. They was on their knees, an' the fire lickin' from the embers was a-fryin' their knees an' shins. They was begging God t'forgive 'em an' take 'em back to His lovin' arms onest more. But they won't no hope. Hit was too late. The flames just blazed up all the stronger, an' onest they seen they won't no hope, they bellowed out the filthiest profanities that ever echoed through that dark, dreadful place.

"Suddenly they was a huge gush o'smoke an' flames belching outa th'ground, an' I seen the Devil hissef rise up from the smoke an' flames. He was huge – as big as twenty men - with stinkin' smokin' hair all over his nasty, disgusting body. Friends, if Lucifer was ever the handsomest angel in heaven, he was just as foul an' hideous in hell! He was roamin' around a-grabbin' these poor damned sinners an' a-swollerin' two or three at a time. I could heah their screams as their bones was a-breakin', an' he was a-slobberin' an' a-droolin' blood an' bones all over the place while he was a-reachin' for more. Sometimes he'd vomit up a head or a foot, but the worst was still to come; 'cause in a few minutes the rest of 'em would be digested an' come outa th'other end, an' the whole mess would be re-form in all that burnin', smokin' excrement an' vomit, an' slime.

"Then I seen her. Hit was my *own* deceased mother. Her face was made up like a whore, an' she was stark necked! Even with the hot flames a-lickin' all around her she was a-rubbin' an' writhin' on this bishop who was a-wearin' a miter. He was raisin' up a cup o'wine in a sacrilegious pantomime of the Last Supper. She was tryin' t'pull his vestments off an' was a-reachin' all around t'grab a-holt of his privates, but they was another whore a-pullin' her back an' gouging at her eyes. I couldn't stand no more. Hit won't no dream, an' I could see where I was a-headed. I called out for **JAY-sus** - an' I saw my mother shuddah. The damned in hell looked up at me in silence an' fell tremblin' to the flaming ground.

"Friends, fellow sinners, this heah was real. When I woke up, the fever was broke, an' I was healed body an' soul. Satan had done been beat this time. Satan don't want ya t'believe hit no more than those lost souls did who's already cookin' down there with him condemned forever. Forever – now that's a thought some o'ya ain't considered. Think about th'heat for all eternity! Ya been a-settin' heah for th'best part of a hour. Hit's pretty hot, but 'taint nothin' to the flames o'hell. The blade in that fan's been a-spinnin' an' a-whirlin' around – how many times since we been heah? A thousand? Probably more'n ten thousand. But if hit was a hunnert thousand, or even if hit ran 'till the motor gave out – an' if each one o'those revolutions was worth a century, hit wouldn't be nothin' to all eternity. Just the blink of an eye compared to the endless horrors that's a-waitin the damned. Think o'how bad a blister hurts when ya burn th'end o'your finger. But that gits well in a few days. Now consider your whole body a-fryin' an' a-sizzlin' for all eternity!

"That's what th'Devil has a-waitin' for ya. He's a cunning trap-setter, a master predator, an' his prey is man. He saves his best tricks for the "good people." He ain't worried about the thieves, an' drunks, an' adulterers. He knows he's already got them in his hip pocket. He wants *you*. He wants ya t'believe they ain't no hell. He's done planted all o'his false churches with their false Bible an' their false teachins for t'drag ya down with the damned. He knows your name, an' he shudders ev'ry time ya confess Christ, 'cause salvation comes from faith!"

Throughout Belcher's harangue, he kept glancing anxiously toward the back of the congregation. After about an hour, a small balding man in a checked shirt and blue jeans appeared at the back doorway pulling two wooden boxes on wheels. The reverend stopped abruptly and signaled to the electric guitar in the choir to strike a chord.

"Now friends, this heah is Deacon Fennel Corbin, a man o' the Gospel with a powerful faith. He done come to us from down around Galax, Virginia. Fennel's a man o'faith, full o'the Holy Spirit! Amen, he's a man what's run the Devil outa many a congregation from heah t' Eastern Kentucky an' cleah down t' Southwest Virginia." The small gathering stirred uneasily as the stranger drew the two wooden boxes down the narrow aisle. They were nearly identical, about three feet wide, four feet long, and nearly flat – only about eighteen inches in height. One was stacked on top of the other, which was rigged with a long wooden handle and a set of wheels. The top box revealed a small trap door secured with a wooden latch and three leather hinges. Several men in the pews drew back as the boxes passed down the aisle. Abner Beasley didn't flinch; his hard stare followed the deacon and the two boxes as they rolled to a stop. He turned and faced the silent fold.

Deacon Corbin appeared to be in his late thirties. The blonde hair that he had remaining was combed into a wave. Despite his wiry build he had a noticeable paunch developing beneath the large silver buckle that adorned a thick leather belt. He had a slight harelip revealing rotted teeth when he spoke in a high nasal twang. "Folks, I want t'warn ever one o'ya that ain't right with th'Lord t'hole back from these here serpents when they're turned aloose." One man and his pregnant wife bolted through the back door. Abner Beasley stood motionless, his eyes fixed on the two boxes. Corbin gave little indication that he noticed the commotion, his hand resting casually on the top box. "Now, there's a smart man, my friends. He knows when t'cut his losses. Now, any o'ya what don't believe in what we got heah can turn to Mark 16:17: *'An' these signs will accompany those who b'live. In my name they will cast out demons, they will speak in new tongues, they will take up serpents, an' if they drink any deadly thing, it will not hurt them.'*"

"**Amen!**" roared Reverend Belcher, and a tentative scattering of weak Amens returned from the flock. The scraping of chairs along the wooden floor could be heard as Corbin's hand eased the latch open.

"So there ya have it as plain as day. It don't make no difference what others thank or try t'tell ya; if you're right with God an th'Spirit's in ya, they ain't no reason not t'take ahole o'one o'these heah serpents in th'name o'God, jus lak Moses done in th'wilderness, an' bear witness to th'**powah** o' th'Lord!" With that he opened the trap door and without even looking down withdrew a huge timber rattlesnake nearly four feet long and as wide as a two-inch drainpipe. Corbin held the snake loosely, about eighteen inches from its head. As he drew the length of the dark gray reptile from the box, it curled up his arm and formed a compact ball in his hands, its flat, triangular head raised a couple of inches above its mass. The snake's shiny forked tongue darted intermittently from it mouth as Corbin addressed the hushed audience. He returned the menacing glare of Abner Beasley. "Now, y'all kin see these heah are th'real thing. I got six of em, an' each one's a loaded gun. One bite'll send a healthy full-grown man to th-undertaker in less than half'n hour." The snake's rattles shook for the first time as Corbin squeezed his hand. "Now, I warn ya agin, If ya aint in the Spirit, git back!"

Two men emerged from a middle row and cautiously approached the boxes. Corbin handed the rattlesnake to the first man, who grasped it gingerly, his arm fully extended. Reverend Belcher reached into the second box and withdrew a second rattler only slightly small than the first. He handed it to the second man who passed it on to another worshiper as Belcher reached into the box for another viper. The coils were passed among the congregation. Only one woman touched a snake, and many of the men declined. When a rattler was presented to Beasley, he stood motionless, his eyes riveted on the reptile, his face a study in unsuppressed hate. Jumping Branch's most infamous reprobate took the snake in his hand, almost jerking it from the man next to him, and drew the coiled mass to within three inched of his own nose. Beasley refused to flinch as the serpent's forked tongue probed the short span separating them; his cold eyes met the elliptical pupils of the pit viper. The entire gathering was now staring at him. Slowly an expression of calm descended on Abner's countenance. He squeezed the writhing mass slightly. The rattles began to shake menacingly, but he did not withdraw the snake from his face. Staring aghast, an astonished Mildred Scruggs whispered to her husband, Clem, "I do believe he's in the Word!" Glaring straight at the serpent's head, a mocking expression of contempt covered Abner's face. The congregation was transfixed. The men of God were forgotten, eclipsed by the reckless audacity of the town's most notorious dissolute.

Abruptly Abner hurled the cold-blooded mass against the wall of the sanctuary as snakes were dropped and people scattered. Several chairs were turned over in the melee and two women fell to the floor as chairs blocked their escape. One was bitten on the buttocks, and a man was nipped superficially on the ankle as he made for the door. Throughout the panic, Abler Beasley stood motionless taking the scene in. When the room was nearly empty and he began his slow exit, a small rattler slithered into his path. Beasley calmly pinned its neck to the floor with the back of an overturned chair and ground the heel of his boot into the serpent's head. No one uttered a sound as he impassively made his exit.

- - - - - - - - - - - - - - - - -

Despite Deacon Corbin's warning Maud Shifflett, the woman who was bitten, did not die. For two weeks half of her buttocks was colored a dark purple and swollen to double its already considerable size, but she was released from the hospital after three days. The only long-term effect was the permanent and total loss of feeling on one side of her ass; however, her husband Don asserted her erogenous zone in this particular area was more than sufficient for its purpose. Deacon Corbin recaptured all but two of his snakes – the one Beasley had killed, and another that was last seen slithering up into the rafters. Neither Corbin nor his snake was ever seen again in that part of the mountains. Needless to say, attendance at the church dropped sharply until the dead of winter when the faithful were convinced that no snake could survive in the church where the stove remained unstoked until early Sunday morning. A few worshipers never returned, and for a while Reverend Belcher seemed a broken man. Phil's mother had returned to church the very next Sunday; her faith was never shaken. But neither she nor her boy could escape the stigma of what had happened. Phil, in particular, felt the accusatory bony finger of Reverend Belcher pointed directly at him. And then the nightmares began.

Chapter 19

Phil Beasley dreaded Sunday mornings, but he was even more terrified by the consequences of leaving the church. He had heard the whispers around town about his hell-bound dad. And the good Reverend never allowed his tiny congregation to forget the intense, eternal torment awaiting those who chose to follow his father's path – the absolute hopelessness, the utter despair of all who had thrown their lot in with the Devil and now faced an implacable Judge whose justice was as fierce as it was absolute. After Phil's father left, his mother's determination to raise an exemplary son grew to the point that it nearly consumed her. No sacrifice was too great in assuring his place at the head of his class, as a leader of the young people at church, and eventually as the first ever in her family to attend college. It nearly cost her life, but she succeeded; and on August 29, 1964, assisted by a federal grant from the Appalachian Assistance Fund and an ROTC scholarship, Philip Beasley was enrolled at Fairmont State College in Fairmont, West Virginia.

Fairmont State was Phil's first real exposure to the world outside of Jumping Branch. He found his studies considerably more difficult than at the school where he had excelled back home, but he was determined not to fail, and he managed not to flunk out of school. Eventually his work progressed from acceptable, to respectable, and even occasionally outstanding. He had few friends.

Phil had grown to a young man of unremarkable stature. He was 5'10" in height and slightly on the pudgy side. His walking gait was ungainly – almost a stalking stride with his broad head at an angle ahead of his body. Although both of his parents were fair skinned, Phil's complexion had a darkish, almost swarthy cast. His wide mouth and thin lips had earned him the unkind sobriquet "Frog" among some of his high school classmates, who regarded him as a kook. While at Fairmont he attended Abundant Grace Baptist Church in town – a strictly fundamentalist community but still a far cry from his primitive Pentecostal church back home. Later he became a member and eventually an officer in the Baptist Student Union. Academically he found that he was most successful in mathematics, and through hard work and many long hours with his professors, he earned a math degree four years later. But he distinguished himself most in ROTC, where he attained the rank of cadet colonel, and upon graduation took his commission in the United States Marine Corps.

Much later General Beasley would look back at those four years in a very different way than most recall their college days. For him these were the disconnected years. Lacking the military structure of the Marines and the small town atmosphere of Jumping Branch, he found himself without a social footing. Yes, there was intellectual growth – immense strides considering his background. And it couldn't be denied that there was a broadening of perspective as a result of his exposure to new ideas and cultures. But even that was limited. Fairmont State was local in its scope – most of its students came from within 100 miles of the campus. The student riots at Berkley and San Francisco State – even at Kent State, which was not that far away geographically – might as well have been on Mars. And even at this backwater of conservatism, Phil was considered an outsider. He did not pledge a fraternity, and he was not involved in athletics. Although he excelled in military science, he had no real friends in the ROTC. Even the Baptist Student Union, where he served as treasurer, was not in reality of his denomination.

Phil had six different roommates during his four years at Fairmont, all but two of them freshmen. The last was Wyatt Scarce, another loner of his class with whom he lived for their last three semesters. Neither enjoyed much social life. A victim of his acne-incrusted adolescence, Wyatt's face was scarred with pockmarks, the effect heightened by black bushy eyebrows that fused over a wide nose. Wyatt was only marginally more affluent than Phil, but he was a top student who would eventually earn a degree in dentistry and return to his hometown of Gary, West Virginia to open a flourishing practice until 1992 when a scandal involving improper liberties with anesthetized female patients was aired by CBS on *Sixty Minutes*.

One of the most traumatic experiences of Phil's college years came only a few weeks after he had begun to room with Scarce. Phil had just acquired his first car, a 1953 Dodge sedan for which he had paid a financially desperate sophomore $100 - $50 down and $10 a month for five months. The title would actually be his by the end of the semester. Phil's roommate needed a ride home to Gary, West Virginia for Spring Break, and offered to have Phil as his guest for the week. Financially it was an offer that Phil could hardly refuse. Scarce had arranged a week's work for both of them at the local Kroger's where he had bagged groceries during high school. Two of the regular boys were taking a week off, and the vacationing college students would fill in for the week. It was the best money for a week's work that Phil had earned in his entire life. The days passed by uneventfully until the Saturday before returning to Fairmont. Several times during the week Wyatt had dropped obscure hints about a whorehouse in the coal town across the mountain. Phil had basically disregarded the comments attributing them to his roommate's puerile tendency toward swagger. Finally Saturday came. "Well, what will it be? Are we going to get laid or not?"

Phil was wary. He was twenty years old, but "getting laid" would be a new adventure for him. He had recently had several dates with Janice Southall, a freshman from Huntington, West Virginia, where her father ran the town's largest bank. They had met at the Baptist Student Union. Janice was very petite, barely five feet tall, and almost painfully thin. Her style of dress was tasteful and in the latest mode. Her light brown hair was long, straight, and parted in the middle. Janice had a clear, pure singing voice, which she had developed as a soloist in her church choir back home. She also played the guitar and performed folk songs in the style of Joan Baez. The night before leaving campus, Janice had allowed Phil to reach up under her sweater and feel her small firm breasts, a milestone that he achieved only reluctantly and after patient encouragement on her part. As the couple parked behind the Science Quadrangle in the front seat of his Dodge, Phil slowly moved his hand up the sweater that covered her her midriff. He kneaded the soft Cashmere beneath his hand and felt the pressure of her palm just below his shoulder. He moved his hand up an inch and sensed the tightening of her fingers. As his hand moved across her ribs and cupped her breast, she began to stroke his shoulder forcefully in a circular motion that reached a crescendo the moment Phil slid his hand under the sweater and touched the tiny dark circle of her bare erect nipple. His prospects having reached this point, Phil's enthusiasm for an evening at a mining town brothel was not high.

"I don't know, Wyatt; the thing doesn't feel right. I've saved up more than a hundred bucks this week. Besides, it doesn't seem fair; I've got Janice now."

"Fuck Janice! You drive across the mountain with me, and I guarantee it'll feel right. This is vacation. You're not married or nothin'; the way I see it all bets for this week are off."

"You don't have a regular girl."

"Big shit! Janice will be your regular girl when you get back. You can fuck her eyes out."

"I wish you would watch how you talk about her. She's not that kind of girl."

"Oh, yeah. I forgot she's a saint. And you're the fuckin' Pope or something. Jesus Christ, I'm beginning to think you're a queer."

"Watch it, Wyatt."

"You know what I mean, pal. We don't get a chance like this every day. It's only twenty miles. We'll stop at a nip joint across the mountain. You can come inside with me and look around. If you don't like what you see, or if your conscience is still bothering you after we get there, you can just sit out in the car and wait. It won't take me more than half an hour – an hour tops."

This introduced another dilemma. Phil had never tasted whiskey; in fact, he had tasted wine only once, and then by accident at a friend's wedding the previous summer.

Nevertheless, he found himself waiting in his car that evening for his roommate to emerge from the small, unpainted shack with a fifth of Kentucky Gentleman. Phil started the engine and backed out of the dirt driveway as Wyatt unscrewed the cap and poured a couple of shots into two paper cups. To each he added two ice cubes and two inches of ginger ale. Just outside of town Wyatt told him to turn right and directed him down a dark gravel road that ended three miles later in the back of a hollow. "Shit! We missed it. Turn the fuck around."

"What are you talking about? We didn't pass anything."

"The hell we didn't. I've been back here plenty of times. The whorehouse is about a mile back on the right. The lights must've fuckin' been off; I don't know why!"

Phil turned around, and, sure enough, the driveway was about a mile back. But the long clapboard house was nearly dark – only two dim lights in the upstairs windows were on. "You sure this is the right place?"

"Hell yeah, I'm sure. Only the place is usually lit up like a fuckin' Christmas tree."

"What do we do? Go in?"

"Something's not right. Let's just pull back in the woods and see if anyone comes along." Phil had taken only a couple of sips from the cup since leaving the nip joint. He was surprised that the taste was not bad and that he could feel no effects from the two small sips. He had spilled a little of his drink on his jacket while bouncing over a deep rut in the road. The smell was sweet, not "like the smoke of Hell," as Reverend Belcher had described the stench of the forbidden spirits. He took a long swallow and began to feel warm inside. They waited for half an hour.

"I don't think anyone's coming," Phil said. "Should we go up and knock?"

"I don't fuckin' get it."

"Think they had a raid? Closed it down or somethin'?" Phil's voice was beginning to slur.

"Who the hell knows? I remember about five years ago they was a big riot supposedly when a carload of cadets from Virginia Tecl refused to pay the tab. Some fuckin' dispute over the terms or whatever. One of the whores called her boyfriend, and they was coal miners and Hoakies all over the damn place. Police came in and shut the house down for three months." Wyatt mixed two more drinks – a little stronger this time.

"Whaddawe do?"

"Who th'fuck knows. They's spose t'be a nigger whorehouse across town. I never been there, but I hear some o'the the Virginia Tech assholes are regulars."

"I don't know 'bout that. I don't feel good about messin' with that stuff. Sounds like it could be *real* risky to me. Maybe we should f'rget the whole thing."

"I think I know where it is. Let's ride over there and see what's goin' on."

Before they finally got there, they had made a half dozen wrong turns. Wyatt finally had to ask directions from a stooped over black man who was obviously under the influence. The place was a different layout than the previous establishment. Five tiny trailers in a sort of a cull-de-sac at the end of a short deeply rutted dirt road. Each had two doors with wooden stoops leading to separate rooms. There was very little space to park and no place to hide. The whole area was brightly lit by a mercury vapor light. Phil backed his car as far back as he could next to an old Chevrolet station wagon – a "woodie" that someone had painted green. Wyatt handed him another drink. "Do we just go up th'steps an'knock?" Phil slurred.

"Let's just watch a minute. I don't see nothin' but niggers."

"You said the Tech guys go here all the time."

"Shuddup an' keep your eyes open. I wanna see someone white."

Several times they saw a door to the nearest trailer open, and a large black man wearing jeans and a loose flannel shirt looked out. Finally he came down the steps and walked slowly toward the car. "Start th'fuckin engine," Wyatt hissed, but it was too late. The man was at the passenger's window.

"You college boys lookin' to buy some pussy?"

"How much?" Wyatt asked as he took a long gulp from his cup.

"Depends on how much you got t'spend." He pointed at the last two trailers on the end. "Starts at twenty bucks. Go up to fifty."

"What ya'got for twenty-five?" Phil heard himself say. He felt a sharp elbow to the ribs from his passenger." The man pointed to the middle trailer, a rusted green Fleetwood."

Pay me heah an' ask fo' Pearl. A real nice, young, light-skinned gal. She'll treat ya right.

"Young" is a relative term and is often in the eye of the beholder. Pearl appeared to be about ten years Phil's senior. She was indeed light-skinned. Although large-boned, she was only slightly heavy, and her rather broad face could actually be called pretty with large, expressive eyes. Her infectious smile, revealing a gold front tooth, was encouraging. "What's yo name, college boy?"

"Ben," Phil lied. "Ben Johnson." Pearl was not fooled.

"Well, come on ovah yeah, Ben Johnson, or whoever you is, and don't be so bashful." Phil met her half way across the tiny room. He had forgotten that he was still holding a full cup. "Is you gonna put that drink down, or did you bring some heah fo' Pearl?" Without a word Phil handed her the cup. Pearl took two long swallows and handed the nearly empty cup back. She laughed as her callow john instinctively rotated the lip of the cup around and finished the drink. He turned to place the empty cup on the table, and as he moved back Pearl draped her right arm over his shoulder. He felt her breasts lean against him and then her large right hand at his crotch. "You got a girlfriend, Ben Johnson?"

"Sure. I got one."

"She gotta name, lovah-boy?"

"Alice." He could hardly stammer the name.

"Do Alice treat you like this heah?" Pearl guided Phil expertly toward the small iron bed. He could feel her loosening his belt. "You can call me Alice if you wants. You can even call me her real name."

- - - - - - - - - - - - - -

By the time it was over, Pearl had extracted from Phil his real name – at least his first name, and Janice's name as well. She obliged his clumsy attempt at post - coital small talk with her customary humor, and even told him an abridged version of her life before showing him the door. "You try some a'what you done learnt heah on Janice, and then come back t'Pearl fo' lesson numbah two. I guarantee you she'll 'preciate it."

When Phil got to the car, Wyatt was waiting for him. "You stink!' Wyatt shouted waiving his hand in an exaggerated motion to disperse the odor of Pearl's cheap perfume. "And I can't b'live you went and paid twenty-five bucks! I talked 'em down to fifteen. All I gotta say is you must love that nigger pussy. I been here waiting for half an hour."

Phil was silent as he started the car. Putting the Dodge in gear, he nearly hit a blue Ford parked in front of him. "Better let me drive," shouted Wyatt. "You had too much whiskey, or pussy, or both. We'll never make it back to the highway." After trading seats, Wyatt poured what little remained of the fifth into two cups, but when he offered one to Phil, he found him slouched in the seat, unconscious.

The next morning Phil awoke with a fierce hangover. In addition to a brutal headache and an unquenchable case of cottonmouth, his whole body ached as if he had fallen from a two-story window. He allowed his roommate to drive back to campus. "You'll want a shot of penicillin from the infirmary when we get back."

"What for?"

"You're kidding! You don't want to be shovin' that root o' yours into Janice after you got a dose of the clap. Need to give it a week or two to clear up." Phil only shook his head painfully. Out of embarrassment, he skipped the trip to the infirmary; however, the impending symptoms never surfaced. But that Sunday night the nightmares resumed – only more hideous and vivid than before. He could see the Reverend Belcher astride his black horse, its nostrils flared, as the clergyman looked down over the smoking abyss. He could feel the steep ground of the declivity giving way beneath him as the preacher shouted.

"You've mingled with the Infidel. You have sown your seed among the heathens as the faithless Jew joined with the Canaanite woman! Now, meet your master!" Behind the preacher he could see Janice crying in the dust. She wore a wedding dress that was becoming soiled by the dark brown grime. The snarling dogs with the yellow eyes clamored past her knocking her off her feet. Phil extended a craven arm toward her. "Help me! Make me my heart pure as snow!" The dogs with their snapping fangs trampled Janice, and she could not move. Beneath him was the flaming abyss. Janice was shouting something. Her tears, blackened with dust and soot, were streaming down on her grimy white dress. Belcher's voice could be heard shouting hoarsely over the din of the bawling hounds. And a new voice from below. It was the dark guttural laugh of a woman, and below him he saw her. It was Pearl, the light of the flames gleaming from her gold tooth as she laughed and wiped the sweat from her dusky brow and gestured enthusiastically. "Come on ovah heah, Lovah-boy. Pearl's a-waitin fo yah."

Chapter 20

Max straightened up as the foreman rolled the blueprint that had been laid out on the makeshift table and returned it to the tube. The sun bore down with a ferocity uncommon for late September, and Max could feel the sweat gathering and dripping beneath the sweatband of his hardhat. He removed the hat and sunglasses and wiped his face with a clean handkerchief. Both his white shirt and the blue paisley tie that he had loosened too late were now drenched. Was it the heat or the sheer daunting reality of what was transpiring before his eyes? Two saw horses and a sheet of exterior plywood had held the final conceptualization of his thirty million dollar career gamble. The abstract. But all about him the hard physical reality of what he had set into motion was beginning to take shape. Strangely, the sight of what he had unleashed was both satisfying and unsettling. The earth-moving equipment had been gone for weeks leaving an enormous gaping scar in the alluvial earth that ran along the James River. Not since the 1700's when President Jefferson commissioned this very Kanawha Canal, at that time a 200-mile engineering marvel along the James, had the river bottomland withstood such an assault. Max had prevailed upon the architects and landscapers to spare the row of massive silver maples along the canal's bank. They had held out against the ravages of "100 year" floods that had been arriving with alarming frequency – six since Hurricane Camille in 1969. Max would not be the agent of their demise.

His hospital would be built to withstand similar flooding that could be expected perhaps every five years or so. The price of Max's strategic location would be the occasional inconvenience of a shutdown while riding out the high water. The architects had succeeded in creating a building that would be both functional and aesthetically imposing. The main floor would sit well above the flood plane. The massive footers had to be set extra deep into the musty walnut colored bottomland. Not a trace of Virginia's infamous red hardpan that had frustrated generations of farmer and gardeners but would have provided welcome stability here. Four towering cranes were positioning tons of steel beams into place overhead as easily as Max had assembled Lincoln Logs as a child. Already the outline of the building was becoming discernable.

Max climbed back into his Rover and pulled out onto Huguenot Road leaving a dark cloud of James River silt behind. When he arrived at Henrico General, he found Colonel Harrington in high spirits anticipating his impending release. Initially his recuperation from the heart attack had been slow and marked by two alarming setbacks including a nasty bout with pneumonia. But recently the Colonel's recovery had accelerated, and his vital signs had rebounded beyond Max's most optimistic expectations. "Who do you plan to stick needles into after tomorrow, Max? Maybe you can round up one of your old grade school teachers to work your revenge on."

"It would never be as much fun without you; besides, your defibrillators are so worn out, I'd be afraid to try them on a new patient – wouldn't make 'em jump the way you did."

"What will you do to amuse yourself?"

"I'll have to admit the place will be pretty boring once you're home."

"Not home – remember? Westham Green."

"Finest retirement community in Richmond."

"Old folks home, you mean. General Beasley couldn't wait a damn month to toss Louise and all my stuff out in the front yard."

"Aren't you exaggerating? I can tell you're really impressed with your successor."

"Don't get me wrong. Hell, I don't even know him, to tell you the truth. Only met him one time. But it's pretty clear how much he values my guidance."

"Don't be too hard on the guy. Obviously he wasn't your first choice – mine either, but that's not his fault. His reluctance to seek you out is understandable under the circumstances – especially with you in the hospital – and no matter what we think, he's here to stay."

"Here to stay."

"What do you mean by that? Are you implying something?"

"I don't know. Not really I guess. He just seems a little peremptory to me. A little too eager to take over."

"That's what he was hired for. I mean, the guy's a general with a distinguished record as a Marine pilot in Vietnam. Generals tend to be on the overbearing side – comes with the territory - but I suppose you have to have a little something on the ball to get that far up the ladder. Give him credit for that at least, and as for *you* calling *him* peremptory - - "

"Yeah, I know. Maybe it's just the colonel in me talking; I could tell you some stories about generals during my time in the corps."

"Oh, here we go. Can't wait to tell me about all the military fiascoes caused by headstrong generals who refused to listen to their subordinates. A little professional jealousy, by chance?"

"Maybe so, but a little deference to my experience wouldn't hurt. It might even make *his* job easier."

"Well, let's give it a little time. I'm sure once he sees you are up and around he'll seek your input. He'd be a fool not to."

"Think so?"

"Think what – that he'd be a fool, or that he would ask your advice?"

"Both."

"We'll see."

"Well, one good thing about your heart attack – it put a hold on that Crawford business."

"Yeah, I'm amazed I didn't come up with this strategy sooner. Next time I need to come up with a dilatory tactic, I'll have this in my repertoire. All I need to do is have a massive heart attack and my problems are over – at least until I'm on my feet again."

"What did his lawyer say?"

"Marvin?" He had no choice. Daniel Marvin may be a loser socially, but he knows how to win in court. You can't ignore his record. Even if he could have proceeded while I was laid up, it would have been a mistake on his part. He would have forfeited too much sympathy and legal leverage. This guy means to take us all down – me, the academy, anyone he can implicate. He doesn't mind waiting."

"So you think this delay could actually help his case?"

"Maybe not. They say Father Time can be the best defense attorney of all. But I'm sure he'll use his time to see who else he can involve. The more he can splatter or intimidate, the better his chances of getting someone to break ranks and win the case for his client."

"Maybe you should think about that."

"I'd die first. I've put a big part of my life into the academy – my best years, really. There's no way these people are going to take what this school's done and reduce it to nothing. I thought about it for weeks; I'm taking them on all the way."

"General Beasley – is he with you on this?"

"I'm not asking his permission. Like I told you, I've only spoken with him the one time."

"Don't let all of this get to you. Concentrate on your recuperation. I just looked at your chart; your numbers are looking really good. You should be your old self in no time. Poor Louise, she's the one I feel sorry for."

"That supposed to be a joke?"

"See you later, Colonel. I've got real patients to look after."

"Give them my sympathy."

"You've really got a way with words, Colonel. I'll stop by tomorrow before you leave."

"*Brad*, Max."

"What?"

"The name's Brad. And thanks for all of the care and the concern. I mean that, Max. I know all you've tried to do for the school this summer while working overtime to get your hospital off the ground. Not many would have done that. And there's no way Louise and I can repay what you've done for us personally."

"Forget it. Where would I be if it weren't for you and the Academy – and for you?"

"Well, I really appreciate all you've done. I just want you to know that."

"Sure, Brad. See you tomorrow." Max looked back as he left the room and motioned as to ask if the Colonel wanted the door to his room closed. The Colonel shook his head and clicked the TV on with the remote.

Chapter 21

Long before Point of Fork Military Academy opened for its 143rd session, General Phillip Beasley was securely in command. He had moved into the President's House during the second week of August a week before the football team arrived for pre-season. Formal installation was scheduled for Alumni Weekend, on the third week of October. It was to be a sumptuous affair with all of the military pageantry and many dignitaries including James Gilmore, the Governor of Virginia, in attendance. Also on that weekend, during the biannual meeting of the board of directors, the General planned to unveil his master plan for leading the academy into the millennium. The theme would be, "A City on a Hill." Chosen for both its geographical and biblical relevance, the term was intentionally paradoxical in its connotations. Both the imagery of isolation as well as notion of shedding light unto the world appealed to Beasley's concept of the academy's mission for the Twenty-first Century and beyond.

In communications with his administrative staff during the summer, General Beasley had gone to considerable lengths to pay due deference to his predecessors and their accomplishments. But he left no doubt that he would not allow the academy to rest on its laurels. He had an agenda, and he made it clear that he had no intention of concealing his plan from anyone. The underlying themes behind all of his programs would be modernization, communication, financial stabilization, and spiritual revitalization.

Two days after his arrival General Beasley called Ed Alley, the director of grounds, to his office. Alley had first come to the academy over twenty years earlier as an assistant to the Commandant, Lieutenant Colonel Bristow. A large barrel-chested man with a handlebar mustache and a receding hairline, he walked with an easy, almost swaggering gait. Having retired as a captain in the army, he was seen upon his arrival as someone whose military background could eventually make him a likely successor to Bristow. Within less than a year, it became clear that Alley was not suited to the day-to-day dealing with adolescent boys, and he was re-assigned to the Maintenance Department. Two years later he was made head of that department, where he proved to be an excellent supervisor. Alley's style of leadership was much better adapted to the personnel there, and he was instrumental in initiating and carrying out the long process of upgrading and maintaining equipment. Gradually he had brought order to a crisis-ridden department whose previous course of action was typified by responding to one emergency after another as they came up. He established a system of regular periodic maintenance for buildings, grounds, shops, and equipment. The academy's fleet of over twenty vehicles was serviced on a regular basis. A revolving schedule of retiring three vehicles every year was initiated, and over time most of the heavy equipment (ancient army surplus of Korean War vintage) was replaced with new or at least functional machinery.

It had been no easy task. In addition to having to wrestle with Colonel Harrington every year for additional funding, Alley had learned, out of necessity, to deal with superannuated and jury-rigged equipment and keep things going for years while the department was in the process of upgrading. He was also confronted with a huge backlog of neglected maintenance; for decades the improvements made on campus had been largely cosmetic. And then there was always the delicate issue of faculty housing. It seemed that campus homes and apartments had an uncanny disposition to develop leaks or blow out wiring around graduation time, Parents' Weekend, or whenever demands for manpower an equipment were most critical. Yet in the face of this Ed Alley had succeeded in bringing the department into the modern era.

He had also done one other thing. He had succeeded in making the campus a place that made an immediate statement to anyone who stepped on the grounds. The academy would never grace the cover of *Southern Living* as Woodberry Forest School had in 1983; it wasn't intended for that. Point of Fork was a military school and would always maintain a certain ambience of austerity. But within eight years every cracked sidewalk on campus had been repaired. Every dead or diseased tree or shrub had been removed or replaced. Every broken window, loose brick, or weak handrail had been secured. Worn out linoleum, torn curtains, chipped paint, leaking fixtures, loose doorknobs – whatever needed attention was addressed, and with the help of the Commandant's Department, the grounds were policed so regularly and thoroughly by cadets serving their penalty tours that not a scrap of paper could be found anywhere.

"You're the first person I wanted to speak with here, Ed; have a seat."

"Thank you, sir."

"Ed, I've always been told the first impression is the one that lasts. That goes for people, places, or schools like Point of Fork."

"I wouldn't disagree with that, sir."

"So in a sense you're really my right hand man when it come to how our school presents itself to the public."

"You've got a point there, General. We certainly try to stay on top of things."

"I can see you do. One of the first things I noticed when I took this job was the neatness of the campus and its overall state of repair."

"Well, it's far from perfect. I could show you plenty of things that are not as pretty as they seem. But we're always working to keep everything functional."

"I couldn't agree more; in fact, "functional' is a good way of putting it. But now I want to move beyond functional to the next level. If we are going to be a City on a Hill, functional isn't enough. We want Point of Fork to be a showplace. A place where visitors can see Christ's hand at work. A place that reflects His creation at His place. I want Point of Fork Military Academy to speak out to the world – to make a statement. Can you help me, Ed? Can we build a City on a Hill?"

"We can do whatever you say, General. You've seen our books; you know there's only so much money allocated - -"

"You don't need to worry about that. Never doubt the Lord, Ed. The funds will be there if it's His will, and I believe it is. All I need to know is that you are with me on this."

"General, I've put over twenty years into this school, and I have at least five more years 'till retirement. The people here at Point of Fork are special folks to me. You'll see that soon yourself if you haven't already. I don't know a man on your payroll –

maybe one or two exceptions - who won't go the extra mile to make this place work. We have good men here, and I can tell you straight up that you can count on their best work. As long as we're given the means necessary to do the job, we'll - - "

"Don't doubt the Lord, Ed. The means will be provided. As long as we honor Him, He'll honor us. I've got major programs that I plan to start on soon, but my first project is a modest one – one that needs to be taken care of right away."

"What have you got in mind?"

"We don't have a conference room anywhere on campus."

"The president's dining room downstairs in the mess hall is used for that."

"I know, but we need something more formal and readily accessible to the administrative staff – something designed specifically for that function. You know the two large offices right next to mine?"

"You meant the Guidance Department."

"Exactly. If you took the wall out separating the offices and re-opened that old fireplace on the end, the room could be re-furnished to make a handsome conference room."

"Well, I suppose it could, but I don't know where you would put the Guidance Department. And I'd have to check the fireplace. I'm sure it hasn't been used in fifty years or more. You know these old buildings; it's probably a fire hazard."

"Let me worry about the Guidance Department, Ed. That's my job. I'm sure you would have to get the chimney relined, but we can do whatever we have to in order to bring it up to code."

I think that wall between the rooms may be a support wall. It would be a pretty big job to - -"

"Check it out and give me an estimate of what it would take. I've scheduled a meeting for two weeks, and I'd like to have the conference room ready."

"Two weeks. Even if the wall's not a problem, it would take half my crew - -"

"Better get on it then. I plan to have a large table and furnishing delivered in a week or ten days. I've already talked with Basset Furniture, and they've agreed to give us a deal."

"Those people are pretty-much high end. You might want me to contact some of the people we deal with. I think they can come up with some quality furnishings that would serve our purpose nicely."

"Not our purpose – His purpose. If we're going to be a City on a Hill, we want to have the best. I already have it picked out."

"Alright, sir. I'll see what we can do."

"I know what you can do if you set your mind to it. Two weeks. That's what it's going to be."

Chapter 22

Ed Alley left the president's office shaking his head. Two weeks! His best men were over on Faculty Row replacing the front door to #5. Except for the Bradys, Vernon and Lynda Philpott were the only remaining couple who had not moved off the Row to the larger faculty homes on campus. They had remained childless, and perhaps because of that, or more likely because of their peculiar tastes and interests, they had never become assimilated into the school's community. Vernon had thrived though, notwithstanding his detached or aloof relationship with his colleagues. The photography business had proved a financial bonanza, and his *Tae Kwon Do* club was even more lucrative clearing over $10,000 a year for him in profit from private lessons and the sale of equipment. Vernon even profited surreptitiously by the academy's "no cars" policy for cadets by allowing them to park their cars on the sly for $20 a week in his carport. The Philpotts lived frugally and had invested well. In addition Vernon had taken full advantages of the academy's generous professional development program that funded all course work toward teacher recertification or advanced degrees at any of the nearby colleges or universities.

Vernon had earned his MS in Chemistry from UVA with designs on a Ph.D. in that field, but when he was not recommended for that program, he transferred to the university's School of Education where he had nearly completed his Ed.D. Originally Vernon had hoped to parlay this degree into an administrative appointment at the academy, but over the years he had come to realize that as an outsider of the "academy family," the likelihood of that strategy's coming to fruition was remote. Plan B was to take his degree elsewhere as soon as it was completed. He had saved enough money to purchase a substantial home and could find a suitable position at another private school, in a public school system, or possibly at a small college.

Philpott had few friends at PFMA. Most suspected, with considerable justification, that any friendly overtures on his part were selfishly motivated and would ultimately lead toward some ulterior end. One of the few who failed to recognize this was Dunston Brady, who was impressed with Phillpott's classroom antics, which included charging cadets 25 cents to be excused to the restroom, and occasionally raising a test grade for any cadet who would crawl on the floor from the back of the room and lick the linoleum all the way to his desk. Vernon had become friendly with him years ago on the night he saw Dunston help his indisposed wife up the steps to their apartment. Philpott fancied himself a subtle seducer – and a careful one – always ambiguous enough in his advances to leave a back door escape in the event that the object of his advances took offense. Rae Ann, no novice in the field of flirtation, recognized his designs immediately but had no interest in the sneaky little redhead with the shit-eating grin.

This is not to say that Rae Ann's interests had never ventured beyond her husband. She had been hit on a number of times – not by academy staff but by students, and she did little to discourage their flirtations. For years persistent rumors had circulated regarding her "more than professional" relationships with some of the more outgoing cadets. It began quite innocently. During her first year at PFMA Rae

Ann was asked by Colonel Harrington to sponsor a social committee to organize the dances that he had recently instituted at the academy. The result was the Fortnighters Club, which held monthly dances in Alumni Gym and also provided transportation and chaperones to off campus dances every month or so at girls' boarding schools such as Foxcroft, Stuart Hall, or Madeira. The highlight of the year for the Fortnighters was the Scabbard and Blade Ball, which was held on the third weekend in April. For two weeks members of the club were allowed to report to the gym after Study Period and put up decorations for the ball. Coach Wagner, a team player even when it hurt, tolerated this inconvenience with as much good cheer as he could muster. His one perennial complaint as Athletic Director was that the Fortnighters, who faithfully worked overtime to prepare for the event, and who were responsible for the cleanup as well, were always conspicuous by their absence on the following Monday, leaving a two day job for his gym crew before the field house could return to normal.

The 1986 Scabbard and Blade Ball was one of the biggest ever, especially for Rae Ann, who had prevailed on Butch Slay, the club's president, to book Bill Deal and the Rhondells for the event. A band from Rae Ann's salad days in Richmond, the Rhondells were enjoying a minor Renaissance during the nostalgia craze. More or less intact following their leader's release from prison, they mixed old standards such as "Be My Baby" with the more current hits. It took some persuading on her part.

"I don't know, Mrs. Brady; none of us have ever heard of this group. Everyone liked Cellar Rats last year, and we can get them for half of what the Rhondells are asking."

"Trust me on this one, Butch. This will be better than any band we've ever had. You'll be a hero with the boys, and Elena will fall all over you. I promise."

"You think they can play the modern stuff?"

"What do you think I am, your old grandma?" They were hanging ornaments on a Christmas tree for the Holiday Hop. Rae Ann leaned over to place a ball on a branch revealing an inch of midriff as her red sweater rode up her back. Butch had to admit that even Elena Curtis, his girlfriend of two years, couldn't hold a candle to Mrs. Brady in her tight jeans.

"I guess we could at least talk to them and see if they have an opening."

"Better call them before you leave for vacation. They're pretty popular, and I don't mean with "old people" either!"

"You're not old."

"Don't think so? I'm over thirty."

"No way."

"Tell you what. You book the Rhondells, and promise to dance with me when they do 'What Kind of Fool Do You Think I Am.' we'll see who's old."

"Is that a deal?"

"You get Bill Deal, and you've got more of a deal than you can handle."

"Funny!"

"You'll see." She winked at him, and he blushed.

- - - - - - - - - - - - -

Butch Slay was almost a Ted Henning clone. From a prominent family in Lookout Mountain, Tennessee, he was a nationally ranked scholastic tennis player. Butch was a good student, particularly in mathematics. He planned to enter Vanderbilt University the following fall and later join his father's engineering firm. Because of his striking good looks, classmates referred to him as "Robert Redford." Ostensibly this was a term of derision, but mostly the name was used out of jealousy. On the night of the Scabbard and Blade Ball, the theme was appropriately, "Deal Me In." Alumni Gym was decorated in a gambling motif (a concept that would have been anathema years later under the Beasley regime) with giant playing cards suspended from the ceiling. The tables were covered with green crepe paper suggesting a poker game with a royal flush in hearts set at each place. Major Reardon was the master of ceremonies, and Captain Philpott snapped a shot of each couple as they were called through the Arch of Sabers. He stood to earn at least $1,000 for the evening. Many of the cadets' dates were stunning in their low-cut evening dresses, none more so than Elena Curtis. But even she was no match for Mrs. Brady whose dress was split more than half way up her thigh. Dunston, in his dress Greens, looked awkward and out of place. Basically a non-dancer, he disliked going to these affairs with his wife, but since the Fortnighters was part of her job – a part that Colonel Harrington considered important – he always went along and danced the first dance.

Rae Ann didn't have to wait long for her turn with Butch Slay; "What Kind of Fool," was the Rhondells' fourth number. Elena was a good sport as Butch had prepared her for the imposition, but she became increasingly annoyed as the evening wore on and they shared several more dances. Rae Ann danced with other cadets - members of the club and a couple of admirers from the football team that she didn't particularly care for. It was well after eleven o'clock when Rae Ann asked Butch to be her partner as a profusely sweating Bill Deal slowed things down with a sensuous rendering of "The Tracks of My Tears." Elena sat icily and ignored the conversation at her table keeping her eyes riveted to the couple dancing across the floor. She watched his hand on her bare back and saw them linger together as the last notes of the song faded. When Butch returned to the table grinning, he was stunned and momentarily bewildered as he caught a cup of cold punch in the face.

"What the hell's your problem!" he shouted as Elena leapt at him spilling several cups from the table. Rae Ann heard the commotion and ran back to the table to break the couple apart.

"Get your filthy hands off me, you bitch." Elena missed as she tried to slap her rival with a roundhouse right. Losing her balance in her tight dress and high heels, she crashed to the floor. Her dress was soaked with punch. Several cadets, in their bungling attempt at gallantry, escorted Butch and Elena off the dance floor and outside. Neither Butch nor Elena was seen for the remainder of the evening. Dunston rushed to the side of his thunderstruck wife, and within a couple of minutes the mess was cleaned up and the Rhondells were rocking. Rae Ann sat with her husband for the balance of the evening refusing all invitations to dance.

Moments after arriving home, the Brady's phone rang. Dunston answered it. "I'll tell her," he responded, hanging up his phone. "It's the infirmary. There's a sick cadet; you'll have to stay the night."

"Fuck! Did they say who it was?"

"No, but I really wish you'd lay off the swearing."

"You know what, Dunston? You're an asshole. The cadets all call you an asshole, your so-called friends call you an asshole behind your back; I just wanted you to hear it from me for the first time." Dunston stared down at his feet without a word.

Rae Ann changed into her uniform in silence. When she arrived at the infirmary, the cadet officer of the day had already unlocked the door and let the cadet inside. He handed her the key. "Thanks, Andy."

"Will that be all?"

"Sure. See you tomorrow." Rae Ann went back to the admitting room. She went to the water cooler and drew a paper cup from the dispenser. It was then that she was startled to see Butch Slay slumped on one of the couches in the darkened room. She started to flick on the lights, but went first to the couch. He was motionless. She tilted his head back. "You alright, Butch?" When he failed to answer, she sat down beside him. "Are you sure you're sick, Butch? What's wrong? What happened to Elena?" Butch didn't answer; he just shook his head. She leaned and put her arm over his shoulder. A moment later she felt his hand beginning to move up her knee. Two fingers paused under the hem of her dress. She smiled and took his wrist removing his hand. "Isn't that what got you in trouble in the first place?" He looked up at Rae Ann and again placed his hand on her thigh.

- - - - - - - - - - - - -

The following Monday, Colonel Harrington called Rae Ann to his office. "Terrible incident at the ball the other night. I saw the whole thing."

"I don't know what to say, Colonel. Obviously we do everything we can to keep things like that from happening."

"I know, and you do a first-class job. Louise and I really appreciate what you have done with our cadets. You may be aware that before I arrived we didn't even have dances here at Point of Fork. The Baptists wanted to string me up when I started them, but I'm convinced that your program has been a resounding success. Although I believe strongly in single-sex education, I have never thought it was healthy to keep boys separated entirely from the opposite sex with no opportunity to have a normal social life. What you do for these kids is important."

"I appreciate that, but incidents like the other night make me wonder sometimes."

"Don't give it another thought. I'd say this sort of thing is inevitable from time to time. We might as well expect it. I would caution you, though, not to get too familiar with the cadets. I know it's not easy with what you do in the club and all, but I'd maintain a certain distance. Some of these young boys can misinterpret things and get the wrong idea. We don't want that."

"But I didn't even - -" The Colonel raised his hand to silence her protestation.

"I know,' he assured her, "that everything was perfectly proper. You have my complete confidence. I just wanted to touch base with you and make sure that everything is alright from your standpoint."

Leaving the president's office, Rae Ann felt better than she had going in. There was a slight lingering sense of guilt, but she had patched things up with her husband and would make it clear to Butch Slay that there would be no more trips to the infirmary with mysterious symptoms. It was her day off, so she walked across campus toward her town house on the row. Since classes were in session, she was surprised to see the red head of Vernon Philpott coming out of #5. She felt an impulse to avoid him by turning off toward the library, but looking ahead she saw that he was motioning toward her. "I've got something I want to show you; come on in for a second."

"Don't you have a class, Vernon?"

"It's my free period, and next period's lunch. I have all the time in the world."

"Well I don't. Unless this is really important . . ." He fixed her with a sarcastic stare.

"You don't like me, do you, Rae Ann? That's OK; you really need to see this. I can assure you, it's *extremely* important, as you'll soon see. I have some pictures that I just developed last night. I've been going over them all day."

"I don't have time for - - "

"Just for a second. Come in and I'll get them." Rae Ann came inside but declined to sit down as Philpott strolled over to his desk and picked up a large manila folder. He slapped the folder on his hand as he crossed the room and handed it to her. "I enlarged them myself." The color drained from Rae Ann's face. "I have several copies if you'd care for a set."

"What the hell do you want? Money? I don't have any fucking money."

"Who said anything about money?"

"How the hell did you get these pictures? Were you hiding in the infirmary closet like a fucking pervert?"

"I wouldn't say it's fair to use that term – especially considering the source. I'm a professional photographer; with my equipment I certainly don't have to hide in closets to get close-up shots. How do you like them? I'm particularly fond of that last one."

"What do you want?"

"Not money. Believe me, I earned enough that night to cover my time and expenses – even though I did have to stay out an hour or so later than I expected to get these last ones."

"Stop trying to be cute. Just tell me what you want and get it over with."

"Not much, really. Not much at all. I figure if you don't mind giving that kid a blow job, you wouldn't mind - - "

"What? Right here, right now?"

"I figure that would fairly compensate me for my trouble. At least for the present. Later we can talk about a more permanent arrangement."

"There's people around . . ."

"Not a soul. The whole Row is empty. No one in sight or hearing to bother us." He stepped forward and took the photographs. He placed both hands on her head and then her shoulders pushing her down. She was on her knees loosening his belt. She didn't answer when he asked if she would be more comfortable on the couch. The jockey shorts slid down, and Vernon felt her hand parting his legs. Her fingers moved up the soft, red hair of his inner thighs.

Without warning he felt an excruciating jolt of pain radiating from his crushed testicles. A spasm shot like a bolt of lightning up his spinal chord. The pain was so intense that at first he had no power to scream – much less to defend himself. His years of *Tae Kwon Do* were useless to him as she gave his scrotum a second twist sending jets of pain flowing out across his twisted body as he writhed in agony. She gave his balls a final shake and released the sack roughly. He lay convulsing in a contorted knot on the floor. He couldn't breathe, and a wave of nausea engulfed him. His whole body was warm and he felt that he was beginning to slip out of consciousness.

"You do what you fucking want to with those pictures. Show them to my husband, give them to the Colonel; I don't give a shit. You just do that, and I won't have anything to lose. I'll tell everyone who it was that took them and how you tried to blackmail me. Especially the part about how I put your perverted little red-headed ass on the floor!" Philpott didn't answer. He didn't move. He couldn't even look up as she left his living room slamming the door behind her.

Chapter 23

General Beasley's first official meeting with his administrative staff took place at 8:00 AM in the new conference room. The massive mahogany table displayed a prodigious centerpiece of fresh cut flowers in a large Waterford vase. The table was surrounded by twelve matching chairs. Before eight of the places a blue folder was set bearing the familiar Point of Fork crest. Above the table was a massive chandelier styled in the same pattern as the vase, and on the far end of the freshly painted wall the PFMA crest was again emblazoned, spanning five feet across. The linoleum floor had been replaced with red oak parquet, and a silk Persian rug graced the area immediately in front of the fireplace. By 7:55 all of the administrators had arrived. Before being seated they were directed to a smaller walnut table in the corner next to the fireplace where a continental breakfast had been provided. A waiter served coffee from a new silver service. At precisely 8:00 the General began. "Gentlemen, I would like to open this meeting, as we will begin all future deliberations, with a prayer. Chaplain Findlay, if you please."

The elderly gentleman stood and bowed his head. "O gracious Father in Heaven, we thank thee for this day, this school, and the people gathered here today seeking to do your work at this very special place. We thank you for the opportunity to labor in your vineyard. We ask that you will bless our meeting here today; give us wise counsel as only you can – that our work may be pleasing in your sight, that our harvest may be bounteous, and that all we do may be for your glory. For we ask this in the name of your Son, Jesus Christ, and for his sake. Amen."

"Thank you, Chaplain. Gentlemen, let me take this opportunity to thank all of you for being here this morning as we open a new school session and as I begin my first year as president of Point of Fork Military Academy. I have already met several of you, I have spoken with most of you over the phone, and I have written to all of you. I want to begin by expressing to you, the people with whom I shall be working most closely, how much I appreciate all of the efforts you have put forth over the years to bring this academy to the status that it enjoys today as the preeminent school of its type in the nation. Many of you have served this academy for well over twenty years, and the fruits of your labor speak for themselves. I am looking forward to working with each and every one of you. I can promise you that in dealing with me, 'what you see is what you get.' I am a very direct, up-front type of administrator; I have no hidden agenda. My feelings are not hurt easily, nor do I take offense at your comments or constructive criticism. I don't want "yes-men." By the same token, you will find that I will never hesitate to come to you when I see things that are not to my liking. If something doesn't look right to me, you will hear about it from me directly, and we will work together to make it right.

"As I look out on this beautiful campus with its wonderful facilities, I can't help being struck by the great strides this school has made in its first 142 years. The contributions that this academy and its alumni have made from the time of its humble beginning are astounding. Much of the credit can be attributed to your efforts. But as I look toward the future, I am equally struck by the challenges and tasks that lie before us. We live in a changing world, gentlemen; and if Point of Fork is to maintain its position of leadership as it approaches its sesquicentennial, we must not allow our academy to be left behind. We wish never to forget the values that brought us to our current status in the field of secondary education, but let us never become so complacent that we fall behind the learning curve in the ever-advancing progression of educational theory in a modern world. Change, just for the sake of change, is reckless and often counter-productive. But ossified and outdated concepts of education, while they may have been productive in years past, will not answer the needs of today's students who will be competing in tomorrow's world. We must be careful never to relinquish the good in what we have set forth thus far, but failure on our part to embrace new areas of advancement will ultimately relegate us to the second tier of private schools. During my tenure as your president, Point of Fork Military Academy will not find itself becalmed in the backwaters of secondary education.

"So in order to forestall that eventuality I am setting forth the four initiatives that I have outlined in the material before you, but first I ask that you look closely at the PFMA crest on the cover of the folder before you. You will notice that the Latin inscription, *Abuent Studia in Mores*" is now replaced with an English slogan – one that all of our cadets and their parents can read and appreciate: "A City on a Hill." This approach will serve us well. Not only does it distance us from the secular humanism of the former motto; it also looks toward a future that this academy must welcome if it is to fulfil its mission in the twenty-first century."

The men at the table looked quizzically at each other as they opened their folders. Rick Wagner glanced at Buck Bristow and caught the raised eyebrow. In going through the document page-by-page, it became clear that the General's plan entailed a wholesale revision of much that had been in place for years. Much of his thrust in the first area of modernization encompassed the second area of communication. Although the academy had begun using portable computers in a few of the classrooms in the 1980's and had expanded the program to include a six-tower server providing Internet, e-mail, and extensive academic services across the campus, there were still instructors, particularly some of the older ones, who had never ventured out onto the information highway. The training in technology that had been encouraged for years would now become compulsory. Computer technology would become a universal component in all classwork, and would be used almost exclusively for reporting grades and for daily communication within and between the various departments. Someone conversant in these fields would be brought in to oversee this initiative and facilitate its implementation.

Furthermore, communication between the academy and its various constituencies, particularly parents and the board of directors, would be expanded to create greater involvement in the operation of the school. General Beasley was perplexed at the academy's general lack of concern in this area. "If we are to carry out our mission for those whom we serve, how can we fail to seek out the input of our clientele and the people who are charged with directing our efforts? A report card every six weeks doesn't get it, gentlemen – not in today's market. Not with today's tuition and the tuition they will be requiring in years to come. Today's parents are consumers, and they expect and deserve more from our instructors. It's our mission to see that they get it." The General tied this point to the third issue of financial stabilization.

"The same goes for our board of directors. The tradition of a biannual gathering of old alumni for a pork roast and an afternoon of reminiscences is no way to run a school in the nineties. We need more from our board than rubber stamping a handful of proposals they haven't half looked at in the morning before a football game. I am seeking people who are willing to give of their time to provide the type of leadership that can take us into the next century.

"I also shall expect the board to give more freely of their financial resources." Several heads looked up around the table. "Do you know that there are eleven individuals (I won't mention names) who have served on our board for over five years and have given less than a thousand dollars to this academy? Six haven't donated a dime in recent years. I have to ask how serious their commitment to our school can be. Stewardship is a concept that implies sacrifice. This academy has been blessed, gentlemen. The Lord has allowed it to survive and even thrive in the face of fiscal policies that, if left unchecked, would lead to the eventual degrading or even the economic collapse of our school. I've gone through the books thoroughly and have seen the numbers, and I know where the lines on the graph converge. Point of Fork Military Academy may appear to be fiscally sound for the moment, but I can assure you that, on its current path (without significant increases in tuition and funds from other sources), this academy is headed toward a financial meltdown." Jerry Butler, the academy's treasurer, looked around the table in utter bewilderment.

Beasley then turned to the issue of spiritual revitalization. Citing the academy's founding by the Baptist church, he noted a gradual retreat from the school's original mission. "Much of what we deplore in society today is the direct consequence of American's rejection of the Christian values on which this nation was founded. When

God was taken out of the schools, the performance of those schools began to plummet by every measurable standard. That's no coincidence, gentlemen, and I'm sorry to say that Point of Fork has not been immune to the insidious infestation of modern atheism either." Chaplain Findlay met his eyes. "Oh, I know that's a strong term, Chaplain; but when you look at our faculty, our curriculum, and our general way of life on this campus, can you honestly say that we are living up to the Christian standards that those men set forth when the school was founded?"

Chapter 24

Max was in the back yard with Brett when Johanna called from the patio. It was Ron Frazier on the phone. He knelt on one knee placing his index finger firmly on the top of the football. "One last kick, son. Then inside for supper." The boy took three steps and struck the ball firmly with his right foot. Max smiled and shook his head in amazement as the end-over-end flight of the ball formed a perfect parabola straight over the fence and halfway into the yard next door. Brett and Max had been therapeutic for each other during the months since Justin's death. It had been more difficult for Johanna who had become increasingly withdrawn. Max had made an effort to block out the pain with activities designed to keep the family occupied with as many outings and activities as his time would allow. But he found it difficult to elicit much enthusiasm from his wife, and increasingly he began to notice that Johanna was spending time alone in the house away from both him and Brett.

"What's up, Ron?"

"Just calling to update you on things here at the academy."

"The kids haven't burned the place down, have they?"

"No, not yet. I guess they're settling into the new regime here just like we are."

"And how's it going?"

"Well, the new guy has come on like gangbusters, but we're all holding up OK."

"Yeah, well, I suppose that's to be expected any time there's a turnover like this –

especially with a general, and all."

"Sure. I guess you're right, but I don't think anyone anticipated the changes to be so sudden or that sweeping."

"You don't sound too enthusiastic, Ron; have you spoken to Colonel Harrington about it."

"Not a word. Has he said anything to you?"

"No. In fact I haven't spoken to him since we discharged him a week ago. I called a couple of times and got Louise, but he was resting and I asked her not to disturb him."

"Frankly, I'm surprised."

"What do you mean? Is there something going on that he would have mentioned?"

"A lot. And I don't mean just school policy. Did you hear about Crawford's lawsuit?"

"No. When's it coming to trial?"

"It's not. Beasley called Marvin this morning and agreed to settle."

"You're kidding! At the board meeting I thought we had decided to call his bluff and fight it all the way."

"That's what we all thought, but apparently the General has other ideas."

"It'll make the school look like shit when the papers get it. Beasley can't want that."

"No, but I'll bet he's decided that the school can take its lumps and cut its losses. Besides, this didn't happen on his watch. He won't get the blame."

"I don't know that it happened at all. What's Colonel Harrington saying about it?"

"That's why I called you. You're as close to him as anyone; we thought he might have spoken with you."

"Well, if it just happened this morning, maybe the Colonel doesn't even know. But I doubt that. Beasley wouldn't just do it without saying anything at all to him. Not unless he was just going to hang him out to dry. He wouldn't do that, would he?"

"Hard for me to say. He's only been here for a few weeks, and so far I can't read the guy at all."

"OK, Ron. Let me call the Colonel and find out what he knows. I'll get back to you as son as I have something." Max hung up the phone and dialed Harrington's number at Westham Green. There was no answer. Supper was on the table.

"What did Ron Frazier want, Max?"

"He called about the Crawford lawsuit. Seems that General Beasley's going to settle the thing."

"Well, maybe that's the best thing. Just end the thing and go on."

"Could be, but I'm surprised he didn't bring it up before the board. Seems to me that we should at least have some sort of input. And I'm concerned about how it will affect Colonel Harrington. Don't forget – he's named in the suit too – along with Buck

Bristow."

"Sometimes I wonder if that board and the school aren't taking up too much of your time. I mean, you have your practice and your new hospital. And I hope you're not forgetting the family in all of this. These have been tough times for Brett and me. You have all of your little projects going on to keep you occupied – it's been hard on us."

"I know, Johanna. You're right. Maybe I shouldn't have let him talk me into serving on the damn thing in the first place. Of course, I had no way to know about . . . the other."

"About *Justin*! You can say it. About *Justin* getting *killed* in a bus wreck!"

"Easy, Johanna, you're right."

"You're damned right, I'm right. Our family's never really grieved since Justin died. You've had your work and your hospital project and your damned academy board. Brett and I don't have shit. We need you, Max; maybe you owe it to us to get off that board." Max looked across the table at his son who was staring down at his empty plate. He had tried to spend some time with Brett every evening after work. He wanted to point out that he had tried to get Johanna involved with all of their activities, but he knew that would not be fair. He was trying to think of a way to put an end to the quarrel until he and Johanna were alone when the phone rang.

- - - - - - - - - - - - - - - -

It was Kay Alexander, the triage nurse at Henrico General. They had been trying to call him for some time, but the phone had been busy. "It's Colonel Harrington,

Doctor. He was brought into emergency an hour ago with a massive heart attack."

"What are his signs now? Have they started a catheter?"

"I'm sorry, Doctor Jarvis, he passed away just after he arrived. There was nothing we could do for him." Max froze for a moment. He removed the phone from his ear as if to hang up but did not.

"Kay, are you there?"

"Sure, Doctor."

"Is Mrs. Harrington there?"

"Right down the hall. Shall I get her for you?"

"No, tell her I'll be there in ten minutes." He hung up the phone, mumbled something to Johanna who had gathered what had happened, and hurried out the door.

It was early Saturday evening, and already the emergency room was filling up with accident victims, several of them reeking of alcohol. Louise met him in the waiting room; her face was ashen but otherwise she seemed composed. Max embraced her for a second before she gently pushed him away. "Louise, I'm so sorry. I just heard."

"I know, Max. I've talked with Dr. Phillips; there's nothing you or anyone else could have done."

"I haven't talked with anyone. I don't even know what happened. I felt pretty good about him last week when we released him."

"Oh, he's been upset for days. Ever since that new General decided to pull the rug out from under him."

"The Crawford case?"

"Then you knew about it."

"No. Not at all. I just heard less than an hour ago."

"Well Brad found out on Monday. Beasley told him, and he never got another decent night's sleep. I never trusted that man from the first. If you ask me, he might just as well have stabbed Brad with a knife."

"Well, I doubt that really had anything to do with - -"

"Don't tell me! You told me yourself to keep him calm, and then this new General comes along and tries to put - -"

"All I mean, Louise, is that we have no real way of knowing what triggered the attack. He's been in bad health for a while. It could have been anything. Blaming Beasley isn't going to help you or anyone else. The bottom line is we just don't know."

"You may be right, Max, but I knew Brad pretty well. This thing just ate him up. I just felt so powerless. And Brad was so testy. Wouldn't let me call you."

"I wish he had although I doubt that it would have made any difference. Maybe we'll know more later. What difference does it make at this point anyway?"

"You're right, Max. I'll go back and see him for a minute and then go home."

"I'll go in with you unless you'd rather be alone. Then I'll drive you back."

"You're a dear, Max." They stayed only a couple of minutes. Colonel Harrington appeared to be the picture of composure. Amazingly not a hair was out of place, and even his color was remarkably flush. Max wondered if someone had taken a few moments to tidy him up. He couldn't help imagining that Harrington might sit up and ask what all of the fuss was about. Max helped Louise into the car and pulled out of the lot.

"I'll have someone bring your car back tomorrow morning."

"I appreciate that, Max. You're too kind. Brad had some papers he wanted you to have. Something he was planning to give you. If you'll come in for a second, I think I know where they are."

Max took the papers with him when he left Westham Green. When he got home, he took the envelope to his study. He started to open it but tossed it on the table instead. He had had enough for one day; he felt dead. For the first time in weeks he wanted a drink. He went to the bar to pour a stiff Jack Daniels. The bottle was gone. He looked in the box in the cabinet. He was nearly certain that only one of the six bottles had been opened since Christmas – possibly two, but he doubted it. The box was empty. He looked upstairs toward the bedroom and shook his head sadly. In the corner of the cabinet he found a half-empty bottle of Scotch – not his drink, but it would do.

The next morning Max was out of bed before six. Brett and Johanna would be up within an hour to get ready for 8:30 Mass. The Sunday paper was on the porch, but Max went directly to his study and opened the envelope from Colonel Harrington. There were four letters inside. The first was a copy of a letter the Colonel had sent out to six former cadets. All of the alumni had been in school with Max, and he had known three of them well. Harrington's letter was seeking information about Crawford, Captain

Reardon, and anything that could shed light on the alleged secret society. It was obvious that he had chosen people with whom he felt close enough that he could rely on both their candor and their confidentiality. Two responses were in the envelope. The fourth letter was from a Major General Alex Tillman of the U.S. Marine Corps.

Max opened a letter from a Nathan Bowles, now a CPA in Lexington, Kentucky. Max remembered Bowles as a quiet classmate whose main distinction was that he had taken six years to graduate. A good-natured kid, he had become so familiar with the faculty and staff that over time he had somehow knew whatever was happening on campus before most of the staff did, and by the time he graduated he had acquired a key to virtually every lock on campus. Even Colonel Harrington had sent for Bowles early one Saturday morning after locking himself out of his office. But this time Bowles had little in the way of useful information. He did recall hearing rumors when he was a cadet about a secret club called The Brotherhood of the Sword. It was supposed to have involved Captain Reardon and a bunch of "weirdo cadets," as he recalled. While a cadet he had assumed that the rumors were true. But over time he had decided that the stories were probably malicious rumors – the ubiquitous type relating to unpopular students and instructors.

The second letter was in an airmail envelope bearing the name and return address of Luis Carbonell. Max opened it.

> October 2, 1997
>
> Dear Colonel Harrington,
>
> How good it is to hear from you, Sir! I wish only that the occasion were a more happy one. I am please to

tell to you that my family and I are well. You have never yet met my wife, Maria. She is a law student (much better than I was). We are very happy and hope one day very soon to raise a family. Maybe you will see some more Carbonells at PFMA! Our export business, as you know, is doing quite well. I would like to say a bigger donation to the school will be coming. I know it should be. We'll see what can be done!

About Crawford I can add almost nothing. He was my roommate for a short time, and I remember that he was kicked out for stealing a watch. That's all. He was not really a friend. I don't know about him and Captain Reardon. Just the rumors is all.

I wish I could be of more help.

Sincerely,

Luis Carbonell

P.S. The new President, General Beasley, do you know him well? Maria met him before when he was stationed at Guantanamo. She was very surprise to learn that he was made the new president there. I hope he will do well for the school.

Max reread the postscript and went to the final letter. The note from a General Tillman had arrived only two days earlier and was obviously in response to an inquiry by Harrington regarding General Beasley.

October 29, 1997

Dear Brad

No, I really can't say that I know Phil Beasley very well at all. I recall that he was in Vietnam about the same time I was, but he was flying F-4s off the *Enterprise* in the Gulf of Tonkin while my outfit was in country. I'm told that he was a good pilot; I understand that a lot of his promotions go back to his service there. But the guy is not well liked by anyone that I know. In fact a couple of officers have told me that the corps was more than glad to be rid of him when he signed on with your school. This is only hearsay, you understand; I've hardly even met the guy, and he really left no impression that I recall. But you wanted the low-down on the guy, and that's all I know.

If you really want to get to the bottom of it, you might contact Lt. General Jack Fleming or Major General Donald Jefferson. I think you know the former. To put it bluntly, they don't like him. I'm sure they would be happy to fill in all of the details that you want. Tell them I said to call or write.

Glad to hear that you are recovering well! Give my best to Louise.

One final piece of friendly advice – enjoy your retirement! The hell with Point of Fork. You did a splendid job for which you can be justly proud. If Beasley is any kind of man, he'll do fine resting on your legacy. If not, screw him!

Semper Fi!

Alex

Max stuffed the letters back into the large envelope. Brett and Johanna were still upstairs. He went up to find his wife still in bed. "Time to get up, Johanna. I'll wake Brett up." She rolled over and squinted at the sunlight streaming in the room.

"What time is it?" Her voice sounded hoarse.

"Almost seven. We gotta hustle to make 8:30 Mass."

"You and Brett go ahead. I don't feel well."

"What's wrong, do you think you have a fever?"

"I'm just beat, Max, and I've got a splitting headache. You and Brett, go; I'll be up when the two of you get back."

When Max and Bret returned from Mass, Johanna was just dragging herself out of bed. "I'm going by the Hospital for a couple of hours, Johanna. I'll swing by the Peking Duck for some take-out on the way back."

"I don't mind cooking. I think there's a roast almost thawed in the fridge."

"No, you get your rest. See you about one."

"You don't have rounds today, do you?"

"No – just checking on a couple of patients and a few other things."

"You mean that academy business, no doubt."

"Well, yeah, that too. Just a couple of things I need to check out."

"Of *course*."

Max grabbed the envelope and headed for the door. By the time he had checked his patients and gotten to his office, it was almost noon. He decided to call Dan Marvin at home. He introduced himself as a member of the PFMA board. Marvin did not sound impressed. "OK, Jarvis, I know who you are. What can I do for you?"

"Well, I heard that you and General Beasley have come to an agreement in the Crawford case. I wonder if we could discuss that."

"I have nothing to say to you. You can discuss it with your board. I don't see why you need to call me."

"Well, I'm also calling on behalf of Colonel Harrington."

"The *late* Colonel Harrington."

"Then you already know."

"It's my business to know; I'm an attorney. By the way, Jarvis, what business is that of yours? Are you representing the late lamented Colonel Harrington's estate? I could have sworn you were a sawbones, not a shyster."

"No, just a friend. I haven't spoken with General Beasley yet, but I'm concerned about Mrs. Harrington. All I want to know about the settlement is whether it includes him and Colonel Bristow. Frankly, I'm worried about Mrs. Harrington's exposure to this." There was a significant pause.

"You've got good cause to be concerned. To be perfectly candid, I could care less what happens to that academy up there. They can take their toy soldiers and their flags and banners and go marching off into Kingdom Come for all my client cares. It's Bristow and *especially* Harrington that are going to answer to me."

"Colonel Harrington's dead. You know that."

"Yeah, but the last I heard, his assets are very much alive."

"What's the deal, Marvin? Sounds like it's personal to me."

"Oh, I'm taking care of my client's interests – don't worry about that. The settlement we've arranged with the school is a handsome one. Crawford will be set for life, thanks to your Colonel's negligence. I made sure of that."

"Then it's a done deal?"

"As far as the academy's concerned."

"Doesn't the board have to approve it?"

"A mere formality. Your board's semi-annual meeting will rubber-stamp it this fall. That's a lot faster than going to trial. By late November Mr. Crawford will be a wealthy man."

"Then what's the point of dragging the others into it? Whatever problems you may have had with the Colonel are beyond redress at this point; he's obviously out of the picture."

"Tell you what, Jarvis. I don't tell you how to treat your patients. How about leaving the lawyer work to me. You stay away from my client, or I'll have your ass in jail. Just stick to your doctoring if you know what's good for you. Or building that fancy new hospital of yours. Seems to me you have more than enough to do just trying to keep your patients here with us among the living."

"That's a really tasteful comment, Marvin; it really becomes you. Shows your class!"

"Oh, I'm really hurt! Richmond's most promising young physician has called my comportment into question! Well, just so we understand each other I'll lay the whole thing out for you. I had no use for Harrington when he was alive and I have no use for him dead - except to serve the interests of my client. I'm sure his widow is a fine Southern lady, but that's not my concern. When I'm done with her, she can live out the rest of her days in the poorhouse for all I care. And based on what I know of the case, that might not be too far-fetched."

"What do you mean by that, Marvin?"

"See you in court, Jarvis."

Chapter 25

Phil Beasley's senior year at Fairmont was by far his most fulfilling in all respects. Having spent most of the previous summer completing his ROTC basic training for the Marine Corps at Parris Island, he returned to campus in the best physical condition of his life. There he was distinguished as one of a small handful of recruits who had also been selected to attend Navy flight school after graduation. Phil returned to Fairmont with his naturally dark complexion tanned to a deep bronze, and he had shed fifteen pounds from his pudgy frame since the previous spring. His stocky, compact physique could almost be called muscular. Early that year he was elected treasurer of the Baptist Student Union, and over Christmas break, he went home for a week with Janice to Huntington, where he convinced Mr. Southall to give him his daughter's hand in marriage. On Saturday, the day he left to return home, it was agreed that the wedding would be postponed until after Phil had completed his tour of active duty in Southeast Asia.

On his way back from Huntington, Phil stopped for gas in Gary. He did not contact Wyatt Scarce. It was 6:30 when he called Pearl. "Why, Phil Beasley his own sef! I declaih, I ain't heard from you *or* Ben Johnson since las spring!"

"I've been away at summer camp."

"You *is*? What they beet teachin' you? Archery an' merit badges an' sech?"

"Not kids' camp - Marine Corps camp. Basic training at Parris Island."

"I know, honey. I was jus foolin' wit' you. You done already tole all about it las May."

"I thought so. Listen Pearl, OK if I come over to see you tonight?"

"Why, 'coase it is. You know you's always welcome heah at Pearl's. I always got time fo my college boy! Jus one thing."

"What's that?"

"Wait till aftah 9:00. I got to go see my sistah fo a little while. Her chile's sick an' she needs to go out fo an hour or so an' pick up a few things."

"OK, it's 9:00 then."

"Right. 9:00, an not befo. See you then."

Phil picked up two hot dogs at the local Tastee-Freeze and drove across the mountain. He stopped at the same nip joint that Scarce had shown him the year before and purchased a fifth of Kentucky Gentleman. He had several hours to wait. He pulled off the road near the bottom of a coal elevator and drank nearly half of the bottle in the dark. He would save some for Pearl. A full moon was beginning to rise over the mountains into the clear winter air. He watched several dozen cars pass before he turned the key and headed for Pearl's trailer. She smiled broadly, showing her gold tooth, and waived at him as he drove up.

Phil was back on the road by 11:30 headed home to Jumping Branch. Physically he was feeling no pain, but as usual, he was already beginning to feel guilty. He switched on the car radio and began to turn then dial looking for a station. Several faded in and out weakly until he reached 1170 and picked up the clear, strong signal of WWVA. The waning twangs of a steel guitar tapered into the night, and a familiar voice came over the airways.

That was Jim Reaves, friends, with "Four Walls," and this here is your ol' coffee drinkin' nighthawk, Lee Moore, beaming out over 38 states and half of Canada from right here in Wheeling, West Virginia, home of the Jamboree. This last segment of the post-show program is brought to you by the good folks over in Middletown, Pennsylvania who remind you men that if you're really serious about making good money in a high paying profession, you need to send 'em that letter right away. That address again is:

> Truck Drivers School
> P.O. Box 111
> West Harrisburg Pike
> Middletown, Pennsylvania

I'll have that address for you again in a minute, but now here's a number by David Houston that's rose all the way up to number five on the charts.

> *La-ast night, all alone in a bar room*
> *Met a girl with a drank in her hand*

She had ruby red lips, co-al black hair

And eyes that would tempt any man

Then she came and sat down at my table

And as she place her soft hands in mine

I found myself wanting to kiss her

For temptation was flowing like wine

And I was a-all-mo-ost persuaded

To strip myself of my pride

A - all-mo-ost persuaded

To push my conscience aside . . .

    Phil pulled off the road to relieve himself. Even in his inebriated state he realized that the temperature had dropped to well below twenty degrees. The moon was almost overhead now, small and shining like a new quarter. The night seemed almost as bright as daylight. Phil stumbled off into the frosty trees, nearly tripping over a fallen maple, but he reached out to a nearby hemlock and managed to steady himself. It seemed to take several minutes to empty his bladder. He was shooting a stream uphill, and the steaming urine flowed back to his shoes. On his way back to the car, he could hear the disk jockey sign off. The sharp air seemed to have sobered him up a little, but soon after he slid back into the warm car and pulled onto the road, he began to feel tight again. He tried to concentrate on the news broadcast, something about President

Johnson's upcoming State of Union address, the but his mind kept running back to Janice and his act of carnal betrayal with Pearl. How many times, now, had he done it? Would she ever find out somehow, and how would it ever end? He could feel a tear making its way down his right cheek as the *Midnight Gospel Hour* came on the air. The first number was "He Called Your Name" by the Dismembered Tennesseans:

> *Upon the rugged cross of Calvary*
> *'Twas there my Precious Savior cried*
> *"Forgive them, for they know not what they do"*
> *O sinner, friend, for you he died.*

> *His hand is gently knockin' on the door*
> *Outside He's waiting' to come in*
> *His heart is breakin' as he waits for you*
> *To wash you free from ev'ry sin.*

Phil pulled off onto the side of the road. He couldn't drive. Between the tears, his conscience, and the effects of the alcohol, he was totally incapacitated. He thought of Janice, and he hated himself. He looked with disgust at the bottle on the passenger's seat. There was still some Kentucky Gentleman left – maybe two inches. He started to toss the bottle into the woods, but instead he unscrewed the cap. He took a long swig and felt the hot, soothing liquor flow down his throat. He climbed out of the car into the frigid air. Almost instantly his bare hand felt numb as he clutched the slick, wet bottle. He began walking. The tears seemed to be freezing on his cheeks. He passed a small house with Christmas lights still turned on. Probably a miner's shack. Out front, almost on the road, a crèche had been placed. It was rustic and simple, probably put there by a child. The Baby Jesus was an old toy doll; Mary and Joseph were larger dolls dressed up to look like the Child's parents. Horses, cattle, and sheep from a toy farm set were scattered around. There were even two pigs that the Holy Family would never have touched. Phil looked at the bottle and hated himself. He hurled the bottle, smashing it on a rock face across the road. Immediately a light came on in the shack. He quickened his pace – almost running for a fifty yards until he was out of breath. He came to a railroad crossing.

Phil turned right and began to stagger up the tracks. He noticed that his feet had become numb as he concentrated on his footing while skipping every other railroad tie. The effect was hypnotic – temporarily forestalling the unrelenting torment of Janice and her dusky rival that intruded on his psyche. He came to a trestle that crossed a broad gulf with swift bolder-strewn river about thirty feet below. He stopped and looked down. For a moment he experienced a sensation of vertigo as though he were falling into the chasm. He listened intently for a faint rumble that he momentarily thought he had heard. Was it a train? He dropped to one knee and saw a bright light like the headlight of a locomotive, or was it the moon reflecting off the stream below. He knew that he was disoriented as he began to scramble back toward the edge of the brink. He could not tell which direction the sound was coming from. It was still a rumble, louder now, and then there was the distant sound of hounds in full cry with the pounding of horses' hooves now growing more distinct. Phil scrambled to the edge, threw himself onto the embankment, and cowered. It was the Reverend Belcher. He turned the blinding white beam of a coon-hunting lamp on Phil as his quarry drew back. The dogs were snapping as Phil slid back onto the precipice. He could smell the stench of smoking flesh. He was falling.

When Phil awakened, the sky over the mountains in the east had begun to turn gray. He was still lying within ten yards of the trestle. His head was exploding, and his throat was raw, but he could not feel his hands or feet. He looked at his watch. It was almost six, but he had no idea how many hours he had lain in there in the cold. He walked past the crèche and noticed that the Christmas lights were still on at the house. Back at his car Phil found his keys still in the ignition. He started the car and began driving. He stopped at the first gas station he found open and got ten dollars worth of gas. He bought a large cup of coffee and a BC powder. He asked to use the restroom. In the tiny, fetid room he nearly jumped at the touch of his still-icy fingers on his penis. He noticed a rubber machine on the wall. "Should have had one of them last night," he thought as he flushed the filthy commode. He went to wash his hands, but there was no water.

When he got home to Jumping Branch, Phil found the house empty. His mother was probably at his aunt's for after-church dinner. She had had indoor plumbing for almost a year now, and Phil was grateful to have a shower before falling asleep on the sofa. When his mother came home at 3:30, Phil found that his hands had finally thawed. He did not appear to have frostbite as he had feared, but he was now sweating and too dizzy to stand. His mother was shocked to find that he had a temperature of

103. The doctor prescribed antibiotics, but Phil was slow to recover, and he returned to Fairmont State a week late for his final semester with a fairly serious case of pneumonia.

- - - - - - - - - - - - - - -

Less than a year after graduation from Fairmont, Captain Phil Beasley had completed flight school in Pensacola, Florida, and was aboard the *USS Enterprise*. He was flying protection along a 200-mile perimeter around the carrier in the Gulf of Tonkin as well as bombing missions into North Vietnam. Before enlisting in the Marines, Phil had never been 200 miles from Jumping Branch. See the world! By Christmas he had shot down his first MIG and was dodging antiaircraft fire and SAM missals in bombing raids over Hanoi. Phil had gained the reputation as a fearless pilot who never turned back and would engage the enemy almost to the point of recklessness. Several times he had steered his F-4 over heavily protected targets and dropped his payload long after the other pilots had turned back. He was admired, even by his detractors, but he was not popular. Few socialized with Phil, and even fewer cared to fly on his flight.

Shore leaves to Da Nang were infrequent on the *Enterprise*, and as often as not, Phil opted to stay on board. He had no friends to go with, and he knew too well how he would respond to the prostitutes and b-girls that he was sure to encounter there. It was always the same. He would walk the streets alone for hours, speaking to no one. Eventually he would purchase a bottle of whiskey – they had Kentucky Gentleman in Country – and for ten dollars he would end up screwing a Da Nang whore. Then back to the bottle and the familiar guilt trip. In the end he couldn't wait to get back into rotation on the *Enterprise*

Phil's daring in the cockpit appeared to be in marked contrast to his staid approach to all other aspects of his life. Elsewhere he was anything but a risk-taker. His pious demeanor and his colorless personality made him an outsider among his fellow officers. Yet it was this same single-minded approach that made him cautious and sensitive to the prevailing expectations of those in authority over him that also made him a stalwart warrior at the stick of a fighter-bomber. It was not that he was fearless; often he was petrified. But he was even more fearful of straying from the prescribed course. Everything by the book. Orders were orders, and he had neither the audacity nor the imagination to countermand his duty as it was laid out to him. Plus he was a truly gifted pilot. Ask anyone on the *Enterprise* about Captain Beasley: "He's fearless. He's got the best flying instincts and reflexes on the wing. He's a dumb prick."

Beasley's most harrowing mission came on the morning of March 8, 1969. He had flown fifteen missions in the past eight days, a record for him. Phil arrived for the briefing at 2:00 AM. On his flight was a Lieutenant Carl Evers. Carl was twenty-four and had been married to his high school sweetheart since his junior year at Virginia Tech, a fact that he then had to keep secret as a member of the Corps of Cadets. This became problematic during their senior year when Sally, an English major at Hollins College, became conspicuously pregnant. By graduation the birth of their daughter was only two months away, and Carl hardly got to meet Melinda before shipping overseas. Family and law school would have to wait.

By 6:00 Beasley had loaded his gear, checked his maps, and completed his preflight preparations. The four F-4 bombers had been advised to expect heavy resistance near their target, a SAM site located about twenty kilometers north of Hanoi, but the bombs were delivered on target almost without incident. The wing had reformed and taken a supposedly safe bearing when someone picked up two MIGs approaching at two o'clock. Almost immediately Beasley had one straight in his sights and fired the AIM-7, but the missile undershot as the MIG climbed. Suddenly he found himself being sandwiched as he detected a second MIG advancing below him. As he maneuvered to dive below the second MIG, the sky bloomed with flack. *God! They don't care if they take out two of theirs just to kill me*! SAMs were all around, looking strangely familiar like the telephone poles that lined old Rout 14 back in Jumping Branch. He heard someone shouting "Mayday!" on the radio as a SAM whizzed by. The sky was dense with flack, and he saw nothing but fire on both sides – he couldn't tell whose –*Please, God, not me!* – And amid the chaos and cacophony he thought he heard the hoarse, familiar cackle of Reverend Belcher's riotous laughter.

The radio was silent as he climbed out of the flack and turned for home. There was no sign of the MIGs. As the wing regrouped, he saw that Evers was missing. He tried the radio but he could get no response. Finally CROWN was contacted, and a search was called in. He landed at 8:15, and by 10:30 it was obvious that Evers was gone.

Later that afternoon Beasley went through Evers' personal effects – a common precaution before sending them home to the families of the deceased. As expected there were no love letters or pictures from girlfriends he may have met on leave. On Evers' desk was a letter that he had written to his wife only hours before.

Dear Sally,

Two more months! I can hardly believe that we're this close! Flying bombing runs is a tough way to pay for law school – and it won't, but at least we'll have a start when we get to Charlottesville. I think that with your job at Albemarle High School we can suck it up and get by. That's if Melinda's crying doesn't keep me from studying!

Believe me, I'd give anything to hear that voice right now – or yours after all this time. I can't tell you how much I miss both of you and how much I envy you seeing Melinda taking her first steps.

Thanks for the pictures. Please send more as soon as possible. Keep me in your prayers – as I do you, and thank Father Cummings for the prayers and kind words at Mass every Sunday.

Got to go now – big mission tomorrow early. But don't worry, I know how to take care of myself.

All my love to both of you!

Your husband, father, and daring pilot,

Carl

Beasley folded the letter and placed it in with Evers' other belongings. It was hard to believe – *Carl Evers in hell.*

Chapter 26

It had to be the most asinine thing he had ever done in his life. He knew for a fact that he was making a mistake when he walked out of the door after dinner. "Where are you going, Max?"

"To the office. I need to go over the account with American Hospital Supply." He looked back at the house as he started the engine. Ten minutes later he was on Franklin Street headed into the Fan District, a part of Richmond's inner city that had been unevenly restored at odd intervals to semi-respectability or above. Although some areas of the Fan remain derelict, the Federal and Georgian style townhouses on many blocks are as grand as ever and attract a young and affluent clientele. At 205 Shields Street stands Joe's Inn. Initially a humble fixture, since 1958 its trendy reputation has grown over the years with the area's chic Renaissance. Max walked inside and immediately spotted Frank Crawford siting alone in a dark corner nursing a Heineken. A half-eaten Greek salad was pushed back across the table. Max walked over to the table and sat down. Crawford looked up. "I know you. What are you doing here?"

"Can I buy you a beer, Frank?"

"Just started this one." Max motioned to the waitress and ordered a Bud Lite. "You want to talk about Point of Fork."

"You read my mind, Frank. You don't mind, do you?"

"As a matter of fact, I do. I've said all I *ever plan* to say about that shithole for the rest of my fuckin' life. Said it to my lawyer, said it to my shrink, said all I'm *gonna* to say from here on out. But I'll tell you this, Jarvis; I've fuckin' said enough. Enough to set me up for life. Enough so I can drink as much of this shit as I want to, every night if I want to, without some asshole heart surgeon having to buy me a beer. If I could manage it, I'd sue their ass 'till the fuckin' place closed down for good, but since that's not possible I suppose I'll have to settle for making their lives as miserable as I can. Just like they did mine."

"A noble undertaking, Frank. It must make you proud."

"Whatever. And you can tell your Baptist general that the Heineken Breweries in Holland want to join me in personally thanking his fine institution for financing my alcoholic addiction down here at Joe's Inn. I only wish that our great war hero, the late Colonel Bradley S. Harrington himself, were here to see what a fine upstanding man he and his school has made of me."

"You're a pitiful excuse for a man, Frank. Do you really think the academy is to blame for all of your dysfunctions?"

"Oh, that's right. I forgot – must have had too many beers for Chrissake. This is the part about how we make our own breaks in life. Isn't that what Chaplain Findlay told us every Sunday? Pull ourselves up by our own fuckin' bootstraps and don't blame anyone else for our own failures. How in the *hell* did I forget? And what was the other part? Oh, yeah – if you have faith in the *Lord* and live by the *Holy Word*, why shit! – You'll receive all you pray for and more! You'll have fuckin' *eternal life*! Kind of makes you feel good inside, doesn't it?"

"Why are you so bitter, Frank? Believe me, I didn't come here to preach to you. I could care less what you do with your life. But I sure as hell don't see how Point of Fork is responsible for whatever problems you think you have, and I *know* that Harrington's widow never did anything to you. Why are you after her?"

"Didn't come here to preach? Did I hear you right? Why, of course you did, Jarvis. You don't even have to *try*. Just your fine example is sermon enough; you don't even need to open your damn mouth. Why, just seeing you sitting across the table from me is an inspiration – coming to the rescue of a down-and-out derelict and a poor widow! Shit, it's just like back at the academy. What a credit to your fuckin' school. Just feast your eyes on that suit! And I'll bet that tie you're wearing would set a guy back a good two hundred bucks. And those shoes you got on! Plus, look at you; I don't think you've even touched that beer in front of you, and here I'm ready for another. Let's see, how many's that for me now?"

Max stood up. "I can see you're in no shape to talk."

"You're right," Crawford sneered. "Thanks again for reminding me. Nothing like the voice of reason to remind us social rejects to do what's right. How did I get along all these fuckin' years since you were my squad leader?" Max turned to walk away when he felt Crawford's hand come down on his shoulder. "Please sir! Don't walk away from me, sir; I need *guidance*!" Max turned and Crawford grabbed his tie pulling him back across the table. Both beers spilled, and Crawford fell back, pulling Max by the necktie on top of him as the table toppled. Max was now in a rage, knocking a second table to the floor as he yanked Crawford to his feet and sent him staggering toward the bar with a vicious right cross to the face. He threw Crawford to the floor, knocking three patrons from their stools, and was pummeling him when two police officers pulled him off. Both men were taken into custody and booked.

It was almost 3:00 AM before Max's lawyer had him released. Max had not called Johanna, and when he arrived home at 3:15, everyone in the house was asleep. Max didn't even attempt to go to bed. He took a shower and dressed for work. He looked in on his wife who was dead asleep. Max got a Diet Pepsi and started to pour it into an empty tumbler he found in the sink. It had been rinsed, but when Max sniffed inside, the smell of bourbon was unmistakable. He sat down at his desk and waited for the paper to arrive. At 7:10 the *Times Dispatch* landed on his porch; the story was on page two of the local section.

Local Physician Arrested in Tavern Brawl

Richmond - M.T. "Max" Jarvis, a prominent Richmond heart surgeon, was arrested last night with a second patron of Joe's Inn after a violent altercation that caused an estimated $1,000 damage to the trendy establishment located at 205 Shields Street in the Fan District. Both were charged with disorderly conduct. Jarvis, the chairman of the Virginia Cardiac Care Center, a state-of-the-art facility recently under construction on Huguenot Road, could not be reached for comment.

Also charged was Francis M. Crawford, of 411 Cambridge Street. Crawford, who recently settled a multi-million dollar lawsuit against Point of Fork Military Academy, indicated that he would file charges against Jarvis, his alleged assailant. Crawford, who has a list of nearly a dozen previous arrests in the area, indicated that he and Jarvis had been classmates at the academy during the 1970's and that he had been attacked after being confronted about his recent litigation against the school.

Max folded the paper. He could hear Johanna and Brett coming downstairs.

Johanna's face appeared to be white and swollen. "What time did you get in?"

"Late. After midnight."

"No shit! It was after *two o'clock*. That "office work" must be keeping you pretty well occupied. Seems like that "hospital account" is keeping you going late into the wee hours. What did you say her name was?"

"Take it easy, Johanna. Hold it down until Brett's gone. We've got real trouble. I'll explain later."

"I can't wait to hear this!" Brett came down and poured a huge bowl of Captain Crunch. Sensing the tension in his parents' silence, he gulped down the cereal and was outside waiting for his ride within three or four minutes. His parents' unspoken but relentless anxiety had grown increasingly oppressive to Brett since Justin's death, and recently Brett had sought to escape their tacit hostilities whenever he could avoid them. As the Farinholts' station wagon pulled away, Johanna turned a cold eye to her husband. "OK, Max, let's have it." Without a word he passed the article across the table. Johanna took almost five minutes, obviously reviewing the article several times. "I wish it *had* been some bitch. At least you would have been acting your age."

"I had no idea, Johanna. How was I to know the guy was going to practically tackle me?"

"You really want to know how all of this could have been prevented? Well, let's start from the fucking beginning. How about a little honesty? You run out of the house last night with some fabrication about work at your office. Then you proceed out to some bar to start a fight with one of your former classmates at that damned academy.

Hell, that school's taking so much of your time you can't even be bothered with Brett or me."

"Now hold on! You know that's not fair."

"Oh no? Well, look where it's gotten you. How are your financial backers going to react when they read this? How about the hospital, the dream that was supposed to be the great crowning achievement of your professional career? I'd say that's pretty much history. In fact if I were you, I'd be worried about your job at Henrico General; that could be gone too."

"You have every right to be pissed. I'll admit I deserve this, but you know I was just trying to do what was right."

"No, you weren't. You were trying to be a hero. You were trying to be the white knight who comes riding in to save the world. It's image, Max. Isn't that what it's always been about? You being the basketball star. *You* being the famous heart surgeon. *You* building the state's greatest cardiac facility. And *you* coming to the rescue of that damned military school you always romanticize over. It's you, you, *you* - not *us*. Bret and I have needed you more than ever since Justin, and you have chosen to retreat to your own little kingdom – leaving us to fend for ourselves."

Max denied it, but he knew his wife was right. It was the same old story. He could never leave well enough alone. "*Impulsive behavior*," isn't that what the shrink called it when they sent him off to military school? Probably a more clinical name for it now considering the bucks those boys pull in. *Obsessive/Compulsive*? Hell, *he* should be suing the academy – they were supposed to cure him of that! But he was never satisfied. There always had to be something else. Some new escapade out there – some grand mission. He had to be the hero. It *was* about him. Not his family, not his marriage, not even the hospital or the academy – *him*! And in the process, he had managed to destroy a family and a career that most people would have sacrificed anything to have attained.

Max got to his office at 7:45. There was a message to meet with Dr. Schofield in his office immediately after rounds. He knew going in what the meeting would be about. Ellis Schofield listened patiently as Max explained what had transpired at Joe's Inn. "I understand what you are saying. You didn't go there to pick a fight."

"Right. The paper makes us sound like two drunks in a tavern brawl. There was only one guy picking a fight and only one drunk – Crawford. In fact, I don't think I even touched the one beer I *did* order."

"No, but apparently you somehow managed to get it all over you – both figuratively and literally."

"I can't deny that, but *he* was the one who got physical. I couldn't believe it when he grabbed my tie and pulled me over on him."

"I'm sure that's exactly the way it happened, Max. But you used poor judgement. It was a serious breach of discretion to even be in there with him under those circumstances. You knew how unstable he was. His attorney had already warned you to stay away from him; you should have listened."

"When the facts come out, you'll see that - - "

"When the facts come out, our hospital's reputation will already have been compromised. At that time we can determine what your status with will be. Until then I'm putting you on paid administrative leave. Dr. Featherston and Dr. Moro will absorb your duties for now."

When Max returned to his office, there was a message to call Spencer Copeland at the bank. Sure enough, the bank was putting the project on hold until Max's status was resolved. It seemed unlikely that construction of the hospital would proceed until new investors could be brought in and Max's name was disassociated from the project.

Max sat at his desk. There was nothing there for him to do, but he felt no inclination to go home and share the latest developments with Johanna. When he thought about her mental state, there was no way to exclude his own contribution to her disorder. What had happened to Justin was fate. But his lack of support after the tragedy was inexcusable. His preoccupation with his own aspirations, whether they involved his surgery, the hospital, or the academy, had served as a distraction, blocking or at least blunting his sense of despair and loss. It had worked for him, but it was not shared with Brett and Johanna. He had saved himself but left them to deal with their grief alone. Some hero.

Chapter 27

When Rick Wagner met with his football staff on the eve of pre-season practice, he had every reason for optimism. The Titans were coming off of a 7-3 year, its worst record in ten years, but that team had been extremely young, dominated by sophomores with only one significant player graduating. Almost the entire stating defense was intact, and the offense had lost only one starter, Sylvester Crumpler, who had garnered All-State honors at center and signed with Ohio State. That loss was somewhat mitigated by the infusion of four talented newcomers including two massive linemen who had transferred in from a large programs in Texas. Wagner and his staff were convinced that PFMA was ready to recapture the State Championship. Rick was passing out playbooks to his staff when he spotted General Beasley in the doorway. He invited him in. "General Beasley, I'd like to introduce you to our football staff. I hadn't expected you to be with us tonight, but we really appreciate your interest. You have an open invitation to stop by anytime."

"Thanks, Rick, I'll plan to take you up on that offer. Gentlemen, I always like to open every meeting with a prayer. Would any of you care to oblige?" Mike Allen, the head JV coach, responded with a short generic prayer asking God's blessing on the school, the players and the coaches over the course of the coming season. The General smiled and addressed the men in the room.

"Men, other than my administrative staff, you are the first group I have met with in my new position here at the academy. I'd like to tell you the same thing that I told them.

I consider it a privilege to be with you here at Point of Fork Military Academy. I consider the academy to be a City on a Hill. And we are the stewards whose responsibility it is to labor here in the Lord's vineyard. Let me be direct. For better or worse it's a fact that our athletic program is the school's most visible point of reference in the minds of many of our alumni and prospective patrons. I hope Point of Fork goes 11-0 this year and wins the State Championship. I'm new here, but from all I've learned about the team and its tradition, I feel that I have every reason to expect that. But I'm also here to tell you that even if you go 0-11 you have no reason to fear for your jobs. At least not for this year." There was a ripple of self-conscious laughter. "What I want, and expect, and *demand* is an athletic program that reflects the Christian philosophy and commitment on which this academy was founded. If PFMA is to be a City on a Hill, its message to the world must shine forth from all of its programs – military, academic, and athletic."

"Gentlemen, I want everyone associated with our school to understand that we are evangelists for Christ every time we walk into a classroom, or through the barracks, or onto the athletic field. We all have to be on the same page with that. We want to win here at PFMA, but we want to win for the Lord. I liked your prayer, Coach Allen. I'd like to see every practice begin with a prayer; our cadets need to see that. It goes without saying that profanity by the players *at any time* should not be tolerated by the coaches and should be dealt with immediately and appropriately. I might suggest a one-game suspension for the first offense. I trust there's no need for me to point out that Point of Fork will have zero tolerance for such language from its teachers or coaches anywhere here at the academy.

"I want our parents, our fans, and our opponents to understand that when Point of Fork takes the field, we are not just winners on the gridiron. We want to represent ourselves and this academy as winners in the Crusade for Salvation. Anything less than that will be marked down as a loss in my scorebook. You have my best wishes for a successful season, coaches. If you play by the rules, I know you will be victorious. I look forward to being at practice from time to time and, insofar as possible, at all of your games."

Coach Wagner thanked the General. As soon as Beasley left the room, Rick set up a depth chart and started to fill in the probable stating offense. He wrote in Bill Birkhead for tight end and stopped abruptly. He turned around and stared at his staff. "Based on what he said, I don't know if we'll have eleven players to put on the field for the first game. We might have to get the tuba player from the band to fill in at quarterback."

General Beasley had inherited a veteran staff. Ron Frazier, Buck Bristow, and Rick Wagner had all come into the administration through the school's academic ranks. Jerry Butler had taught math at the academy for six years before going back to school to earn his MBA. He returned to Point of Fork as Assistant Treasurer. Chaplain Ed Findlay, was a PFMA alumnus. Under Colonel Harrington the school's administration had remained small; most of the faculty and staff had raised their young families together on Faculty Row and had maintained close personal ties with the faculty. Salaries were uniformly low, so (with few exceptions) rank conferred little status or jealousy among friends and associates whose bonds had been so intimate through the years. The same continuity characterized the teaching staff. The yearly turnover was always low. Despite the many quirks that manifest themselves in people living so closely together, the school had somehow fostered a genuine sense of family and easy familiarity among most of its staff. Children raised at Point of Fork often remained close friends long after leaving for college and marriage. Even social misfits such as Vernon Philpott, Dunston Brady, and John Reardon were tolerated and assimilated if not totally accepted. Every family has a skeleton or two in its closet.

August 25 was the opening day of pre-school meetings, and Pleasants was the first to arrive for breakfast. He had spent the last two weeks of vacation with his sister in Charlotte, and he was returning with a tale to tell. He did not have long to wait as he was soon joined at the accustomed table by Taliaferro, who flung his tray down in a clatter of disgust. "I see that our dining establishment hasn't improved on its breakfast cuisine." He gazed despondently at his tray of runny eggs and then to Pleasants' tray. "What's that – a sausage?"

"You tell me."

"I believe it was so-designated on the menu, but I declare for all the world, it appears to be a big fat dick!"

"I have no use for it. Care to indulge your appetite?"

"Need you ask?" And with surprising celerity he plunged his fork lustily into the offending member, conveyed it to his tray, carved it into three greasy morsels, and dispatched it in as many bites.

"I can see that you brought your appetite back with you," Pleasants remarked.

"Well, I have to eat *something*, but I must say this nauseating spectacle is enough to induce a fast of forty days." He glared malevolently as the families began to file in. His eyes fell on Rae Ann Brady. "Look at that strumpet! I have to wonder how that pusillanimous mouse of a husband can keep her satisfied."

"Oh, she stays well-satisfied; you can be assured of that," offered Pleasants rolling his eyes. "I'm told she is of a most generous nature, although I'm not sure Vernon Philpott would be in accordance with that characterization."

"And would you look at that hussy, the Reverend's Mrs. Findlay."

"The help-meet of our chaplain? I'm surprised at you, Jubal!"

"Oh, she may look sweet and play the role of the pious spouse, but don't be fooled."

"How can you press such calumny on this fine Christian woman without hard facts, if you'll excuse the pun?"

"Trust me, Shelby. She may look sweet and compassionate, but those are the most dangerous ones. Give her the opening, and she would cut your balls off."

"Well, I have some news." Taliaferro raised his head. "We have a new scholar of some renown entering the corps this fall."

"A jock, no doubt."

"What else?" His name is Luther Franklin, quite a basketball star at East Mecklenburg apparently, and the *Charlotte Observer* has run a number of articles on his departure for greener pastures."

"I trust that their loss and his eminent matriculation here will assure us of many a glorious winter evening."

"And the gratifying spectacle of supplicant coaches from all over to our venerable gymnasium."

"By all means remind them to genuflect upon entering our illustrious temple of sweat. How is it that our campus is to be graced with Mr. Franklin's august presence? Did we have to delve into the teachers' pension plan to purchase a new sports car?"

"Oh, I don't think he could fit into one of those. The paper says he's 7'2" and weighs almost three hundred pounds. I understand his academic statistics are not so impressive, though. Plus he seems to have run afoul of some of the local *gendarmes* although the charges were dropped. It's all in the articles; it appears that some of the faculty at the high school even had the temerity to try and interfere with his basketball career. A little issue of academics."

"No doubt all of North Carolina's in mourning over our gain."

"It's all here in the articles. You can read all about it."

"I can't wait. And little do I doubt that this sterling lad will be scheduled into my Senior Government class."

Taliaferro's speculation proved prophetic, and two weeks later the towering bulk of Luther Franklin was wedged into the largest desk on the front row of his third period government class. Cadets had been issued their first evening's assignments, and

Taliaferro opened class with a few general remarks on the previous night's reading. "Gentlemen, you read a chapter last night outlining the three branches of government. Can anyone refresh our memory as to what these three branches could be? Yes, Mr. Stokes?"

"Legislative, executive, and judicial."

"Very good. And Mr. Webber, would you be kind enough to edify us regarding the composition and function of the legislative branch?"

"Yes, sir. That would be the Senate and the House of Representatives. Basically they write the laws."

"Basically, you are correct, Mr. Webber. And Mr. Dooley, could you tell us something about the executive branch?"

"That would include President and his cabinet."

"True enough, and the Vice President. But what do they do, Mr. Dooley?"

"I guess they approve the laws that the Congress makes."

"Fine, one of the main functions of the President is to ratify bills sent by Congress, but the duties and prerogatives of the executive branch extend far beyond those parameters. We'll go into that in some detail later. Now what of the judicial branch? Mr. Franklin, perhaps you can enlighten us as to the function of that branch of government." The question drew a blank stare. "Mr. Franklin?"

"I'm not sho what you's axin'."

"What I'm *axin* is your views on the judicial branch of the government; surely, you have some familiarity with the legal system." The hulking student's eyes dropped.

"You means da po-lice an' th'coats? That what you talkin' bout?" His eyed his new adversary with distrust.

"Sure, Mr. Franklin, tell us what you know about the courts."

"I donno that much 'bout 'em. I only been in dere onest – las summah."

"Then perhaps you can tell the rest of us how the system works – based on your personal experience." Franklin's eyes narrowed and his face hardened.

"I ain't got no complaint. Said I done beat the shit out my hist'ry teachah aftah school fo' makin' fun o'me, but dey ain't got no proof on me an' done found me innercent, whilst th' po bastard I spose t'done assaulted is still in th'hospital wit fo broken bones."

What Luther Franklin lacked in diction he more than made up for in straightforward candor. The plain-spoken senior earned his "gentleman's C" in Government as well as all of his other courses. He averaged 21 points and 14 rebounds at PFMA, and after a two-year stint with Dean Smith's Tar Heels, he was the first-round pick of the Denver Nuggets. But even in that rarified air on the other side of the continent, he never forgot his friends back in Virginia. After signing his second lucrative contract as well as a shoe deal and various other endorsements, Franklin donated $250,000 toward a learning resource center at Point of Fork.

Chapter 28

Max had done almost nothing but eat and sleep for two weeks – and very little of that. His instincts for self-preservation had been frustrated at every turn. He was out at Henrico General. Soon he would have no regular income, but his mortgage payments would be coming due on schedule. Construction had been halted on the hospital. Spencer Copeland at the bank was breathing down his neck. His partners wanted him officially disassociated from the project – the sooner the better. *His* project – he reminded them. And worst of all, Johanna. No support, no communication, nothing. He couldn't blame her; as always he had gone off on his own without asking anyone and done what *he* thought was right. She was never consulted or made to feel a part of the planning; by what right or logic should he count on her support now that he had managed to lay waste to everything? She looked awful, her drinking was becoming more evident, and their rift was beginning to take its toll on Brett. Max had hired Louis Murray as his attorney to oversee the complexities of his entanglements with Crawford, the bank, and his partners. Plus Murray handled divorces – a consideration that Max tried to suppress. Above all, Murray had warned Max *not to do anything* to exacerbate the situation. "Give me a week to make some inquiries and see what real options you have. You stay put; if you don't rock the boat we may be able to salvage your career and even your project – *maybe*. But for now just leave *everything* to me." Fat chance.

The PFMA board of directors was scheduled to meet during Alumni Weekend on the afternoon following the Staunton Game. Johanna had urged Max to skip the function in light of all that had happened, but Max was determined to go. He had even called Tom Hatch.

"You're out of your mind, Jarvis. No way!"

"It's the *only* way, Tom. I've got to know."

"*Why* have you '*gotta know*'? Haven't you carried this shit too far already? Your name's been plastered all over the newspapers, I understand your career's shot, and God knows what this is doing to your family."

"That's just it. There's no logical reason for me to turn back now; I'm too far in, so I might as well push this forward to the end. I've got nothing to lose at this stage of the game, and at least I'll know the truth."

"Great! And what do you think the knowing the truth will accomplish for you at this point? Let's say you prove that Crawford's a liar – that this Brotherhood of the Sword, as he calls it, was the product of his deranged imagination. What have you accomplished then? Will it save your hospital? Will it reconcile you with Johanna? Will it do anything to unseat this new asshole of a president that you seem to detest to the point of ruining your life? Even if you're right, what do you hope to get out of this?"

"You say you know a way into the tunnels?"

"*Knew* the way – fifteen years ago. Hell, they've added a dozen buildings since we left; for all we know, the tunnels might not even *be* there anymore."

"But you remember where the opening was."

"Sure, I guess so. Five or six of us met there almost every night for a smoke. Used to walk all through there. Lots of nice things you learn at military school."

"Meet me Friday night on the track. Wear dark clothes. I'll be next to the pole vault pit at midnight. I'll bring two lights."

"This is really beginning to sound like the Hardy Boys. Listen, Max, this isn't some Disney movie; we're adults, and this is real life. You should listen to what your friends are saying about you. They say you've totally lost it, and I'm beginning to believe them. This isn't rational."

"I left rational behind a long time ago, Tom. Rational can't help me now. I need answers that I can't get by playing the game and following the rules. I'm using my own logic. It's the only way."

"You've totally lost it."

"You may be right, but I've got nothing to lose at this point."

"Yeah, *you've* got nothing to lose, but how about *me*. I still have my family and career that I haven't screwed up yet. I make a lot of damn money twisting kids' teeth straight; I don't need to get myself into the same fix you're in."

"You won't. I've got it all figured out. You'll be safe torturing your patients back in Knoxville, and no one will be the wiser."

"Tell me, Max, did you have it all figured out when you met Crawford at that bar?"

"Listen. We meet at midnight. Take me to the tunnel – the grate that's unlocked."

"The one that *was* unlocked fifteen years ago! The hasp was loose. They're sure to have found it by now. There may not even *be* an opening now. They could have a building standing there. We don't even know if those tunnels exist anymore."

"OK – we get there and there's no opening. That's it, then. No harm – no foul. We just turn around and go home, but at least we gave it our best shot."

"And if it's there?"

"Then it's up to you. You can come with me if you want, you can stand guard outside the tunnel, or you can get in your car and drive back to your motel."

"They're all right. You're insane!"

"Then you'll help me?"

"Like I said, you're nuts."

Max had been standing on the track for twenty minutes. It was 12:15, and his eyes had become accustomed to the dark. Finally he saw a dark-clad figure emerging from the murky gloom, and soon he was able to discern the shiny dome and familiar grin of Tom Hatch. "A little early for the board meeting," he whispered.

"Glad you still have your sense of humor; we may need some cheering up before this is all over. Are you sure you want to go through with this?"

"Hell, yeah! Why else would we be out here in the middle of the damned night?" There was a long silence.

"Well - - I guess I owe you one. Now we can call it even."

"Owe me one?"

"You could say that."

"Call *what* even? I don't know what the hell you're talking about!" Another pause.

"Remember the poem about The Three Gents?"

"You? How the hell did you get in there? I had the only key. The tunnels, my friend; you'll soon see. One of the entrances was right under the ditto table."

"Start marching, asshole! Where's the open grate?"

"Just let me get my damned bearings. It wasn't that easy to find even then. We need to go back behind the parade ground toward the rifle range."

"What the hell was the tunnel doing out that far?"

"Supposedly the new gym was going there eventually."

"Well, then the opening may still be there. The field house is beside the football field – where the old armory used to be."

"Unless they built something else there."

"I don't think so. That area's all grown up in shrubs and pine trees. They play paint ball back there now."

"Good luck on us finding it, then."

"Let's get started." They crossed the track and walked in the dark along the tree line skirting the open area of the campus. The white pines that now bordered the parade field were nearly twenty feet tall. Many were nearly a foot in diameter. Tom led

Max back into the thicket and began to wander around.

"It's all different now. Even if the grate were here, I don't think I could find it."

"Put one of these headlamps on. See if the light helps."

"And bring the night watchman down here? No thanks."

"That old Sergeant Makepeace never caught anyone in his life. He's probably been asleep in the guard room for an hour by now."

"I'm sure Makepeace is long gone to that great guardroom in the sky. He must have been eighty when we were here. They've probably got whole crew of night watchmen by now. *Young* guys with infrared cameras."

"Right – and GPS equipment to pinpoint vulnerable spots on campus in case the Chinese try to storm the academy! No doubt they're watching us right now."

"Just keep the light off. We're pretty close to the place."

"How do you know?"

"It was almost at the bottom of this hill. If it's still here, it would have to be between where we're standing and those old oak trees. I remember them."

"How about behind those shrubs?" The blackberry bushes were nearly impenetrable, but the two men worked their way through the briars. Max tripped on the grate, and nearly fell. It was almost completely covered with vegetation."

"Here it is." They pulled back the weeds and rotting boards that had apparently been placed there years ago. Max yanked on the grate and cleared the debris away from the lock. He saw the crusty green Yale still in place. "Shit! It's locked."

"It was *always* locked. Try the hasp." Max grabbed a piece of wood and slipped it between the hasp and the frame of the grate. The hasp came up easily.

"We're in!" Max lifted the grate and set it in the weeds. He stood up sweating and puffing, but grinning at his erstwhile classmate. "OK, Tom, this is it. You've done everything you agreed to – *more* than you ever agreed to. You can turn around now, walk back to your car, and be safe in bed by two o'clock. I'll see you at the board meeting tomorrow morning." Tom looked at his friend's lunatic grin and grabbed one of the headlamps.

"Let's get going. You'll be here until daybreak trying to find the old gym by yourself."

Max climbed down the eight rungs of the iron ladder. As soon as he was at the bottom, he turned on his headlamp and waited for his accomplice. Tom switched on his headlamp and looked around at the dank walls. It had been a dry summer, and the cement floor was dry in most places. "We weren't so high-tech back in those days. All we had was candles or rolled up newspapers to light our way." Tom led the way down the long tunnel, pushing aside cobwebs that clung to the moldy walls.

"Where does this thing hook up with the rest of the system? It seems like we've walked a mile already."

"Not really. Distances just seem longer down here in these narrow corridors. We're almost at the first junction." About twenty yards ahead, the corridor formed a Y. Tom looked up and saw another grate. "This is the first junction. That grate was always locked. We're right under the main quadrangle. The flagpole is almost directly above us. The left fork goes up to Heritage Hall. The other eventually works it way back to the old gym." They followed the right fork.

"Are you sure you know where you are going?"

"This place hasn't changed at all. I could do it blindfolded." They passed through two more connections before taking a tunnel that forked to the right and ended after about thirty yards. "OK, Max, we're here. This ladder takes us to the old boiler room. Assuming it's open and the door to the gym's not locked, you'll have your answer in a couple of minutes."

"Think we should turn our lights off?"

"No need to as long as we stay in the basement." There were only four steps leading up to the basement. The old grate opened easily, but the door from the boiler room into the old gym was locked. Max gave it one shove with his shoulder, and the hinges gave way.

"We're in!"

"OK, now what?"

"We look for evidence."

"Like what – you think Reardon left a scrapbook of naked boys?"

"We should be so lucky! I guess what I'm *hoping* to find is nothing."

"*That's* why you dragged me out here? You can't prove a negative. You don't know who's been in here over the years. They could have cleaned up all of the "evidence" years ago."

"Look around, Tom. I doubt if the place has been touched."

"And what if you *do* find some kind of proof? A smoking gun. Where the hell does that leave you?"

"I guess I'll have to go to Crawford and apologize to the poor bastard."

"What exactly are we looking for?"

"Crawford described a ritual. We're looking for cigarette butts, candle wax, soft drink cans - -"

"Shit, Jarvis – *we* had candles and cigarettes when we were in here; I told you that."

"Did you guys bring in soft drinks too?"

"Hell, I don't remember. Probably. It was fifteen fucking years ago!"

"Mountain Dew? Marlboros?"

"How the hell should I know? They were pretty popular brands."

"How about ping pong paddles? Did you play table tennis down here too?"

"Let's have a look around."

The boiler room was next to the showers. Across from the showers were the locker room and a hall leading to the pool. The doors to the lockers were all open with the exception of #1, which was still padlocked. Max turned the beam of his light down into the pool. "Holy shit." Four tables were standing on the pool floor, and about a dozen folding chairs were stacked against the wall at the far end. Looking down, they could see melted wax on all of the four tables. Cigarette butts were strewn along the edges of the pool as though they had been swept aside. Next to the folded chairs was a large metal trashcan with a top on it – what Max and Tom used to call the GI can as cadets.

"You going down there?" Max shook his head sadly and didn't respond for a few seconds.

"No. I think I've seen enough. I wish to hell I hadn't found this. I feel like I want to puke."

"Well, you brought me all the way out here in the middle of the night. I'm going to check this out." Tom climbed down into the shallow end of the pool and began to pick up cigarette butts, holding them up to the light. "We're ten for ten, Jarvis – all Marlboros." Max leaned against the wall as Tom opened the top of the GI can. He extracted a crushed soda can and held it up to the light. "Bingo! Mountain Dew, buddy – almost mint condition!"

"That's enough, Tom. Let's get the hell out of here; this place is beginning to give me claustrophobia." Tom climbed out of the pool.

"Sorry about the bad news, Max." They walked past the lockers. Tom glanced at #1 and stopped in his tracks.

"No way."

"Come on, Max. You mean you're not even curious?"

"It's a locked locker, so what?"

"It's *one* locked locker. The others are all open."

"One locked locker – so what?" Tom yanked on the door. It was firm.

"You got a screw driver?"

"I didn't bring any tools. Let's get out of here."

"I left my keys in the car. You got any?" Max handed him a small ring of keys.

"I'll guarantee you none of them will fit." Tom shoved the end of a house key under the bottom hinge and began to jimmy it up. "Hey, you'll break the - - "The hinge snapped off, and Tom was able to pull the bottom corner out. Applying leverage, he popped the screws of the upper hinge and tossed the door aside with a loud clatter.

"Look what we have here!" Tom removed a Bible – King James translation. There were a couple of cartons of Marlboros – one unopened. Several legal pads with rosters, minutes of the meetings, and copies of the ritual. He handed them all back to Max who hardly glanced at them. "What's this? Look here, Max – this is too good to be true." Tom handed back a paddle and then a handful of Polaroid photos. "Any of these guys look familiar? Max stared at the first picture. It was a kid – maybe fifteen years old - being struck on the naked buttocks with a paddle.

"That's Reardon with the paddle. The kid looks kind of familiar; I don't remember the name."

"Me either. How about this one?" It was of a boy – about the same age – in his jockey shorts trying to make a muscle."

"That's Williamson." Tom shuffled through the stack of photos.

"No butt-fucking yet. I think Reardon was a closet-queer or else he kept the good pictures somewhere else for his private diversion - - Hello!"

"Don't tell me! What you got?" Tom scrutinized the photo more closely before handing it to Max. It was of a powerfully built youngster in a muscle pose wearing nothing but a jock strap. His entire body was glistening brilliantly as if it had been oiled.

"Recognize him?" Max stared in disbelief, but there was no doubt. It was Luis Carbonell. The two men gazed at each other without a word. A muffled noise startled Max.

"What's that?"

"Shit! I think someone's coming!" A light shone dimly from around the corridor, and instantly the two men froze like cadets of fifteen years ago caught with a skin magazine. "There's nowhere to go. I believe we're fucked."

Chapter 29

Tom was half-right. Sergeant Makepeace had indeed gone on to his reward years ago, but he had not been replaced by a crew of night watchmen – only one – Captain Hadley Lamar Honeycutt. Honeycutt was in actuality Makepeace's third replacement, his two immediate predecessors' careers having been truncated due to varying degrees of chronic alcoholism, petty thievery, corruption, or simple indolence. Honeycutt was cut from a different cloth; despite his idiosyncrasies, he proved to be more than satisfactory for the job. For one thing, he had a passion for his assignment; he worked at it. And as Commandant, Lieutenant Colonel Bristow was willing to excuse a little over-zealousness in light of Honeycutt's unwavering devotion to his responsibilities.

Captain Honeycutt, at 48, was still in excellent physical condition. A compact man with a dark complexion and a constant five o'clock shadow, he had retired in 1973 as a Sergeant in the army military police. He now relished his position as the head of campus security at PFMA – even though he comprised a department of one. His business card, which he would readily produce on nearly any pretext, read: Captain Hadley Lamar Honeycutt, U.S. Army, Retired, Director of Surveillance and Security, Point of Fork Military Academy, Columbia, VA 23068. Honeycutt, while a master of stealth when the occasion warranted, also believed in presenting himself as a conspicuous presence on campus. He had attached a large halogen spotlight to his 1977 Jeep, whose intense beam easily penetrated the curtains of barracks rooms, slumbering faculty homes, and other campus buildings all hours of the night brilliantly illuminating the entire targeted area. At times of international crisis, Honeycutt intensified his efforts – constantly scanning the CB for indications that the academy might be marked for a terrorist plot. He considered PFMA as a ripe target for such a machination by Iran, Iraq, or other truculent states. Halloween was also a special occasion for Captain Honeycutt. Although trouble from outside never materialized, he attributed that impeccable record to his constant state of vigilance. On the last evening of October he strategically deployed a dozen selected cadets around the campus perimeter as well as certain other vulnerable locations inside. This detail was affectionately referred to as the Narc Patrol by the corps because it was invariably composed of Honeycutt's regular snitches.

It was a pre-Halloween training exercise of the Narc Patrol that doomed Max and his co-conspirator. Cadet Corporal Jason Starkey had nearly fallen asleep at his post defending the flagpole when he noticed a light shining up through the grate. He notified Honeycutt by walkie-talkie, and the Director of Surveillance and Security was on the scene within seconds. He called the cadet stationed in the guardroom and ordered him to contact General Beasley and inform him that unknown intruders had breached the campus perimeter and infiltrated the campus. Then, after calling in his detail to stand guard at the flagpole and using his master key to unlock the grate, he began his descent into the tunnel.

Several times in past years Honeycutt had ardently petitioned Colonel Harrington to allow him to carry a revolver while on rounds. These appeals, despite his impassioned and painstaking rationale, were firmly rejected. He had done no better with Beasley, but this didn't deter him from keeping a 357 magnum in the bottom of his locker in the guardroom. Now he earnestly wished that he had ignored his superiors' shortsightedness and was better armed for this confrontation. He had no way of knowing whom he was challenging nor how many they were. Armed only with a flashlight (only slightly less brilliant than his mobile spotlight), he rounded the final corner and threw a blinding beam at the cowering suspects. When it became clear that the intruders presented no threat, Honeycutt was emboldened to order the two culprits to place their hands on the wall while he searched unsuccessfully for identification. He then informed them of his position at PFMA, even handing each of them his card, and told them that they were now officially in his custody.

Tom and Max tried every contrivance they could think of to extricate themselves from their quandary, but to no avail. Beasley had been sent for; this was going straight to the top. "General, these suspects claim to be members of the board of directors. I don't know about that, and I don't care. All I know is that they were both apprehended in the underground tunnel system. I'm fairly sure that their penetration was detected by my men before they could carry out whatever sabotage they had in mind."

"Thank you, Captain Honeycutt, for a job well done."

"If you would like for me to ascertain their identities, we can run a check on them tonight."

"No, I know who they are; that'll be all."

"I haven't had time to check the tunnels for explosives. I'll dismiss my cadet detail and carry that out myself. Or if you want, I can call in the Sheriff's office."

"No, that won't be necessary. Thanks again – that'll be all."

"As you wish, sir."

While Honeycutt was re-locking the grate, Beasley and his two board members walked in silence to the President's Office in Heritage Hall. "OK, Jarvis, want to fill me in on the meaning of his escapade, or shall I ask Mr. Hatch?"

"Just doing some checking, General."

"You're going to have to do better than that, Jarvis. Let me be clear; I'll lay my cards right out on the table. I know you don't like me. I don't know why that is or what I could have done to arouse your enmity, but I *can* tell you this: the feeling's mutual."

"It's not about who likes or dislikes who personally;" Tom interrupted, "it all comes down to - -"

"Just let me do the talking for now, Hatch. I have always been aware that Jarvis was trying to undermine my work here, and I don't know where you come in, but the way things stand now, I'm holding all of the cards, so I call the shots."

"Alright, what do you have in mind?"

"I'll be blunt. As President of Point of Fork I have to answer to the board – you and twenty-six others. In the few months that I have been here, I have already exercised my authority to appoint three members replacing those whose terms expired last summer and Ted Hampton who passed away."

"With *your* people, no doubt," Max interrupted.

"If you want to put it that way. All appointees must be approved by the remaining board committee, as you know, but that hasn't been a problem. The men I've selected are good Christian men. Men with the evangelical zeal and vision to carry out this academy's mission into the Twenty-first Century."

"So you're stacking the deck with folks who think just as you do."

"People who share my vision."

"And that is?"

"I've never made a secret of that. Point of Fork has been mired for too long in the past, a past that stands between what it is and what it is destined to be - a City on a Hill."

"That past you speak of so disparagingly is what handed you a $100, 000 a year job at one of the most successful prep schools in the nation. I wouldn't be in too big a hurry to dismantle what we have now until you learn your way around. A lot of good people have dedicated their careers to what we have here."

"Whatever you say, Jarvis; I'm not here to debate educational philosophy with you, and frankly you are hardly in any position to challenge me on that or anything else."

"OK, so what's the deal? Where do we go from here?"

"That's up to you. I can pick up the phone and have the Sheriff's Department here in fifteen minutes. Given the dismal state of your current litigation, I don't think you need any more negative publicity or other problems. Hatch, I don't know how you got involved with this debacle, but I seriously doubt you want any part of that either."

"OK, you've made your point," Max interrupted, "You've got us by the short hairs;

what do you want?"

"Both of your resignations – that's first. The board meets tomorrow before the game; I want them signed and on my desk by 10:00 AM."

"Tomorrow morning?"

"That's right. You two don't seem to worry about the hours you keep anyway. I don't care how you do it – hire a courier if you have to - but get them here by ten or I'll have both of you prosecuted to the full extent of the law. Neither of you need that – especially you, Jarvis."

"Anything else?"

"Two things. First, after tomorrow morning, I don't want to see either of your faces on this campus again – ever. And before you leave, you are going to tell me what you were up to sneaking around on campus tonight." Max told him the whole story. He described their entry into the tunnels, told him what they had been looking for and what they had found. Everything. Except the photos; they were still in his back pocket.

Chapter 30

Point of Fork led Staunton Military Academy 14-7 at halftime, but the visitors ran back then second half kickoff and scored twice in the fourth quarter for a resounding 28-14 upset in front of an Alumni Day crowd of over 3,000 Titan fans. For Coach Wagner the defeat stood as a paradigm of a season fraught with frustration and disappointment. While many coaches would be satisfied with a winning record of 6-4, this final tally was far below the team's lofty pre-season expectations. And 6-4 was certainly not commensurate with the academy's proud tradition in athletics. For the second year in a row Point of Fork would not be going to the playoffs. It had been a tough year all the way around – the kind of year in which alien thoughts of quitting intrude into the subconscious of even the staunchest of coaches – people who would never entertain such notions under normal or even the most trying of circumstances.

The season had started well. The team began 3-0 capped by a 31-7 trouncing of Woodberry Forest, the defending state champions. Then the lineup began to be depleted. General Beasley had made good on his promise to be a regular at practice. On the Tuesday following the Woodberry game, Warner found a notecard from the General taped to his locker door. Over the signature was a succinct note: "I'll not tolerate blasphemy by our players on our practice field. You are directed to enforce the Christian principles of this academy. Forbes and Calhoun – one game suspension."

Dillon Forbes was the team's starting quarterback. A 6-5 junior with a rifle arm, he was also a standout in basketball and track; and with SAT scores and a GPA almost as lofty as his passing statistics, he was projected as a top Division 1 football prospect in two years. At 260 pounds, Truman Calhoun started at middle linebacker and was considered the cornerstone of Wagner's defense. Also a top student, Calhoun had already committed to Florida State. Wagner called the two players into his office and informed them of the suspension. "I'm committed to uphold and support the academy's policy, Dillon, not just to coach football; can you understand that?"

"Sure, coach. I understand your position, but I honestly don't know what I did!"

"Apparently you were swearing out there in practice. I didn't hear it or I probably would have said something, but someone did; and the school will not ignore that."

"I may have said 'Jesus!' when Tolliver blindsided me after the play. Was *that* it?"

"I don't know. I'll find out."

"And you still won't say who turned on us."

"Sorry, that's confidential."

"But, Coach," Calhoun pleaded, "I don't think I even cussed. I sure don't remember it."

"Fair enough. You deserve a straight answer, and I'll have it for you tomorrow. See me at the morning break, but the suspension stands."

Rick found General Beasley in his office the following morning. "I issued the suspensions, but the boys want to know exactly what they did."

"Forbes took the Lord's name in vain. In Calhoun's case it was not quite so irreverent, but we need to be consistent – *zero* tolerance for cursing in any form."

"What did he say?"

"He used the "s" word; he said, 'What the s,' when Taylor hit him after the whistle."

"He said 'Shit' on a late hit? We're suspending the kid for *that*?"

"Watch your language in here, Coach Wagner, and understand where I'm coming from. We'll have *no* swearing here of *any* kind here on my watch. *Zero* tolerance – have I made myself clear? One game suspension for the first offense, three games for the second, and if it happens again they're out for the season. I'm sending a message, and if you don't feel that you can convey it for me, I'll find a coach who can."

Forbes came back from his one-game suspension and was 12 for 14 against E.C. Glass with two touchdown passes and no interceptions. He also ran the ball over on a bootleg from four yards out in the closing seconds of the game sparking a 31-28 victory. It would be his last game in a Titan uniform. Four days later Wagner found another of the now-familiar notecards stuck to his locker. Forbes' name was on it. Wagner had faithfully executed Beasley's policy throughout the season even though he considered it too Draconian. A firm disciplinarian, he met with the team and read them the riot act concerning the new policy. He even issued two suspensions himself to key players during the course of the season, so the team was particularly watchful of their language – particularly when the coaches were in earshot, but in the heat of the moment there were occasional lapses. Calhoun made it through the rest of his senior season without incident, but the team was never at full strength on game day. Once, in a 21-7 loss to Thomas Jefferson, the whole defensive backfield had been decimated. On several occasions the suspended players maintained vehemently that they had been misheard or misreported. Eventually it became obvious to the team who the "snitch" was, and although Wagner steadfastly refused to confirm their suspicions, fierce resentment ensued. Forbes turned in his equipment after his second suspension, and as word of his plight leaked out, a throng of other prep schools made it clear through subtle overtures that there would be a place for him on their rosters the following year. The lucky winner would be Dematha High School in Washington, DC.

After the Staunton loss the Titan locker room was silent. Forty minutes later Wagner and the coaches met with the disconsolate players in the team room. There were the usual bromides. It *had been* a winning season – 6-4 overall. And the team had been confronted by a profusion of difficulties and distractions. But no excuses or platitudes could assuage the team's overwhelming sense of bitterness – not just for the unexpected losses but for the sense of betrayal. After dismissing the team, Wagner and his staff were in no mood to celebrate, but they and their wives had made reservations at The Abby in Richmond. After a dinner of prime rib and a couple of drinks, the mood began to lighten; and a few drinks later, the melancholy had totally lifted and tongues were loosened. There were few kind words for Beasley, and by 11:30 when they left the restaurant, Rick's wife Ann had to drive him home.

Rick had a hangover the next morning, but he was the scheduled as the lector at St. Mark's Episcopal Church, so he dragged himself out of bed and got his family to the service on time. After lunch he was beginning to feel normal. Later that afternoon Rick went by his office to tidy up some post-season details. The light blinking on his computer indicated that he had e-mail. It was a curt message from General Beasley.

"Coach Wagner, I must meet with you. Report to my office at 9:00 tomorrow."

"I wonder what the hell *he* wants."

Chapter 31

Max blew the ink dry from his dated signature and reread the text above: "I hereby tender my resignation from the board of directors of Point of Fork Military Academy, effective immediately." He looked at the clock. It was 7:20, and he had still heard no movement from upstairs. Recently Max had assumed the responsibility of waking Brett in the morning. He had no job to go to, and Johanna rarely stirred before mid-day anymore. He trudged up the stairs and found Brett still asleep in his room. Grabbing the nerf football on the floor, he heaved it at his slumbering son, smacking him on the butt. "Up and at 'em, Tiger; don't want to be late for practice!" Brett was on his feet in a split second. Max couldn't help admiring the burgeoning youth. "The kid's going to be six feet before he's thirteen," he mused.

"You taking me to practice?" Brett asked.

"Not today, son; mom will have to drive you. I've got to get away early for the Staunton game at Point of Fork," he lied. Max had not spoken to Johanna about his adventures the night before. He had not conversed with her at all. No doubt she would be elated at his severing all ties with the academy, notwithstanding the circumstances. That discussion could wait. He went to his room and gently shook Johanna, catching a sour whiff of bourbon as she rolled over. "What time is it?"

"Seven thirty. Brett needs a ride to practice in an hour."

"What's the problem with you taking him?" Her voice was foggy and her tone sounded testy.

"I'm going to the Staunton game."

"Thought that was at one o'clock."

"It is, but I plan to meet with a couple of guys this morning."

"Figures."

"What's that supposed to mean?"

"You might as well *move* to the fucking academy – enroll for a postgraduate year for all I care. I mean, you've got no job, you have no interest in Brett or me anymore. All you seem to care for is that stupid school. It's become your fucking life!"

"Hold it down, Johanna; Brett's in the other room?"

"Since when do you give a shit about Brett? Or me? Or *anyone* but yourself? You haven't given a moment's thought to our family for months. Ever since Justin died you've retreated into your own little world. Well, I've got news for you; if you want to go off to the academy and relive your glory days, you'll have to do it on your own. Brett and I have *our* lives to live, and if you don't want to be part of it, I guess we'll have to go on by ourselves!"

"That's unfair."

"Oh *is* it? When's the last time you did anything but worry about that school?"

"I don't have much else to do at the moment."

"You got that right! And why's that? Bingo! Good ol' Point of Fork!"

"You're distorting everything. I'm working with Murray to try to get things back on track."

"Is that right? And who were you with last night? Murray?"

"It's a long story. I'll explain it all tonight when I get back."

"I can't wait!"

Max went downstairs. Brett was pouring cereal in a bowl; although he averted his eyes, it was clear that the boy was upset. Max placed his hand on his son's shoulder and squeezed. "Have a good practice, son. Mom will be down in a few minutes to drive you."

"What's the matter, Dad?"

"With what, son?"

"You know. You and mom."

"It's nothing to worry about, Brett. You know we've all been through a lot in the last few months with Justin and with me not working."

"Is mom an alcoholic?"

"Of course not, Brett. That's ridiculous. What would make you even think that?"

"She doesn't seem to want to do anything anymore. You guys are always fighting."

"Like I said, son, it's a tough time for all of us. I just wish you didn't have to go through it."

"Are you guys getting a divorce?"

"Absolutely not. You can quit worrying about that. I promise things will be looking brighter before long." Max grabbed his son by the shoulder and pulled the boy to his side.

"You sure?"

"Like I said, there's no way!" Max looked at his watch and made for the car wishing desperately that he could believe his assertion.

Once headed west on Route 6, he picked up the cell phone. Murray answered. "It's not even eight o'clock, Max. What's so important?" Max filled him in on the details of the night before. Murray was livid. "You got some kind of financial death wish, Jarvis? Here I'm trying to clear away your growing legal entanglements, and you're adding new encumbrances faster than I can get you out. If you just had an income, I could drop all of my other cases and retire on your cases alone!"

"Don't worry. You'll get paid."

"Sure I will. Listen, Max, and *pay attention* this time. You deliver that resignation to Beasley on time this morning. That's the *one* good thing coming out of all of this. Then you march your ass off that campus and drive home. That's it! No more contact with Hatch or anyone else until I tell you. *Nothing*. Got that?"

"Loud and clear."

- - - - - - - - - - - - - - - - -

General Beasley came directly to the point. "Rick, replacing personnel is never a pleasant job, but it's one that I've had to get used to over the years."

"That how you earned your stars in the Marines?"

"No need to get insolent with me, Rick. It's nothing personal – comes with the territory. And the answer to your question is yes. Unfortunately I had to deal with it in the service just as I must here."

"OK – lay it out."

"You have served this academy well for a number of years."

"About thirty."

"And there's no denying your contribution and devotion to this school. That's why I'm offering to allow you to stay on in P.E. – at least for the remainder of the year. You know I don't have to do that. We don't have tenure here, and your contract says sixty days' notice."

"You're all heart, General."

"Drop the sarcasm. The point is this. I've met with the board, and they've given me the green light to proceed in my plan to completely revamp Point of Fork and bring it into line with my vision of what this school could be in the Twenty-first Century."

"It's been pretty damn good for a century and a half already."

"Don't swear in my office, Wagner. That's the very type of deportment that's costing you and those who share your views their jobs."

"Don't tell me! Who else's head is on the chopping block?"

"That's not your concern."

"I've got a pretty good idea."

"Let me be frank. There's a culture here at the academy that's resisted everything that I've instituted this year."

"The "old guard?"

"Call it what you will, but I'll tell you this. No one is going to stand between me and the mission I was called here to carry out."

"You've only been here a few months. Give it a chance. The people here are as dedicated and as competent as you'll find anywhere. And they can be flexible if you just give them a chance. Most of our people have been in education here for a long time; they could probably teach you a thing or two if you would just listen."

"I was brought here to lead. We're building a City on a Hill here at Point of Fork, and everybody in the canoe has to be paddling in same direction. We *don't* need to hear reports about our personnel getting loud and disorderly in a Richmond bar after a football game. That's not the message we're trying to send. Those who want to help me carry out the Lord's work are going to fall into line. The old culture at Point of Fork has no place in this school's future; we all have to be reading off the same page of music."

"Sounds like what you're describing is a bunch of yes-men."

"No, just simple cooperation. And not going behind my back to try to undermine policy."

"No one's doing that."

"You must think I was born yesterday. I hear what's going on. Two weeks before last Saturday's meeting I knew there was a movement afoot to derail the Crawford settlement, and I know exactly who on the board and the staff are behind it."

"It's bad policy, General. Plus it exposes Bristow, Louise Harrington, and God knows who else."

"That's not the academy's concern. My job as a steward of the Lord's resources here is to protect the interests of the school. Marvin was ready to settle with us, but because of a few objections, we now have to conduct an internal study."

"What's the problem with that? Your deal may have been expedient from your standpoint, but it would have hung a lot of good people out to dry. *Loyal* people who have devoted their lives to this school and who don't have the school's resources to resist Crawford and Marvin."

"Again, not my concern. My concern is the academy."

"Those people *are* the academy, General. That's what you don't seem to understand. It's not the bricks and mortar. It's not the computer center or the athletic facilities. *People* are what has made this school what it is. You need to get that through your head."

"We have nothing further to discuss, Rick. You are my Christian brother always, but you are not the right person to lead our athletic program or our football team. I've given you your options. If you so choose, you can stay on in theP.E.department. Let me know by the end of the week."

Chapter 32

In the two weeks following Wagner's demotion, rumors of impending firings ran rampant throughout the Point of Fork community. Beasley deflected questions related to this at the Friday faculty meetings, but most at the school were anxiously waiting for the next shoe to drop. These speculations were substantiated by faculty members with connections to the academic world outside. For years Vernon Philpott had canvassed the nation applying for various administrative positions in private and public education. Recently he had spoken with Dr. Allen Croston, his advisor for career development at Virginia Commonwealth University. "How about your own school, Vernon? They're looking for administrators."

"In what areas?"

"Quite a few apparently. But your president is only interested in a narrow range of candidates."

"What do you mean?"

"Well, he prefers people with terminal degrees. That Ph.D. after the name is important to him. And then there's the religious question."

"What are you talking about?"

"Well, the word here is that your general's first question is always the same, 'What's your personal relationship with the Lord?'"

"You're kidding!"

"No, and the answer had better be the right one. If you're not washed in the blood of the Lamb, he's not interested."

"I find that hard to believe, even for him."

"You'd better believe it. And he doesn't just leave it there. I had a candidate last week who told him he was a member of Grace Street Baptist. Your general actually called the pastor to check and see if he attended regularly. When Reverend Holly could not substantiate it, the guy was rejected."

As Beasley's agenda drew into clearer focus, other changes of policy and philosophy were becoming more distinct. On several occasions Jerry Butler, the academy's treasurer, had confided that the new boss was, "spending money like a drunken sailor." There had been many recent expenditures on "eye-wash." The general had hired several new people for the maintenance department and a landscaper to spruce up the campus. In raising funds for his many projects, Beasley was so relentless that targeted donors hated to see him coming. Every school function from Alumni Weekend to Parents Day was to be a fundraiser, and the pressure to "provide for God's work" became so fierce and frequent that patrons and alumni began referring to Beasley as the "Dollar General."

Not all of the changes were well received. Not only the unprecedented expense but the style and taste of landscaping had come into question. For Alumni Day alone, over $5,000 was rumored to have been forked over on chrysanthemums and further beautification of the campus. Cadets complained that the place was beginning to look like a convent. More than one alumnus had expressed outrage that over twenty of the grand old elms on campus had been cut down. Beasley asserted that the old trees were diseased, and that leaving a few healthy ones would not have looked symmetrical. Louis Gallagher, a UVA professor of economics, was outraged. "Those trees have been infected with Dutch elm disease since I was a cadet. They looked fine last spring. The thing that *really* pisses me off is what they replaced them with. Those Bradford pear trees are fine for a gas station or the parking lot of a mall, but not on a campus. They'll grow up in five years and then start to break apart and look like shit. That's why they call them the popping pears. At least they could plant some real trees!"

Other transformations were afoot lending credence to the suspicion that the academy was headed for a major overhaul inside and out. Throughout its history Point of Fork had made an ardent effort to evade the stigma of a "glorified reform school" that had affixed itself to most military academies. For decades Major Stuart Slife, the director of Admissions, had followed his guideline that he would not accept a candidate whom he would not be comfortable having as his own son's roommate. The school was willing to get by with less than full enrollment if necessary in order to maintain certain basic standards. Point of Fork was no Philips Exeter, and some misfits inevitably slipped through the cracks each year, but they rarely lasted for long in the system. Students with poor academic records but good potential were considered acceptable. These often became the academy's best success stories. But there were three criteria that Slife had adhered to absolutely: 1) a prospect must currently be in good standing (not expelled or suspended) at his present school, 2) he must not have a police record or upcoming litigation with the courts, and 3) he must not have been treated in any type of psychiatric or drug rehab program.

Beasley assailed that policy on several fronts. Even before his appointment had been made official, he had communicated to Slife that he wanted to increase enrollment for the next year by a hundred cadets.

"There are problems with that, sir. Not only do we lack the beds or classroom space, but our other facilities, not to mention our faculty, will be stretched beyond the limit. And even more importantly, we would have to take in kids that we really don't want here."

"What do you mean, 'don't want'?"

"We have all we can do just finding enough prospective students who fit our cadet profile."

"Then change the profile if you have to. We are in the "life-changing" business. If the Lord sends us a lad who's a little rough around the edges and we can save him, then we are fulfilling our Christian mission."

"I'm afraid that if our pool of inquiries remains what it has been, we're talking more than 'a little rough around the edges.' I'm not sure you really want to take some of these guys. If we're not careful, we'll start losing our good kids."

"That's what I'm paying you to do – to find suitable candidates. We need a hundred more this September. That's the bottom line. If you can't get them, I'll find someone who can."

On Alumni Weekend a vague sense of dissatisfaction among the cadets, faculty, and administration was observed by several alumni. Beasley inadvertently brought this to a head the following week at the pep rally marking the beginning of winter sports. It was a crisp autumn evening. The cadets were happy to be away from their studies for an hour or so to raise a little hell. A giant bonfire had been erected for the occasion, and General Beasley had instructed all faculty and staff to be present to support the cadets and their teams. Hot chocolate and s'mores were served around the blazing conflagration that sent huge sparks swirling into the inky sky. "Prometheus," the PFMA Titan stalked back and forth working the crowd. After the band played and several skits lampooning the faculty had been performed, the winter teams were introduced along with the traditional bravado. Then Beasley stepped forward to address the boisterous mass of cadets.

"Gentlemen, I wish all of you great success in the upcoming athletic season. I am sure that you will carry out the storied tradition of PFMA in splendid style. And it is to that end that I have the pleasure of addressing you on this beautiful evening that God has made for us. As the world looks forward to the coming of the millennium, I cannot help but consider that term in both its historical and spiritual context. Our school stands on the threshold of a new beginning in so many ways, and as we look back on our great tradition of a hundred and fifty years, we also look ahead to the future and the promise that lies before us.

"To mark our new beginning in athletics, I am exercising my authority by retiring the team mascot of the past and replacing him with one more in keeping with our revitalized Christian mission. The Titan was a pre-Olympian pagan god of ancient myth. He has served his time. I now give you a true champion of Christian history. I am pleased to present to you the Point of Fork Crusader!" And in a pre-arranged choreograph, a new mascot donning a blue helmet and breastplate rushed from the darkness brandishing his sword and shield to slay the hapless Titan. As directed, the band broke into its new theme of "Onward Christian Soldiers" while the Crusader pursued his overmatched adversary and dispatched him with his sword.

Beasley's pantomime did not elicit the wild applause he had anticipated. As the PFMA Crusader set upon his venerable predecessor, he found himself the target of a half-dozen well-placed marshmallows and a chorus of obstreperous boos. Continuing his assault, the Crusader found that he was meeting more resistance from the pelting of sticky missiles than the staged opposition of his doomed foe. The incensed crowd was becoming a rancorous mob, and the tactical officers in their ranks were finding themselves powerless to stifle their boisterous opposition. Finally, as the victorious Crusader towered in triumph over the fallen Titan, he caught a scalding splash of hot chocolate in the face expertly heaved from somewhere in the crowd. The unruly mob broke into a thunderous ovation as the mighty Crusader covered his face, dropped to one knee, and had to be led away.

Visibly disconcerted, but ever the gamesman, Beasley proceeded undiscouraged. He cleared his throat and again spoke into the microphone. "I am also pleased to report that the Lord has answered our search for a new athletic director, and he has come to be with us here tonight. He's a man whose athletic and spiritual credentials are beyond reproach. A man of great athletic accomplishments, and a man of God. A witness to Christ's saving power." The General motioned, and a huge figure advanced forward from the night. Dunston Brady looked in bewilderment as his ashen wife shot both hands to her face. "Gentlemen, it is with great pleasure that I present to you our new athletic director and football coach. Please make welcome a former football All-American from N.C. State and current ordained minister, Lieutenant Colonel Nick Zunich!"

Chapter 33

News of the change was in all of the local papers, and within days two letters appeared in the *Richmond Times Dispatch* editorial page. Both condemned the firing of Wagner and expressed dismay at rumors of the wholesale transformations at the academy. Beasley's pointed response was immediate.

Point of Fork is marching ahead

Editor – *Richmond Times Dispatch*:

I regret that the recent developments instituted at Point of Fork Military Academy have elicited such acrimonious protest. I would offer by way of explanation, however, that the academy's mission has always been founded in the Christian faith. That is, and will remain, the driving force of my tenure at this historic school. Perhaps there are some few, even among our alumni, who do not understand or appreciate that. To them I make this reiteration of the school's founding philosophy, but for this I offer no apology.

I should like to address the issue of change. Yes, we are in a process of massive renovation, not only of the academy's physical plant but also touching certain issues relating to policy. Both have been areas of need that have been neglected for too long. Change, even necessary change, is something that tends to meet with resistance, and I suppose that this is just a phase that has to be gone through when new and innovative concepts are introduced to old institutions. In my experience here I have found that this is to be expected even though in my occasional frustration I am reminded of several jokes along this line concerning light bulbs. The Lord's work is not always well received.

To our critics, I simply ask their forbearance as we proceed through a process that at times may seem difficult or unfamiliar. Point of Fork Military Academy will not live in the past. We are marching proudly ahead into the Twenty-first Century. I would remind our critics of the words of Shakespeare, "Be not the first upon which the new is tried nor the last to put the old aside."

General Phillip A. Beasley
President, Point of Fork Military Academy

Four days later the following response was at the top of the editorial page.

Facts are facts when they are right

Editor – *Richmond Times Dispatch*:

It was kind of General Beasley, Point of Fork's new president, to enlighten us alumni and the world at large on the academy's new-found devotion to its mission. So this Tennessee hillbilly would like to be the first to thank him. I can also appreciate his frustration with the resistance he has encountered when it comes to accepting new ideas. I would beg the good general's indulgence in these matters, however, and suggest that he maintain his sense of humor with those light bulb jokes that he alludes to in his letter.

If he finds us a little slow on the uptake or short of the cutting edge, perhaps it is because we are so concerned with the past that we check our facts before proffering them up to the public.

I am sure that even many of the general's relatives back in West Virginia could have told him that the quotation he attributes to Shakespeare can be found nowhere in the Bard's writing. Shakespeare penned many memorable lines, but these are not among them. When I was a cadet at Point of Fork, I was taught that these famous words were written a century later by Alexander Pope in his "Essay on Criticism."

Also General Beasley will find that the meter of this familiar heroic couplet flows better if quoted exactly as the author wrote it:

"*Be not the first by whom the new are tried,*

Nor yet the last to lay the old aside."

Thomas R. Hatch, DDS, PFMA '72
Knoxville, TN

The General was not amused, but there was little that he could do about Hatch at this point. He and Jarvis were plainly lined up against him and had already become an annoyance. But both were off of the Board to Directors now and would soon be replaced with others more sympathetic to his vision. There was not much that Hatch could do to harm him, and Jarvis was fast becoming a pariah everywhere – a nuisance perhaps, but no real threat.

General Jack Fleming was now stationed at the Marine Corps University in Quantico, Virginia – only fifty miles away. Max reached him using the home number that had been filed in Col. Harrington's papers. Fleming had not heard of Harrington's death. He acknowledged that he had known Beasley but was wary of talking about him to a stranger. "You say you were a friend of Brad's, Mr. Jarvis. Even if it's true and you are trying to look into this for his widow or his school or whatever, you have to appreciate my position. I can't just talk over the phone to someone I don't know and start bad-mouthing a fellow officer."

"But you *were* stationed with him."

"Yeah, for eighteen months. In Guantanamo."

"Whom can I contact there? If you could just give me a name, I could call him."

"Try a her."

"A what?"

"Nothing. So long, Mr. Jarvis."

Max didn't move after the General hung up. "A *her*." He looked at the letter to Colonel Harrington from Luis Carbonell and dialed the long distance operator.

"Hello?" A woman answered.

"Hello. This is Max Jarvis, Luis' friend from Point of Fork. Is this Maria?"

"Yes, this is Maria. Pleased to talk with you, Jack; Luis has told me so much about you." Despite her accent Maria seemed to have a better command of English than her husband who had been educated in the States.

"Don't believe everything that reprobate tells you, Maria; I'm really a pretty decent guy. My mother will still vouch for me – that's one on my side at least."

"Oh, no. He tells me you're the best."

"Could I speak with him, please?"

"He's still at the office or on his way home by now. I can give you the number, or he can call you back."

"Let me have the number, and if I don't get him he can call me here at 804 – 288-1176. I need to get some information about some guys we went to school with."

"How's Point of Fork doing these days? Luis doesn't keep in touch much anymore."

"Well, that depends on who you ask. They have a new president, General Beasley. I believe you may know him." There was no response for several seconds.

"Yes, I met this man quite a few years ago. He was stationed in Guantanamo, and he used to fly in here when he was on leave."

"How did you happen to make his acquaintance?"

"It's a long story."

"You don't happen to have any old photos showing him locked up in the clink or coming out of a brothel, do you? I could sure use them now," Max joked. There was no answer. "Maria – are you still there?"

"I'm here. I'll have Luis call you when he gets home."

Max got the number at the office and hung up. Maria's initial warmth had cooled noticeably toward the end of their conversation. Max shrugged and tried the number Maria had given him. There was no answer. He began to review the letters that the Colonel had left him. He was certain there was something in there that Harrington wanted him to pursue. It was almost six o'clock, and Brett's basketball team was playing its season opener at 7:30, but Johanna had not started supper. He found her upstairs. "Are you planning to go the game tonight?" She was well into her second or third bourbon.

"No, I'm not feeling well."

"OK. I'll make supper. Shall I bring you anything?"

"No, I'm going to bed." There should be some hot dogs in the fridge. We have some french-fries in the freezer you can heat up." Max and Brett finished dinner. Still no call from Carbonell. Max called upstairs to his wife.

"I'm expecting a call from Venezuela, Johanna. If Luis Carbonell calls, tell him I'll call him when I get back." There was no response.

- - - - - - - - - - - - - - - - - -

Brett started at forward. From the opening tip-off, the morose, troubled youngster of late completely vanished – as though he had never existed. Brett was the old Brett – stealing the ball, running the floor, passing and scoring with the effortless grace of a natural athlete. Max had never enjoyed a basketball game more. For a couple of hours his troubles on all fronts were lost in the sounds of the crowd, the hollow thump of the ball on the floor, and the squeaking rubber soles of Nikes against the hardwood as players got back on defense. The buttery smell of pop corn and the familiar dank pungency pervasive to every gymnasium on the planet combined to transport him, if only for a brief time, to a world where there were no creditors, no angry partners, no lawyers – and no imperious generals or zoned out wives. Max breathed easier and more deeply than he had in weeks; he felt as though an anvil had been lifted from his shoulders and even joked with some of the parents in the crowd. Once, as his son snatched a rebound, passed off, and raced down the sideline on the fast break, Max actually found himself jumping to his feet and shouting – a typical Little League dad. But on his way home, the cares that had seemed to melt away returned to settle on his shoulders even more oppressively. How had he allowed himself to get drawn into the mess that he had created? What had he sacrificed in the process? And was there any way at this point to reclaim the life he had squandered?

When Max got home there were no messages on the answering machine. He dialed the office number that Maria had given him. No answer there. He decided to call Carbonell at home. Luis was friendly as always but did not show much enthusiasm in response to his old classmate's inquiries. "I'm just not into that anymore, Max. Point of Fork was a great start for me, and I appreciate Colonel Harrington and all, but I have my life here now. I really don't need to get mixed up in all that conflict back in Virginia."

"Tom Hatch is with me on this."

"Yeah, and look where it got the both of you."

"You've got a point there, but look, Luis, I'm sure you know a lot about what happened with Reardon and his club. You could really help us."

"What do you mean? I don't know nothing about no club."

"I think you do."

"What makes you say that? I got a feeling this conversation's gone far enough, Max."

"Tom and I – when we were searching around in the old gym – we found some pictures."

"So?"

"You were in one of them, Luis." Max waited for a response. There was no sound for almost ten seconds. Then a dial tone.

Max placed the receiver back on the phone. *Guess I blew that one*, he thought; *nothing new there*. He decided to mix a drink, something he rarely did alone. Returning to his desk, he took out the envelope that Harrington had left him and began to leaf through the letters again. Twenty minutes passed, and then the phone rang.

"Max, this is Luis again."

"Luis! We must have been cut off."

"No, I hung up on you. Sorry, Max."

"Hey, I can understand your misgivings about - - "

"Listen, Max. I wasn't into none of that queer stuff; you know that. I wasn't even in that club."

"Luis, you don't have to explain - - "

"No, but I *won't* to. This thing's been eating at me for years. You know how Reardon was always hanging around the wrestling team – taking those pictures, all that."

"Yeah, sure. I heard all the rumors. What about it?"

"Well, you know my English ain't so hot."

"Neither's my Spanish. Big deal."

"Well, it was a big deal for me. I was in Reardon's French class. Everyone had to pass the foreign language requirement, even the Spic Patrol."

"I'd almost forgotten that wonderful term of endearment."

"Not me. Anyways, there won't no way for me. I was trying to learn French through the English, and I didn't half-understand the fuckin' English."

"So how does that all tie in with the Reardon's club?"

"Reardon, he toll me he could help me with my French. That's how he got me up to his apartment up in "A" Company."

"What did he want? Did he try to bugger you?"

"No. I don't think he was really into that. He just liked to look."

"So what happened?"

"This is real hard. He wanted pictures. He said I didn't have to strip all the way down to nothing. He said that it was just art."

"And the oil?"

"Yeah, I know. It makes me sick to think about it. That's why I've stayed away. I knew some of those pictures had to be floating around somewhere, and I didn't want none of this getting out."

"Sure, I can see that, but you didn't do anything wrong. This was blackmail plain and simple."

"Yeah, I know, but still . . . "

"Listen, Luis. You don't have to worry about me letting any of this out. It's really of no value anyway. Beasley's going to pay off Crawford, and that'll be the end of it. I really need something that can nail *him*. If I could nail that bastard - -"

"Crawford?"

"No. Beasley."

"You really hate the guy."

"He's an asshole. Plus he's taking the school apart piece by piece. I'd do anything I could to nail his ass."

"I think I may be able to help you with that."

"You?"

"Well, not me exactly. Maria can. She has some pretty good shit on the guy. I known about it for a while, but I didn't want to get involved and bring out that other stuff."

"I don't need to say anything about - - "

"Whatever. I don't care. I'm tired of having it hanging over me."

"What do you have in mind?"

"You never met Maria."

"No, but I spoke with her tonight. I've heard all about her. A beauty queen?"

"And the best woman. You'll see. I haven't been back to Virginia since we graduated – was afraid to. I need a vacation. You really want to screw this Beasley guy?"

"You don't know how much!"

"Think I'll get a room in Richmond and show Maria my old school. We could get together and talk about it."

"No way! You'll stay here with me and my family. We have a big house – at least for the time being until the bank takes it back. Just set a date. My schedule's open."

"Let me check a few things. I call you back in a couple of days."

Chapter 34

In the weeks following Alumni Day, Beasley's plan for a City on a Hill gained momentum. Devotionals were mandated at the beginning of each class day. Faculty attendance at chapel services on Tuesday evenings was also made compulsory. And a school-wide revival was scheduled for the first week of December. Homework would not be assigned during that week so that the evening study period could be given over to chapel sessions conducted by the noted visiting evangelist, Sonny Hockaday. This news played to mixed reviews. The cadet corps, anticipating a week without homework, was in almost universally support of the revival. A significant part of the faculty felt that a whole week was an excessive intrusion on the academic program, but others greeted the news more favorably. The PFMA staff had always retained a large number of Christian fundamentalists, including several of the academy's best instructors. Several others who were on the outer fringes toward sanctimonious extremism took Beasley's initiative as an opportunity to evangelize more vigorously, but the majority were less aggressive in their piety. Their proselytizing had always been carried out through their sincerity and example. The General's program did draw several new Faithful out of the woodworks, and the most dramatic conversion was none other than Vernon Philpott.

Hockaday was a compelling speaker, and he found the cadets to be a good audience. On Monday evening he began with a graphic narrative of his own spiritual odyssey from a life of riotous dissipation to salvation through the blood of Jesus Christ.

He told of his childhood reared in a "good Catholic home." He described his father, the wealthy lawyer who regularly attended Mass and received the sacraments only to cheat his clients at every turn and who would not allow dinner to be served until he had tossed off his first two evening highballs. Hockaday described his high school years in detail: MVP on the basketball team, 1600 on the SAT, and voted most likely to succeed by his classmates. Yet, he said, something was missing in his life; he was somehow empty – not fulfilled. Then he told of his college life – more of the traditional trappings of success but tainted by rampant sexual excess. This degenerate lifestyle he delineated in sensational detail. Then marriage to the Homecoming Queen and a lucrative contract with a Fortune 500 firm. Yet still his life was bereft of meaning. Then Hockaday told a lurid narrative describing the night that his life struck rock bottom. How, with bitter tears streaming down his wretched face, he had placed a loaded pistol to his temple, fallen to his knees, and shouted, "Lord, I don't know if you even exist, but I'm at the end of my rope. If you are there, speak to me somehow before I pull this trigger and end it all right here." He told of the indescribable feeling of love and warmth that washed over him as he dropped the firearm and became a soldier in the army of Christ.

The audience was spellbound as the evangelist told of his new-found calling in life. How at the age of twenty-four, he walked away from his six-figure salary and dedicated his life to the Lord's work. And as the evenings progressed, he went on to describe the deceptions the Devil employs in order to ensnare young lives and seduce them toward an eternity of unmitigated torment. In rapturous terms he contrasted the unsurpassed bliss of heaven, to the despair and anguish of those hopeless souls forever consigned to the excruciating sufferings of hell. "None of us knows the time or date of our final demise on this earth. Scripture tells us that death comes like a thief in the night. My own father, who followed what he considered a form of Christianity, died in his sleep. He had an 8:45 tee time set for the next morning. He has been burning in indescribable agony for sixteen years, yet all those years of torment are less than an instant compared to the eternity of horrors that lies ahead. Some of you out there may be entertaining the idea that you can continue in your depraved state while you are young and reform your lives later when you are older. The Devil has enticed many a soul to hell on that false promise. How many tormented souls in perdition would now give anything for one more chance at the repentance they deferred for years! Too late they realize that each day away from their Savior hardened their hearts until their repentance became an illusion. How many of the teenagers who died on the highways in the last week had every intention of living for Christ at some later date?"

On the final evening Hockaday asked all of those who were now ready to give their lives to Christ to stand. He reminded them that the only way to salvation was through a real, full-gospel, Bible-preaching church. He invited those whose lives had been changed to come forward and write their names and addresses in a book that he placed before the cross. The aisles began to fill as cadets, some self-conscious and others openly weeping, approached the altar. As the organ softly played "Just as I Am," 236 cadets signed.

As Beasley watched the cadets file down the aisles, his heart swelled with pride, but he was nearly overthrown with emotion when he spied the green uniform beneath a shock of red hair proceeding forward among the multitude. Neither Vernon nor Lynda Philpott had ever darkened the door of a church since their wedding day, and had she been present for her husband's conversion, Lynda would surely have reacted with shocked incredulity. During his days at RPI, Vernon had been exposed to the fashionable principles of existentialism, which permeated that arty school, and now, although his teaching assignment was in the scientific realm, his lectures and discourses were heavily laced with existential philosophy. Early on Beasley had gotten wind of Philpott's agnostic leanings and had added his name to his secret list of faculty and staff marked for extinction. But in the weeks following the revival, he found in Philpott a stalwart ally in the war against those who would defy the academy's destiny as a City on a Hill.

Philpott's conversion was as zealous as it was sudden. The very next Sunday he dragged his wife and two young daughters to Point of Fork Baptist and petitioned for membership. In the classroom he became an impassioned spokesman for the saving grace of redemption to the point that balancing equations and the periodic tables became little more than an afterthought in his chemistry class. In less than a month Philpott's exhortations had become so fierce that two cadets' parents (one an Episcopalian, and the other a Lutheran) had complained to Ron Frazier that Philpott was forcefully trying to convert their sons. But Beasley firmly admonished the headmaster not to interfere with the Lord's work on His campus.

None of this was lost on Pleasants and Taliaferro, the remnant of the Three Gents, who would soon follow their associate, Reardon, into retirement. With the end of their careers looming imminent, they felt somewhat invulnerable to the menace of creeping fanaticism. Sitting with Taliaferro at their corner table in the faculty section of the mess hall, Pleasants was bemused at the spectacle of Vernon Philpott and his family. "Land sakes," he exclaimed in a mellifluous whisper, tapping the timer button on his wristwatch. "I do believe we have a new record! One minute and thirteen seconds to say grace over a plate of meatballs."

"I wish the two brats would choke to death on them!" uttered Taliaferro. "The older one is getting so fat, they'll need to bring her in on a forklift."

"Where's your Christian compassion, Jubal? You know we're indebted to the Philpotts for their new-sprung commitment to the Lord's work here on campus."

"New-sprung ass kissing. That red-headed woodpecker and his slut wife haven't changed a feather."

"Jubal! I'm shocked at your skepticism! How can you be so cynical that your heart isn't moved by the healing hand of salvation that we are experiencing all around us?"

"The only hands I see are the ones crawling up the floor to kiss the ground that pompous ass is standing on."

"Did you say 'arse'? Surely you can't be referring to our leader, the General!"

"General pain in the ass. Look at that line of sycophants flocking up to his table. That praying mantis, Dunce-head Brady, nearly spilled his juice racing to get there first!"

"You're not being fair, Jubal; don't forget, Major Brady's our track coach. He's naturally fast – just like his wife."

"Just look at that Beasley, would you? If he's not careful, he's going to break his neck trying to look up her dress!"

"He's just being courteous as any good Christian would be, trying to make sure she's comfortably seated."

"I'll tell you where he would like to have her seated! I've watched him leering at half the women on this campus."

"I'm sure the good General's above succumbing to the temptation to covet his neighbor's wife."

"Take my word for it. He knows that jackass is over-mounted. He'd gladly eat a mile of Rae Ann Brady's shit just to see where it came from!"

- - - - - - - - - - - - - - - - -

Max had complied with Beasley's stipulation that he not set foot on the Point of Fork campus. Both Johanna and Murray had vigorously reinforced Beasley's dictum that he stay away. When the Carbonells arrived Max explained. "You two are going to have to make the trip by yourselves; I'm *persona non grata* at PFMA these days."

"You mean they kicked you out?"

"Something like that. It's less than fifty miles; you guys go ahead tomorrow and have a look."

"How 'bout Johanna? Maria would like the company."

"You've got a better chance of spotting Elvis on that campus than my wife." Luis looked puzzled. "I might as well tell you, Luis, this thing with General Beasley has cost me just about everything: my job, my dream of building a modern cardiac care hospital, my home, and now probably my family."

"You gotta forget about the academy and start putting your life back in order."

"That would be shutting the barn door after the horses are already out. No, I'm afraid it's gotten beyond that. I should have listened to everyone else and stayed the hell out of this. I've blown it." Maria frowned.

"You know Beasley isn't any saint himself," she said.

"No kidding! I'm convinced he's a damned hypocrite."

"I *know* he is."

"*Know*? What do you mean?"

"Well, he's married, isn't he?"

"Sure. Although I'm told she stays pretty much out of sight except for official occasions. A military wife."

"He was married when he was in Guantanamo too, but that didn't keep him from running around."

"Where'd you hear that?"

"From a couple of my friends."

"It's true!" Luis broke in. "When Maria was competing in those famous beauty pageants we have there, there was always a bunch of American servicemen sniffing around – the big brass – generals and stuff."

"In Venezuela?"

"They flew in from Guantanamo. It's not that far, and the pilots have to log their flying hours anyway to keep up their status. They can come in for a weekend, spend a few hundred bucks, and if they're lucky, get laid." Max couldn't contain his excitement.

"Beasley! Please tell me he was one of the lucky ones."

Maria laughed, "What do you want, Max, a video?"

"Wouldn't hurt. But really, Maria, do you think any of your friends could nail his ass?"

"I can't say. They're all married now, and I doubt we could even get them here. But I'll tell you this; he was one of the regulars. I remember him very well."

"Boy, I'd love to lay that bomb on him." Luis shook his head.

"We really don't have nothing. No proof. And I can't see how we can really make any of it stick."

"Maybe not," Max admitted, "But *he* doesn't know that. If he's dirty, and I'd lay my life that he is, even a bluff might smoke him out."

Maria was not sold. "You're overplaying your hand again, Max. I can see how you got yourself into so much trouble."

"Not really, Maria, not now. What do I have to lose? I've already talked to the people I can trust there – Frazier, Bristow, Ed Findlay - - "

"I remember all those guys," Luis interrupted. "They're still there?"

"Not for long if Beasley has his way. Ron tells me he's gotten word that the asshole's already interviewing replacements for all of them. They're living on borrowed time."

"This General's gotta go!" Luis muttered angrily, but Maria was still skeptical.

"Easy, guys. It's a nice fantasy to contemplate; I'd like to see it too, but it's not going to happen. This guy may be a jerk, but he's no fool. Halfwits don't get to be generals. We've got nothing on the guy that will stick."

Max had to admit that they were probably right.

Chapter 35

Rae Ann Brady knew how to handle General Beasley. Men had been coming on to her for so long that the game had become second nature. The General was no sexual predator in the conventional sense of the term. Even in his flirtations he had never overcome the diffidence that he had shown as an undergraduate at Fairmont State. He was loath to risk rejection, and he also had to consider his place in society. Janice had aired her suspicions on several occasions throughout their marriage, but so long as she could present no real proof, he could always manage to keep her distrust in check. Career was another issue, and here his innate caution came into play. In his flirtations he invariably left himself an escape route. His libidinous forays were so slowly initiated and proceeded so subtly and ambiguously, that he never committed himself to the point that he could be accused of anything worse than bad taste in the event that things went badly. And that was most unlikely since the objects of his predation had invariably been women whose station in life made recriminations imprudent. And this very caution had in fact resulted in a marriage that, with the exception of Pearl and a few Vietnamese prostitutes during his more reckless days, had remained technically (if not emotionally) chaste.

Maintaining this façade had become problematic a few times throughout Beasley's career. He had occasionally found it necessary to re-assign junior officers whose wives showed signs of becoming an embarrassment. And there had been one enlisted man, a Corporal Housley, whose wife had been so indiscreet and overtly receptive to Beasley's subtle dalliance that the corporal made a drunken threat that could have gotten him court-martialed. After a few beers in a local bar, a Private Whitehead had made a remark about the General's over-familiarity with Jennifer Housley. When the corporal responded that he could handle any threat to his marriage bed from the General, the private retorted, "You're out of your league, Housley. How do you expect to get past those two stars?"

"It ain't his two stars I'll be takin' out; it's his two balls that will need protectin." Corporal Housley was discreetly shipped out to Texas the next week.

Almost immediately after the General's arrival on campus, Rae Ann had picked up on his remarkable interest in her management of the infirmary. First he would show up at odd hours with trivial or bizarre questions about the operation of the facility. Later he began to come in to have his pulse checked, but when Beasley opened his shirt and asked her to check for heart palpitations, she brought him up short. "Your heart's fine, General, and I don't think you need a scrotal exam either, but I can check with your wife and ask her how she wants me to proceed." Beasley tried to laugh it off, but his face flushed with embarrassment, and he beat a clumsy retreat. But he did not forget this effrontery, and he soon found an enthusiastic collaborator in bringing about her demise.

It had been many years, but Nick Zunich recognized the former Rae Ann Ralston on his first full day on campus. *I'd know that ass anywhere*, he mused as he watched her walk through the breakfast line. Zunich's wife and daughter would not be arriving for several weeks, and already the former linebacker was beginning to feel horny. His leer was not overlooked by Rae Ann who glared back in cold disgust, nor was it lost on Jubal Taliaferro, who nodded at his table-mate and pointed with his fork at the new AD.

"Would you look at that lascivious beast; I do believe we're in the rut season!" Shelby Pleasants suppressed a giggle and responded.

"Why, Jubal, if I didn't know better, I'd swear that the Reverend Mr. Zunich is entertaining thoughts of carnal knowledge upon our head nurse. I would hate to think that - perhaps he's just worked himself up contemplating her conversion."

"He'd like to convert her, OK. You can rest assured of that."

"In the spiritual sense."

"His animal spirit, as the philosopher so sublimely put it. I'm sure I know where he'd like to put that!"

"I'm afraid he would have competition."

"With that dunce of a walking stick?"

"Not her husband, his esteemed employer."

"You mean our General? Our voice crying in the wilderness – calling the whole damned school to repentance?"

"Calling us to eternal life!"

"I'd prefer to see the buffoon's mortal demise. I'd do anything to stay alive just long enough to dance a jig on his grave!"

- - - - - - - - - - - - - - -

That afternoon Nick Zunich paid a visit to the infirmary on the pretext of establishing new procedures of coordination and communication between the infirmary and the athletic training room. She glared at him icily. "Ms. Vance is in charge of triage; I'm confident she's fully capable of working out those details with your staff. We've had no problems in the past, and I'm sure she'll be willing to accommodate any reasonable requests you present to her."

"I don't appreciate being passed off to subordinates; I'd prefer to deal directly with you."

"I'd rather not." Zunich shifted his massive weight and took a step closer.

"You still don't like me, do you, Rae Ann?"

"Let's keep this on a professional basis, Coach Zunich. What's past is past, and I'd just as soon forget it. I may not enjoy working with you, but whether I do or don't is beside the point. We have to work together, so in light of what happened years ago, I plan to keep our personal contact to a minimum. Even you should be smart enough to understand that."

"I kind of enjoyed our last personal contact." He sneered and moved a step closer. "Tell me you didn't get a little bit excited yourself."

"You're out of your league, Zunich. You're not only a brute, but a dumb brute. Only a total imbecile could be so pathetic. Are you really that asinine? Do you honestly imagine that you are so well equipped that any self-respecting female would overlook the fact that you have a face that belongs on a rhinoceros not to mention a brain to match?"

"You still haven't learned, have you? You're sill the dumb bitch that I remember from that night by the river. Just keep this in mind: I've got some pull with the boss around here. Don't you forget that, or you'll end up worse than the last time." Zunich stormed out of the room overturning an instrument table in the process. Rae Ann stood motionless, not certain if the collision had been an accident. She bent over to pick up the instruments scattered on the floor and wondered what his next move would be.

- - - - - - - - - - - - - - -

Nick Zunich was not a man to wait on protocol. Weeks before his official introduction as the new AD, he had hired his football staff. The two coaches forming the nucleus of his staff had been teammates at N.C. State and also regulars at the Riverside Motel football bacchanals. In relieving the former staff of its coaching duties Zunich had ingratiated himself with Beasley, who saw this as another opportunity to chip away at the "Old Point of Fork Culture." The General was justly confident that their resignations as P.E. instructors would soon follow, opening the way for even more personnel compatible with his vision.

Jerry Birkhead and Joe Pajaczowski arrived on the afternoon following Zunch's confrontation in the infirmary. Birkhead had been a freshman at State during Zunich's senior season. A defensive lineman, he was small by major college standards at 230 pounds, but he was totally fearless and extremely agile for his size. A fierce tackler, he hit opponents with jarring force. After college Birkhead made it to the final cut before being released by the Los Angeles Rams. He eventually played five seasons as a starter for the Hamilton Tiger Cats in the Canadian Football League. Birkhead's career ended after his fourth knee operation, and he returned to Raleigh to complete his degree in Physical Education.

Pajaczowski, a quarterback, had been Zunich's high school teammate in Reading, Pennsylvania. They had been recruited together and both were highly prized by the Wolfpack, but Pajaczowski was never a starter during his brief career at State. In May of his sophomore year, he was dismissed from the university after he was caught cheating on a sociology exam. After a tour in the Army, he had been a truck driver. Although Pajaczowski had never finished his degree and was unqualified to teach, Zunich convinced the General to take him on as a coach and (over Buck Bristow's strong objection) as a tactical officer in the Commandant's department. Unlike Birkhead, who had added a hundred pounds, Pajaczowski had remained fit and looked as though he could still take the snap from center.

The three new coaches held their first meeting on the evening of Pajaczowski and Birkhead's arrival. Zunich had wasted no time in adorning Wagner's former office with memorabilia from his playing days at N.C. State and from Brunswick County High School, where he had previously coached. Centered over his desk was a blown up newspaper photo showing a beaming Coach Earl Edwards handing Nick Zunich the game ball after recovering two fumbles in the 1971 Duke game. Below the mat of tangled hair the imprint of his helmet was still fresh on Zunich's sweating forehead as he received the prize in his grimy, heavily-taped hands.

The new coaching staff was absorbed in X's and O's for over two hours before taking their first break. Pajaczowski glanced at Zunich and then at Birkhead, his neckless colleague. "Let's find somewhere a little more comfortable to talk."

"We still got work to do," Zunich answered, a little perturbed.

"We can work. I just don't see no harm with doing it over a beer or two."

"Pay attention to me, Joe, you better be careful about that. Beasley's particular about the booze; make one wrong move, and you could be outta here."

"You telling me no one here drinks?"

"I didn't say that. I'm just warning you to be careful. You can drink at home, but I'd watch who you drink with and where you stow the bottles and cans when you're done. There's plenty of eyes looking around here." Birkhead was now beginning to look perplexed.

"You sayin' *you* quit drinkin'?"

"No, I'm saying that I know enough to be careful. Let's put in another hour here, and I'll take you down the road to a place I know where we can have a couple of brews."

The Rock A'Bye was located on the south side of the James River in Buckingham County about twelve miles from Columbia. The one-story clapboard restaurant stood on a bluff overlooking the river. This old, modest establishment served fried chicken and other home-cooked fare, and at one time had even booked live entertainment on Friday and Saturday evenings, but in recent years this had been reduced to the second Saturday of every month. Even the two pool tables in the back were rarely used anymore, and on weekday evenings the after-dinner clientele consisted of little more than a few locals who listened to the juke box while washing down their Slim Jims and pickled eggs with Miller draft. The coaches had more than a few beers, and by the time they left, Zunich had to be driven home.

His assistants parked his car in the driveway and walked across the campus to their apartments. It was twenty degrees outside as Nick watched them disappear, but he felt warm in his light windbreaker. He started to go inside, but despite the beers he didn't feel sleepy. He felt horny. It took him five minutes to cross the campus to the infirmary, but neither the cold nor the exercise had sobered him. The light was on. He was lucky; Rae Ann's car was parked in the nurse's space. She was on duty for the evening.

Zunich pulled on the door handle, nearly breaking it off, but the door didn't budge. He looked at the sign above the button next to the door. *Ring for nurse after 8:30 PM.* He walked around back to the service entrance. It was locked too, but by lifting the handle sharply upward the door popped open after a sharp tug. Zunich stepped inside. The smell of disinfectant and medicine enveloped him as he eased the door shut. Walking quietly down the corridor, he checked the open doors to the rooms. No cadets had been admitted for the evening. Zunick walked by the dimly lit nurse's station and down the hall toward the overnight apartment. The door was cracked. He could see her sitting on the sofa watching the Jay Leno Show. Rae Ann was alone in her nightgown. Nick felt a stir in his crotch.

Nick stood motionless. An advertisement came on for Blue Mountain Spring Water, and Rae Ann got up to go to bed. She turned off the TV and the lamp, and crossed the darkened room to the bedroom door. Rae Ann reached to turn on the light, but before her hand touched the switch she felt the full impact of the former linebacker as 260 pounds of lust and aggression drove her reeling toward the bed. Never had Zunich blindsided a quarterback and driven him helplessly to the turf as ferociously as he tackled his unsuspecting victim. The wind had been knocked out of her, and she was unable to shout or scream for thirty seconds. By then Zunich was pumping savagely inside her. In the pitch black she could hear him heaving and grunting hoarsely. As her voice began to return, she tried to scream. "I know you, Zunich! You won't get away with this, you fucking pig!" Zunich responded with two vicious clouts to the face and left her lying unconscious in the dark.

- - - - - - - - - - - - - - -

Beasley was nonplussed when Rae Ann stormed past his Mrs. Stickley and exploded into his office the next morning. "That fucking animal you hired beat the shit out if me and raped me last night!" The blood drained from the General's face as he saw Rae Ann's bruised and swollen face, and he stammered for her to please sit down.

"I'll call the nurse on duty!"

"I *am* the fucking nurse on duty, you asshole! I can tend to myself. What I want you to do is get that pig Zunich off this goddamn campus right now before I call the goddamn cops."

"You're upset. Mrs. Stickley, would you excuse us? Call Captain Honeycutt if you would, and ask him to wait outside. Now Mrs. Brady, what's this about Coach Zunich?"

"He fuckin' raped me last night in the infirmary."

"Your language, Rae Ann. I know you're upset."

"*Upset*! I've been *raped* – by *your* coach! I want the cops!"

"Easy, Mrs. Brady. Let's not act rashly. Tell me exactly what happened."

Rae Ann rolled her eyes. *He'll probably get a hard-on listening to this*, she thought. "I was watching TV and had just headed to my room when that horny beast tackled me, threw me down on the bed, and raped me. Then he knocked me out cold!"

"How did he get in? Did *you* let him in?"

"How the fuck do I know? I didn't even see him 'till he drove me across the room. It was dark."

"Then you didn't really *see* who it was?"

"I *know* who the hell it was! It was Nick Zunich – *your* AD."

"It's hard for me to imagine how you could give a positive identification under the circumstances; you say it was dark. We have a number of cadets here – football players – who are just as large as Coach Zunich. Or it could just as easily have been someone from outside. I seriously doubt that anyone here at our school - - "

"I tell you, I *know*. It was Zunich."

"Whatever you say, but that's certainly not consistent with the man's character. He's an ordained minister of the Gospel. And without your actually seeing him, I'm afraid that in a court of law - - "

"Listen, you fucking bastard, I *know* who the hell it was, and if you're going to let that animal - -"

"Your *language*, Mrs. Brady, I remind you! Did you have the facility properly secured?"

"I already fucking told you, it was *locked*."

"Then if what you say is true, I can't see how - -"

Rae Ann stared at the General, her eyes like laser drilling a hole through him. *He's got to know*, she thought. She raised her hand and pointed a finger directly at his face. Then, without uttering another word, she dropped the hand and stormed out of the room, almost knocking Captain Honeycutt over in the process. The security guard looked in and saw his disconcerted boss. "Yes sir, General. What can I do for you?"

"Nothing, Honeycutt. Never mind; I'll take care of it."

Chapter 36

Max watched the Carbonells' rented Pontiac pull out of his driveway. Brett had already left for school, and Johanna was still asleep. There wasn't much for him to do until 3:30, when he would pick his son up at school and drive him to basketball practice. He went back inside and stacked the breakfast dishes in the washer. The *Times Dispatch* lay unopened on the table. Also unopened in his study was a stack of bills and assorted letters from Murray, his partners, and various business associates who now wanted a piece of him. Inches away on his business phone the light had been blinking for over a week. Max didn't even glance in as he passed by the study door. He walked back outside and hopped into the Land Rover. Pulling out of the driveway, Max had no clue where he was headed, but force of habit took him to Henrico General. A small sign indicated that his parking space had already been reassigned: Dr. Mary F. Hensley. A white Volvo station wagon with a baby seat was parked in the space.

He drove past the construction site. It was deserted; a cold wind whistled through the exposed steelwork. All of the equipment had been gone for weeks. Max slowed down as he drove past Brett's school. By the time he turned back onto Monument Avenue, a cold drizzle had begun to fall. He turned on the windshield wipers and headed into town passing the huge bronze memorials to Confederate heroes. A glistening film of ice had begun to form on the surface of the green statues, still cold from the night before. A block past the Lee Monument, Max took a right, and a few blocks later turned onto a winding lane that took him to the wrought iron gates of Shady Knoll Cemetery. He parked and walked to the gravesite. Grass had nearly covered the ground that had had been exposed only a few months before on the day of Justin's funeral. Red Virginia hardpan had stained the bottom two inches of the headstone where it had spattered up onto the marble. Even now Max struggled to reconcile his faith to the impersonal caprice that seemed to lead to the loss of his innocent son. For some reason he recalled a prayer that he had learned from the nuns as a child and had taught years ago to his young sons.

> *Angel of God, my guardian dear,*
>
> *To whom God's love commits me here,*
>
> *Ever this day be at my side,*
>
> *To light, to guard, to rule and guide*

By the time Max arrived to pick his son up for practice, the rain had ended. Having nothing else to do, he sat in the bleachers and watched practice. Arriving home at 5:45, he was surprised that Luis and Maria had not returned from Point of Fork. Johanna was up but had not prepared a supper. She asked Max where he had spent his day, and he responded vaguely that he had been checking on some business. He didn't have the heart to bring up Shady Knoll. Since the Carbonells would be returning at any time, Max offered to go out to the Peking duck and pick up dinner.

It was 6:30 when he returned. Still no sign of Luis and Maria. Max told Brett to serve himself dinner so he would have time for homework. Finally at 7:15 the Pontiac pulled into the driveway. "Where the hell have you guys been?"

"The academy. Where do you think?"

"Hell, they should have given you a couple of credits; you've been gone almost twelve hours! What did you think, Maria?"

"About what I expected. I've seen pictures in Luis' old yearbooks."

"You didn't run into Beasley, did you, Luis?"

"No, but I saw a lot of old faces – people I hadn't see since I left."

"Like who?"

"Coach Wagner, Colonel Bristow, Colonel Frazier."

"Any news?"

"Not from them – nothing you didn't already told me."

"I'm afraid they'll be history and the place will be on its last legs before long. Beasley's got the bull by the horns now. He's going to have his way."

"Maybe not."

"How not? What have you heard?"

"Lots of things. Nothing definite - just rumors."

"From whom?"

"You remember Major Pleasants, don't you? The Librarian?"

"Major Pleasants of the Three Gents? Hell, Carbonell, he *is* a rumor; you know that. A walking, talking scandal. You can't go by anything *he* says."

"Yeah, but sometimes he was right. I remember that too."

"*Sometimes* – he did keep his ear pretty close to the ground, but I also recall that by the time he had finished expanding and embellishing the story, you had to take the cube root of his version to get some close to the truth."

"Maybe, but I think it's still worth looking into."

"OK – let's hear it."

Luis had quite a tale, indeed – almost certainly too good to be true. And even if it were all true, how could it be proven? Luis was not dissuaded by Max's reservations. "Leave that to me, old buddy. I already called Tom Hatch – we're gonna find out."

"But you're leaving in two days."

"It don't take two days to track this down. Either Pleasants is full of shit, or he knows what he's talking about."

"Even if he's right, he's *still* full of shit. Either way your plan take money to make it work."

"Money I got."

"I don't know, Luis. This time you might have more money than brains. I tried to cross the guy, and look where it got me. I'd hate to think we're placing all our bets on the veracity of Shelby Pleasants. Could be that the smartest thing for you to do would be to walk away."

"Now that's strange advice – coming from you! We'll talk more in the morning."

- - - - - - - - - - - - - - - -

Johanna had left for bed hours before the guests retired. Max went upstairs.

Passing Brett's room, he saw that the light was off. As he often did, Max cracked the door and peeked in. "Dad?" Max went in and sat on the side of the bed.

"I didn't know you were still awake, son."

"I couldn't sleep."

"What's the matter? You got a problem."

"You know."

"Know what? What's the big problem?"

"Everything. First Justin, then the hospital, you and mom, the drinking. *Everything's* wrong, and there's nothing I can do to stop it. I wish I could help somehow."

"Listen, son. These things happen with grownups. It has nothing to do with you. We both love you, and nothing that happens between your mom and me will ever change that."

"Yeah, you say that, but *everything* changed after Justin."

"I know, but there's more to it than you realize. It's not as simple as it looks. There are other things."

"You guys are splitting up, aren't you?"

"I hope not."

"When Justin was here, we were a family. Now that it's just me . . ."

"It's not your fault, son. *Forget* that idea! We miss Justin, but all by yourself, you're more of a son than any parent deserves. Losing your brother was tough on all of us, but for a mother it's different. When a mother - -"

"Is it the drinking? Is that the reason . . .?"

"No, that's just a symptom. It's not the real problem. Your mother's not the problem at all, son; it's me."

"No way! You're the best dad that any kid - -"

"I've tried to be, Brett, but I'm afraid I haven't, and I've been even less of a husband. I haven't been there for you or your mother ever since the accident. I didn't mean to, but now I see I was using this academy business to distract me from my own grief, and in doing that I neglected my family. In the end I managed to destroy my career and the people I love most in the process. No, if I were in your mom's place with a husband like me, I'd get myself smashed every day. She's not to blame, Brett. Whatever happens, it's my fault."

"That's not true!"

"It *is* true. It's the *obvious* truth. And as plain as it is, this is the first time I've really admitted it – even to myself. Now, try to get some sleep, son. I'll see you in the morning."

When Max left the room, he found his wife standing outside. She had been crying. "You heard?" She nodded, still wiping away tears. They walked quietly back to their room. As Max began to remove his shirt, Johanna grasped him in her arms.

"I'm *so* sorry, Max."

"For what? *You've* got nothing to be sorry for. It's me. If I hadn't gone off on this academy thing . . ."

"If you hadn't gotten involved, you wouldn't have been Max – the man I married, the man I fell in love with. The same man I see more clearly every day whenever I look at our son."

"God, I hope not! This whole thing has been so stupid. Look where it got me. Now I've got Carbonell – all the damned way from Venezuela - mixed up in this. That's the trouble, Johanna, just like you said, I don't know when the hell to stop. I'm putting an end to this first thing tomorrow morning."

"An end to what?"

"Luis and Tom Hatch. They think they've got Beasley by the nuts."

"Do they?"

"No, I doubt it. The guy's too smart. He doesn't make mistakes that he can't cover up."

"You need to see it through, Max."

"You can't mean that – not after all we've been through. Look at what I've screwed up already."

"I won't argue that, but look at it the other way."

"Yeah, I know. What have we got to lose?"

"I heard you talking to Brett. We could lose each other. I don't want that. You guys give it your best shot. If you screw up, I'll still be here for you - provided you still want me."   Max was moved with a nearly-forgotten tenderness as he took his wife into his arms for the first time in months.

Chapter 37

Max was on the office phone all the next morning. Luis and Maria took turns using the house phone. When they took a break at one o'clock, Johanna had lunch prepared. "Homemade lasagna! What did we do to deserve this?"

"You guys are going head-to-head with Beasley tomorrow, you'll need to be fortified." Max shook his head hopelessly.

"Like the condemned man's last meal. I wish we were more fortified with provable facts."

"We're getting there," Luis responded.

"Any progress with our beauty queens?"

"I wouldn't count on them, Max. Maria was able to contact two of them. Offered to pay their way over here or just have them sign an affidavit, but they don't want to get mixed up in this."

"You can't blame them. Why would they? So, do we bluff it as far as they're concerned?"

"We might have to."

"The General won't buy that – not without a lot of corroboration, and we don't have much. I followed up the scuttlebutt from the *Enterprise*, but that led to a dead end. How about our star witness?"

"I've got Tom Hatch working on that. He'll call us as soon as he has something."

"That's a *real* long shot."

"We'll see; money talks, you know. How about Mrs. Brady?"

"She hates his ass. I think she's on thin ice with him anyway, so she doesn't have much to lose. She claims one of the General's new guys assaulted her and Beasley tried to cover it up."

"She got any proof?"

"Nada."

"Your Spanish is getting real better."

"Better than my bank account. I don't need to tell you, Luis, if we misfire on this I'm screwed."

"That's pretty much water over the dam at this point," Johanna interrupted. "We're already screwed if we don't beat him on this. I say we go for it."

"Hell, we could end up in jail. I believe she wants me locked up, Luis."

"The thought does have its charm," Johanna laughed.

Max tapped his pen on the table absentmindedly. "Rae Ann Brady said something strange, Luis. She claims her husband may have something on the General."

"Let's not involve Coach Brady. I remember him; he'd ruin a wet dream!"

"Just a thought. She didn't sound like he would cooperate anyway. We don't need him – he's just trouble."

"What we need is for Tom Hatch to come through."

"That would help big time – no doubt about it. Without him we're shit."

"But I still think Crawford's the key, Max. He and Marvin."

"I talked with Marvin this morning. It's pretty simple with him. He's got no confidence in our scheme, but either way he's not risking anything. If this thing goes, he's with us. The bottom line is he'll go with the money."

"I figured that," Maria responded. How about your lawyer?"

"Murray? He says I've totally lost it, but I left him no choice. He's aboard."

"One last thing, Max. Do we know the General's going to be there?"

"I checked with Frazier. He's set up a meeting with him for ten o'clock. The General won't miss it; he thinks Ron's turning in his resignation. He'll be there."

"When you guys show up in his place, Ron might as well resign."

"You got that right. This better work."

- - - - - - - - - - - - - - -

Max parked behind Heritage Hall. He and Luis scanned the parking lot. No sign of Tom Hatch. Max looked at his watch and shrugged. "It's five minutes to ten. I guess we go in."

"I'll wait outside for Hatch."

"He should have been here by now. Without him, we've got zilch." The defeat in Max's voice was palpable.

"Should we wait some more?"

"No. I'll give it my best bluff."

Mrs. Stickley's momentary smile upon recognizing Max turned to a frown. "You're not supposed to be here, Mr. Jarvis."

"I have a ten o'clock appointment."

"General Beasley's seeing Colonel Frazier at ten."

"I'm his proxy."

"You'd better leave, Mr. Jarvis. I like you, but I have specific orders to call security if you ever set - - "

Max was already through the General's door. Mrs. Stickley followed right behind him.

"Mrs. Stickley, call security. Have Honeycutt report here immediately." The General's face was red with ire.

"General, it's going to take Honeycutt a good five minutes to get here; you'd better sit down for that time and listen to me."

"You're in violation of a restraining order, Jarvis, and I know Frazier has to be mixed up in this. I'll have him fired and you in jail within the hour."

"I doubt that. Not after you hear what I have to say." Max tried to mask the uncertainty in his faltering voice.

"You underestimate Captain Honeycutt. I'd say you have less than three minutes."

"General, I'm here to present an ultimatum."

"Oh, you *are*!" the General exclaimed in mock-horror." "You're certainly in no position to do that."

"We'll see."

"And what, may I ask, would compel me to agree to any ultimatum that you might bring forth?"

"Scandal. Exposure. The loss of your cherished reputation as a pillar of Christian principles. Showing you for the pervert and the hypocrite that you are." The General's face flushed a deeper crimson. He pressed the button on intercom.

"Mrs. Stickley, have you reached Honeycutt?"

"He's on his way, sir."

"I'd be on my way to my car if I were you, Jarvis. You're blowing smoke; I can hear it in your voice. I can't fathom how you could be so incautious as to come here."

"I've got all the proof I need," Max retorted, but without conviction. I have a complaint from Mrs. Brady regarding an incident of sexual harassment with your complicity."

"You'll have to do a lot better than that," the General laughed. Strangely his voice sounded slightly relieved.

"There's more."

"*Oh?*" The General's voice dripped with sarcasm. "I can't *wait*."

"Back in Guantanamo – when you were stationed there. We have some girls who will testify as to your conduct in Venezuela. And then there's the little matter of certain indiscretions in Da Nang during your tour on the *Enterprise*." The General stared at Max.

"You're bluffing, my poor inept friend. I suppose you have them all out there waiting to finger me?"

"I can get them." The involuntary tremor in Max's voice betrayed his lack of conviction. He felt as though he were drowning. The General smiled with satisfaction.

"You're way over your head, Jarvis. Excuse me." He touched the intercom again. "Mrs. Stickley, has Honeycutt arrived."

"He should be here momentarily, sir."

Max forged ahead resolutely. "There are two demands."

"Demands?" the General chuckled, unable to contain his mirth. "Please continue. This I can't wait to hear."

"First, of course you settle with Crawford. Seven million dollars."

"*Seven* million? I don't know where you've been for the last couple of months, Jarvis, but they've already accepted five."

"I know, but I had to change the equation in order for them to agree to my terms."

"*Your* terms. And what, if I might be so bold as to ask, are they?"

"They agree to drop then litigation against Bristow and Mrs. Harrington. Plus sign an affidavit clearing me of all blame in the incident at Joe's Inn. He'll swear that I was totally passive and that he was the aggressor."

"Now that *would* be nice for you, wouldn't it, Jarvis? Get your practice reinstated. Maybe convince your backers to start your wonderful little hospital back up again. I'm sure Crawford would say a lot of things for seven million. And doubling the settlement would be great for Marvin. Those people, shall we say, can always smell a buck. But you've got one very small problem, Doctor."

"What's that, General?" There was no confidence in Max's voice. He knew he was beaten. Beasley rocked back in his chair and smiled imperiously.

"You've got nothing. No witness, no evidence, no reliable testimony that anyone would have the slightest reason to believe. Just a few unsubstantiated rumors from years ago and the accusation of a disgruntled employee. I'm sure you would like to see me to resign, and, while I'm at it rescue your ruined life, but not today, my friend. Frankly, I'm disappointed in you, Jarvis. You're a Point of Fork graduate. I would have thought you could have done better than this. Please excuse me again. Mrs. Beasley, is he here?"

"Yes sir, General Beasley, but you'd better come out here!"

Beasley directed Max to the door. Totally defeated, Max walked out of the office and nearly bumped into a grinning Tom Hatch. The General followed him through the doorway, but his swagger faltered and his face drained of color as he caught sight of the large black woman radiantly beaming back at him. Hatch began to say something, but she needed no introduction. She had gained fifty pounds, but the infectious smile with the gleaming gold tooth was the same. Pearl stepped forward. "Why, I do declah! If it ain't o'l Ben Johnson in the flesh! Or should I say Phil Beasley his own sef?" Beasley's knees buckled. Had his former courtesan not caught him in her strong arms, he would have hit the floor. "Don' you worry none, lovah. Ol' Pearl's heah to take care o' you." The General shrank back and gazed around the room in bewilderment. "You can't - - that was before anyone ever - - "

"Easy, chile, Pearl knows you didn't mean no harm." He recoiled as she advanced solicitously.

"The Devil's done this!" he stammered incoherently, as heads turned in amazement. "He's been foaming at the mouth ever since Sonny Hockaday won 236 souls for Christ at our revival. He wants to tear down our City on a Hill! He's a-dragging me down into the pit!"

Hatch grinned broadly at Max and turned to a stricken Beasley. "May I borrow your phone, Sir? Marvin and Crawford are on call in Richmond. Max's attorney has the papers drawn up. We can have this done in a couple of hours."

EPILOGUE

The Board of Directors stood on the platform as the corps of cadets passed in review for the first spring parade. As the last company left the drill field, the board members returned to their families in the grandstands. Tom grinned and shook his head. "Looks like D Company's slipped a bit since our days, Max. Obviously they don't drill for hours on the snow and out in the boiling sun like when we were here."

"Right. Looked like the whole third platoon was out of step."

"Nothing a good dose of Major Maytag couldn't cure!"

"I'm sure they said the same thing back in the seventies when you guys were here." Johanna laughed.

"No way!" Max responded. "Tom's right. The place is getting soft: air-conditioned barracks, phones in the rooms; it's a wonder that they can get the corps onto the parade field at all."

"Well, you boys can address your complaints directly to Colonel Bristow and the others. I'm sure they're grateful to you guys for their jobs."

"You got that right!" Tom agreed. "We've got some muscle around here! And how about the hospital, Max. When's it due for completion?"

"Before Christmas, according to the contract, but who knows? They have a million ways of wiggling out of those penalty clauses. My money's on Easter at the earliest."

"And it looks like we've got another target date to look forward to" Tom winked at Max and nodded toward the bulge beginning to show in Johanna's midsection. "When's the blessed event scheduled to occur?"

"Mid-August." Tom made a show of counting on his fingers.

"The hell are you doing?" stormed a blushing Johanna in mock-indignation."

"Just some calculations. I'm computing back to the weekend we ran ol' Beasley off campus."

"You guys are sick!"

Brett looked puzzled. "What are you guys talking about?"

Point of Fork Military Academy forged ahead into the Twenty-first Century notwithstanding the carping of Max Jarvis and other alumni who, like their predecessors before, aired the traditional reproof that academy was becoming a "country club for effete rich kids." Ron Frazier was named interim president after the abrupt departure of General Beasley, and was appointed president of the academy the following spring. Under his leadership, PFMA withstood the financial setback resulting from the Crawford settlement and maintained its status as one of America's outstanding college preparatory schools. As the academy marched boldly ahead into the Twenty-first Century, so did the people whose lives were touched by the school.

- Luis Carbonell's export business continued to flourish. Maria completed her law degree and was later appointed to the national judiciary in Caracas. Both of their sons attended Point of Fork.

- After eight years in the law firm of Battle and Associates, Ted Hemming left in the wake of an auditor's report on his expense account. He moved to Little Rock, Arkansas, where he joined his uncle's practice with the Rose Law Firm.

- Wyatt Scarce's dentistry license had been revoked in 1992 after the *Sixty Minutes* scandal. Ten years later, after serving one year in prison and making full financial restitution, his right to practice was reinstated. During his year in prison Scarce became a born-again Christian and now serves as the West Virginia chairman of the Promise Keepers.

- Tom Hatch returned to his orthodontic practice and quiet life in the suburbs of Knoxville. He was so exhilarated from his adventure at Point of Fork, however, that he was inspired to try Rogaine. Almost immediately a few sprouts began to germinate, but unfortunately the most he was able to cultivate was a thin patch of short, soft, down. Too vain to stoop to a hairpiece, he was compelled to accept his place among the hairless.

- The Reverend Caleb Belcher's ministry in Jumping Branch never recovered the vitality it had enjoyed before the snake handling fiasco. Although he remained for twelve more years at The Full Gospel Holiness Church of the Risen Christ in Jesus Name, he never really recovered from the disaster. It seemed that something just went out of him that day that couldn't be restored.

One Sunday he simply failed to show up for service, and months later word trickled back to Jumping Branch that he had taken up again with Fennel Corbin and that the two were touring the Appalachians as traveling evangelists. Later that year news came that Belcher had died from ingesting strychnine during a tent revival outside of Harlan, Kentucky.

- The Reverend John Leatherwood resigned in disgust from the PFMA board of directors shortly after the appointment of Ron Frazier as president. He did not abandon his interest in education, however, and was soon appointed to the board at Liberty University in Lynchburg, Virginia.

- Sonny Hockaday is now based in Tyler, Texas and broadcasts *In These Last Days* on over 200 television stations in the US and Canada.

- Buck Bristow remained as Commandant until his retirement from PFMA twelve years later. As Ron Frazier's second in command he was instrumental in restoring the academy's discipline that had plummeted so sharply during Beasley's short tenure as president.

- Less than a week after Beasley's exit, Rick Wagner was reinstated as Athletic Director. Nick Zunich, despite the credible but unproven accusations of Rae Ann Brady, was given the option by Wagner to stay on as head football coach. Outraged at the decision, he hotly declined the offer and threatened a nasty lawsuit. This unwanted controversy was averted when a board member persuaded University of Richmond head coach Jim Reid to hire Zunich as an assistant. In 1999 Zunich was named defensive coordinator, and when Reid moved on to Boston College a year later, Athletic Director Chuck Boone, less than a week before retiring as AD, shocked Richmond by naming Zunich head football coach.

This, his most inexplicable act as Athletic Director, also turned out to be Boone's most unfortunate during his twenty-three year tenure. Four years later a list of over twenty serious violations was uncovered by the NCAA, and the widening investigation, going back over twenty years, resulted in two years' probation for the Spiders.

- Butch Slay lasted only a couple of semesters at Vanderbilt. After flunking out, he traveled west on his Harley to Jackson Hole, Wyoming, where for two years he drifted around as a ski bum and kayak instructor. For several months he was a male stripper and later became the paid companion of a Ms. Leah Silverman, age *circa* 45, of Vail, Colorado. After the death of his father in 1994, Slay moved back to his home in Tennessee using his inheritance to start a small Harley-Davidson dealership. He was the first H-D dealer to advertise nationally on the web, and within two years Butch Slay's Hogs was the largest dealer in the nation.

On January 3, 2000 Slay was at home watching the Fiesta Bowl when the doorbell rang. He clicked the mute button and went to the door. "What the - - Where did you come from?" It was Rae Ann Brady. She had obviously been drinking and had aged some, but was looking as delectable as ever.

"Saw your picture on the web and decided to pay you a call. Care to invite an old friend in for a nightcap?"

"Sure," he stammered, but didn't move. Rae Ann pushed her old paramour aside and sauntered inside taking a place on the couch.

"Offer a lady a drink?"

"Uh, yeah. Sure. But Coach Brady - -"

"I gave myself a millennium present three nights ago. Ditched the bastard at a new year's party after he called me a damn lush and begged me to lay off the booze. Never going back to that fuckin' scarecrow, either.

"The millennium ain't 'till next year."

"Who's counting? Besides, I can't wait that long. Say, did you tell me you were going to get me a drink?"

- Dunston Brady tracked his wife down to Tennessee three months after her abrupt departure and six weeks after Butch Slay had evicted her from his residence. Ignoring Dunston's entreaties, she filed for divorce and returned to Richmond where she cared for her ailing parents. Within less than a year, both parents died leaving her a sizeable estate including the family home on Old Lock Lane.

Brady retired from PFMA that June and embarked on his long-cherished dream of hiking the entire 2100 mile length of the Appalachian Trail from Mount Katahdin, Maine to Springer Mountain, Georgia. He wrote to Rae Ann faithfully every evening and dropped his missives in a mailbox whenever possible. After a two-week hiatus in the correspondence, Rae Ann received a call from Buck Bristow. Dunston's badly mauled and decomposed body had been found by some boy scouts at the bottom of a ravine about nineteen miles from Port Clinton, Pennsylvania. Apparently he had encountered a bear at least as large as the one that had attacked Major Reardon twenty-five years earlier, only this time there was no referee.

- Dillon Forbes enrolled at Episcopal High School for the spring semester of 1998. The following year he led the Maroon to a 9-1 record, their only loss a 31-28 heartbreaker to Point of Fork Military Academy. In that game, featuring Episcopal's potent air attack matched against PFMA's strong ground game, Forbes threw for 212 yards and three touchdowns. But with thirty seconds left in the game, cornerback Jason Suggs picked off a pass on the nineteen yard line ending the Maroon's final scoring drive. Point of Fork ran out the clock insuring a spot on the state playoffs. Forbes signed the following February with Steve Spurrier's Florida Gators.

- Shelby Pleasants returned to Farmville for his retirement. On August 1, 2001, at the age of 66, he obtained his first driver's license. Two weeks later he drowned when his 1994 Oldsmobile inexplicably drove off the Route 15 Bridge into the Appomattox River.

- Jubal F. Taliaferro was scheduled to retire at the end of the 1999-2000 academic session. On the morning of graduation the faculty and staff were forming up to proceed into the chapel. Ron Frazier was standing with the graduation speaker, Chief Justice Rehnquist, at the head of the procession; but Taliaferro, who by seniority should have been near the front of the line, was nowhere to be seen. A cadet was dispatched to D Company to find Major Taliaferro, but he returned and reported that the apartment door was locked and that no one had answered his repeated knocking. "Major Mayta -- Tollavah wont there, Colonel. I knocked and knocked. Couple o' guys on first platoon said they heard a lot o' racket and a huge crash up there about 11:30 last night, but they didn't think nothing of it."

After the diplomas were distributed and the last cars had left the campus, Frazier, Bristow, and Ed Alley went to Taliaferro's apartment in D Company, fearing the worst. Alley jimmied the door open, and the grisly scene before them confirmed their worst trepidations. Jubal Taliaferro, all three hundred pounds of him, lay in a sprawl nearly obscuring a shattered walnut table. Overturned next to him was a platter and two porterhouse steaks, untouched except by the flies now buzzing around the fetid scene. A third steak, half-consumed, lay halfway across the destroyed room, whose state of chaos clearly indicated the tumultuous scene of the night before.

The coroner's report indicated that Taliaferro had asphyxiated by choking on a mouthful of medium-rare steak about the size of a golf ball. Stomach contents indicated that he had already consumed at least two porterhouses. The implications were all too obvious. Major Taliaferro, as was so often his custom, had enlisted the help of Louis Johnson for one final theft from the PFMA mess hall. Sadly, this small larceny was to deprive him of the retirement that he had been anticipating for so many years. Surveying the scene of destruction, one could easily reconstruct the frenzy that had erupted during the old scholar's last desperate minutes of agony in the tiny apartment. The overturned chairs, the broken picture frames, and the splintered furniture told the sad tale of an epic struggle and a torturous end.

- John Reardon's retirement held both surprise and fulfillment. Western North Carolina had changed dramatically since he had left nearly five decades before. The Smokey Mountains were still beautiful, but expensive homes and ski resorts had replaced the mountain cabins and shanties of his youth. The hill where his mother's church once stood had been leveled to accommodate a large shopping center.

  Reardon was welcomed into the newer Mount Tabor Baptist Church, where his experience in education and entertainment led him to work with the young people. At least once a month he took youth groups on trips to Raleigh for fellowship with other churches, movies, or wrestling shows.

- The Point of Fork Crusader – never happened.

- When Vernon and Lynda Philpott filed for a no-fault divorce in 1999, only a year after their sudden conversion, the Point of Fork community was at a loss to comprehend what the cause could be. The motive became apparent six months later when Vernon inherited over four million dollars upon the death of his uncle, Johnny Roventini, in White Plains, New York at the age of 88. Vernon had never mentioned his rich uncle to Lynda, but she would have recognized him as "Phillip Morris Johnny," the pint-sized bellboy who became one of the best-known figures of American advertising. Philpott was Roventinni's sole heir. Standing at only four feet, the "living trademark" was heard making his famous call on some of the most popular radio and television shows from 1944-1968. He took in a salary of up to $50,000, a handsome sum in those days, most of which he invested in Phillip Morris stock.

- Janice Tribble Beasley caught her husband in a compromised situation with a local waitress only three months after their return to Jumping Branch. Following the divorce, General Beasley began to grow his hair long and commenced a series of liaisons with several younger women. He began to order his clothes out of *GQ*, *Esquire*, and *Maxim* and was frequently seen driving around town in his Corvette convertible.

In March of 2002 Beasley was in Hawaii accompanied by Nicole Valentine, a substitute teacher thirty-two years his junior. During a trip to Volcano National Park, they were standing with a small group on the observation walk over the Kilauea crater. The eruption came with almost no warning – only a slight rumble that sent the sightseers scurrying back to safety. The General, who had recently begun to experience a significant hearing loss, was too vain to use a hearing aid. At the moment of the explosion, he was absorbed in adjusting the zoom on his camera and did not hear the rumble until it was too late. The platform collapsed sending him headlong into the fiery abyss. Witnesses to the tragedy reported that the lone fatality may have saved the other tourists. With his last breaths he wildly screamed the warning, "Belcher!" (the local term for an erupting volcano) several times as he plummeted three hundred feet to his doom.

- Pearl Woodson never again heard from her old john after their brief reunion in Heritage Hall. By that time she had been married to a coal miner and out of her former business for many years. The mother of three grown daughters, she still lives in Keystone, West Virginia.

- Of Frank Crawford's seven million dollars, about three million remained after his lawyer, psychiatrist and the IRS had taken their share. With this tidy sum he was able to assume a lifestyle that he had only been able to dream of previously. The issue of Crawford's sexuality appeared to be resolved with his marriage in June of 1999 to Sylvia Gill, a waitress he had met at Joe's Inn. During their honeymoon in the British Virgin Islands, a cough that Frank had developed some weeks earlier became so severe that he had it checked immediately upon his return to Richmond. Chest x-rays and further tests revealed a lung tumor that had metastasized into several vital organs. Frank Crawford died on November 28, 1999.

- Dan Marvin used his cut of the Crawford settlement to purchase a cabin cruiser, *The Deep Pocket*, which he docked in Deltaville, Virginia and cruised to Miami every winter.

- Dr. Marion F. Dunnigan's yield from the Crawford case was much more modest, and two years later she needed every penny of it to fight off a swarm of lawsuits emanating from the public's growing distrust of hypnotic regression both in psychiatric medicine and in the courtroom. Among those winning handsome settlements at her expense was John Reardon.

- Brett Jarvis went on to become an All-State pitcher at Douglas Freeman High School. He turned down several baseball scholarships and a tryout with the Orioles to play ball and pursue a pre-med major at William and Mary. A model son in all respects, his only major disappointment to Max and Johanna was the large tattoo he brought home from the beach the week after graduation from Douglas Freeman High School.

- Bradley Justin Jarvis entered this world at a healthy seven pounds eight ounces on August 6, 1999. His parents and older brother spoiled him so badly that he had to be sent to Point of Fork Military Academy in his freshman year of high school.

Made in the USA
Columbia, SC
24 July 2017